ARMED COMBAT . . .

The voice this time was clearly inhuman, without gender, and cold: "Integration incomplete nonpriority interface negative clearance access deny deny cancel—"

Marito looked stunned. "What . . . was . . . that?"

Dubois was white, awestruck. She whispered, "The ship. The ship's computer is interfering." She keyed the transmitter. "Kevin, fight it. *Fight it!*"

The ship growled around them. Tendrils grew out from the corner where Kahn had vanished, unnoticed by either of them. They stretched to their limit, swinging at the humans just out of reach. They stopped, pulled back, and surged forward again. . . .

ROBERT L. HOVORKA, JR.
DERELICT

ACE BOOKS, NEW YORK

DERELICT

An Ace Book / published by arrangement with
the author

PRINTING HISTORY
Ace edition / March 1988

ISBN: 0-441-14254-0

Ace Books are published by The Berkley Publishing Group,
200 Madison Avenue, New York, NY 10016.
The name "Ace" and the "A" logo
are trademarks belonging to Charter Communications, Inc.

PRINTED IN THE UNITED STATES OF AMERICA

10   9   8   7   6   5   4   3   2   1

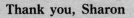

Thank you, Sharon

derelict—*abandoned, adrift, forsaken*

1

Destruction

She was 625 meters long, a hundred at her widest. Long and lean, graceful in a manner unneeded by a craft of space, she was beautiful. The PSL *Goddess* moved away from her planetary point of departure, towards the anomaly that would transport her several-dozen light-years across space. She was proud, powerful, carrying nearly three thousand passengers who were tended by a crew one thousand strong. She was an awesome sight. She was about to die.

Ensign Pamela Dubois straightened her tunic collar and stepped back to regard the results. The mirror reflected a twenty-five-year-old woman, several millimeters over 173 centimeters in height, weight a trim fifty-eight kilograms. Her auburn hair was trimmed short, regulation length, and her green eyes were clear, sharp, inquisitive. She wasn't beautiful in the classic sense, a square jawline causing her to appear harsh. High cheekbones and a vague fold to the eyes created an aura of mystery.

You flatter yourself, she thought.

She tugged at the bottom of her jacket. Styled more for form than for function, it accentuated her modest breasts, made certain her belly remained flat, swelled just enough for her hips. Like many things aboard the *Goddess*, she was as much for show as for work. When she had been a cadet, it had been easier. There hadn't been the constant parading for the passengers. Now she was an officer and a lady, always representing the *Goddess*, her crew, and her owners.

Dubois tucked a strand of hair back into place and sighed. Little more could be done. A glance at the wall clock told her it was time to begin her rounds. Cap in place, she left the officer's lounge.

The portside corridor of Two Deck was empty, except for a single passenger. He walked partly sideways, a loose grin on his lips. As he passed, the odor of alchohol was stifling. It moved with him like a cloud, and she shook her head.

Pleasures for the passengers, duties for the crew.

She logged in at a wall-com and began strolling the deck. Her main function, at the moment, was for show. The ship was rapidly approaching anomaly transition, and the company thought it best that the crew remain in constant sight. However illogical, many of the passengers felt this was the most dangerous portion of the journey. A colorful show of force tended to keep them calm.

Dubois shared some of their anxiety, though hers was purely physical. She was a part of a small minority that could feel the transition. It wasn't crippling, little more than a moment's vague nausea, as if she were spinning in all directions for a fraction of a second.

Her walk took her mind off the coming transit. Not totally pointless, her wanderings kept her within seconds of a garishly striped orange-and-black section of the outer hull. Tall red letters identified it as LIFEBOAT STATION 2-2-7, her duty assignment. The colors clashed with the otherwise peaceful decor, but were required by shipping regulations.

"Excuse me."

Dubois turned, a smile coming automatically to her lips. A teenage boy, escorting a senior, matronly woman, stood behind her. He repeated, "Excuse me, but how would I get to the main passenger lounge?"

"For this section it's on Four Deck, sir." He brightened at the compliment. "The lift is just around this corner."

He nodded. "Thank you. Come along, Grandmother. We don't want to miss the show."

"Don't know why we bother. *I've* seen it before."

The lift doors closed. Dubois grinned. "The show" was the first officer's lecture on interstellar travel. He gave it before each transition. The boy and his grandmother must have boarded at Golden, the planet they were leaving. This was probably his first interstellar voyage.

There wasn't much to see. Dubois imagined that one of the newer, high-gee shuttles had been more to his liking. They made the run in hours instead of days. There was, however, still a large number of people who preferred the "long, slow boat ride."

The situation was not without precedent. A century and a half before the oceanliners of Earth had been retired by the tiny but swift airliners.

Goddess moved with the laborious acceleration of ten meters per second per second. On the average it took her four days to reach a system's anomaly. Her passengers were kept comfortable the entire time by the ship's antiacceleration fields. They scarcely knew they were moving, always living in an artificial one-gravity environment.

Though slight by modern terms, that steady one-gee acceleration had opened the way for man's expansion throughout his home solar system. Journeys that had taken days now took hours; years became days. On one of the first journeys to the solar system's outer edge, the anomaly had been discovered.

It was a point that shouldn't exist, where the space-time continuum wasn't constant. If approached correctly, and at the proper velocity, the anomaly would transport a ship across vast distances in an instant. The classic illustration was of a book lying open on a desk. The corner of one page was a set distance from its counterpart on the other. Close the book, however, and the two corners were pressed together. Step from one to the other, open the book, and the distance had been spanned with only minimal effort. An anomaly closed the book between star systems.

Dubois thought of the distance the ship was about to cover, an insignificant portion of their journey as far as time was concerned. It caused the most fear because it was so unknown. The most fearful would bring up the main lost ships, the ones that had first charted the anomalies, the ones that still were.

What was a nightmare for some was Dubois's dream. The company that owned the *Goddess* also operated the largest deep-space exploration outfit. Dubois hoped to join. She wanted to explore, to face the unknown, perhaps even be the first to contact an alien civilization. Her present assignment, with all its drudgery, was merely a step.

The company felt that its passenger ships were good recruiting grounds, more so than their new torchships. The slow, steady pace of the *Goddess* matched the time and care required by the exploration craft.

Only officers were eligible for interservice transfer, especially into the highly competitive exploration division. Dubois had joined the company's academy and was now serving inboard their ships. Her assignment to lifeboat command was a step on the promotional ladder.

To make better officers of you all, she thought, remembering the manual: "A lifeboat will be your first true taste of command and its responsibilities, especially if there is need to abandon ship."

She smiled. Somehow, despite the *Goddess*'s age, that didn't seem likely.

The clock unwound. Describing a transition was far easier than making one. Vast amounts of power were generated in the final moments before anomaly entry. The ship's field generators were powered up to maxium potential to positively protect the ship and her passengers. The transition fields reached out to find the anomaly, then embrace it.

Dubois looked at the time and braced herself with a nearby handhold. She counted the seconds, her stomach tensing. At zero she held her breath. The flutter came and went, and she knew the *Goddess* was thirty light-years from where she had been.

She exhaled and turned to resume her rounds—

—and found herself floating. From somewhere astern came a low rumbling. She brushed against a wall and could feel it vibrate. It stopped as she regained a handhold.

Training took hold and kept her breakfast down. Alarms were sounding throughout the vessel, and she could hear the emergency bulkheads sliding into place, cutting the ship into individual compartments. A moment later the main power failed. There was an instant of darkness, then the emergency lanterns came on, turning the normally soft-lit interior into glaring light sources and deep shadows.

Dubois knew something had gone wrong in engineering.

The main power supply had been cut, along with all engine thrust (or she would have been slammed against the sternward wall by the continuing acceleration). The null-field was gone, along with the artificial gravity. The ship's fifteen sections were cut off from each other by the automatic bulkheads, each section now with its own power and air supplies. All this could be surmised by her present circumstances. She ignored most of it as being irrelevant.

She pulled herself forward, then flew across a corridor. She caught another handhold, this one at the lifeboat station. She tapped in the access code. Alert lights flashed on, strobing for attention, and the door opened.

Inside, more lights came on, lighting a four-and-a-half meter circular room, a rope strung around its circumference. A single control console came to life as she drifted over to it. Her fingers danced on the touchpad, bringing the lifeboat to life. The hatch covering the boarding tube moved aside, the way to the boat clear.

Dubois stared at the ship's automatic sequencer. Red lights were coming on one by one as the system ran through the evacuation checklist. If all criteria were met without a countermanding order from the bridge, it would be inevitable: abandon ship.

Her mouth felt dry. The sequence completed itself without so much as an amber to break the line of red. Her heart pounded harder as a buzzer sounded. She unclipped a small remote transceiver and put it in her ear, making sure the microphone was attached properly for bone conduction. The earphone hissed for a moment. The words she then heard made it official.

> "Attention all emergency stations, this is the captain. Evacuation procedures are now in effect. Stand by all lifeboats. All damage control parties lay aft. All evacuation teams commence operations, Code Omega, repeat Omega. All . . ."

The orders droned on, but they were no longer relevant to her. Code Omega meant the ship was in imminent danger of destruction.

After a dozen heartbeats she turned to the corridor doorway. Beyond, all she could hear were fearful shouts of confusion.

There was no voice of command, no evacuation team leader sending the passengers towards Dubois's post. They should be out there, rounding up people, searching staterooms. There was no one.

Worse, her assistant, Jon Inns, was missing. He should have arrived on her heels. Where was he?

"Need help?" a man asked from the entrance. He was dirty, his work uniform stained, but at the moment he was a beautiful sight.

"Yes," she said. She drifted towards him. "What happened?"

"Power plant blowout, I think." He grinned, brown eyes twinkling. "I always told Yin number one'd go, but a starman doesn't tell the chief engineer what to do. He tells me and so do you, Ensign. What do you want me to do?"

"Stay right there. Guide passengers inside, to me." She read his name patch. "Buchanan?"

"Right the first time." He was stocky, not much taller than she, but much heavier. His brown hair was as short as hers but dirtier. She guessed he was with maintenance and doubted he had ever talked with the chief engineer. Even before the stains, she could tell his uniform had been a mess, uncreased, and washed just enough to pass inspection—if his shift leader was a friend.

Just what I need, she thought, *another Inns*.

She altered course with a light push on a wall, headed for the boarding tube. Buchanan looked out into the corridor and said, "They're just floatin' around like panicked goldfish. I'd better—"

"Hold your stations!" she said. "Let the e-teams get them."

"There aren't any e-teams, Ensign. Someone's fouled up somewhere." He braced himself to push off, then stopped. "Well, thank someone."

Passengers began drifting up to him. They looked dazed, disoriented by what was happening. He grabbed them expertly and, whispering reassurances where necessary, gently pushed them towards Dubois. She caught them with equal care and showed them where to hold on. She began reevaluating the starman. Perhaps he wasn't another Inns.

Nine passengers were brought in before Buchanan's unseen assistant came into view. He held tightly a barely dressed

woman, cooing in her ear constantly. His uniform was in
disarray, as though hastily pulled on.

Dubois's first thought was to thank him, but anger blotted it
out as she recognized him. "Inns! Where the hell have you
been?"

The petty officer ignored her, continuing to escort the lady.
Her eyes were wide, muscles tight. She was on the edge of
hysterics, beyond panic. Dubois remembered who she was,
Carolina Sims, a woman of questionable charm and limitless
beauty—normally. Terror erased any pretense of seduction at
the moment.

Inns and Sims had been eyeing each other ever since she had
boarded. Their condition of undress told Dubois where her
assistant had been.

The pair drifted by Dubois. Inns guided one of Sims's hands
to the rope and turned to the ensign. His thin face smiled,
indifference plain in his eyes. She hated him, her loathing
made all the worse because she couldn't take the time to kill
him.

She glared at Sims, then refocused on Inns. "Well?"

His smile bent into contempt. Taller than she, he held no
respect for her, rank notwithstanding. She never understood
this but believed it had something to do with her ambitions and
his; he didn't have any, and had nothing but contempt for those
who did.

His uniform was wrinkled, black hair uncombed and
drifting, without weight to hold it. He stared at her over a
pinched nose and replied, "No concern of yours, Ensign."

"'Away from post during an emergency.' 'Failure to report
during same.' I could have you hung."

"But I'm here now, so I doubt it."

"Don't."

"Be thankful he showed up at all," Buchanan said. "We
needed him."

"You're supposed to be my assistant, Inns, walking your
own rounds. What took you—" She looked at Sims. A deep
breath to calm herself, then, "More to the point, get back into
the corridor. There may be—"

She stopped, listening to the bug in her ear. After a moment
she spoke, apparently to no one. The bone-conductive mike
transmitted her words to the bridge. "Boat 2-2-7 operational,
ten loaded." Pause. "Affirmative. 2-2-7, standing by."

She looked at Buchanan. "A special team's coming by in a moment, headed aft. There're passengers trapped there, in and about the rec areas, most of their lifeboats inoperative. Anyone I can spare is to lay aft and lend a hand."

He shrugged, accepting the change as inevitable. "Damn me if I don't get the bitch jobs. First 212, now—"

Inns cut in. "You the jobie who's supposed to fix the lights?"

"Yeah. How'd you . . ."

Inns's leer grew, as did Dubois's confusion. Buchanan grinned in comprehension. "So you're the *man* who kept bitchin'. We thought there was only supposed to be a wo—"

"Cut the bull!"

Nearly a dozen crew members drifted into the intersection, all expertly catching handholds. The leader, a hulking lieutenant-commander, still glared at Buchanan and Inns. "What the hell do you think's goin' on here, a bloody picnic? You two, with me, *now!*"

"Sir," Dubois shouted. "I need one here, in case—"

"I don't care, Ensign. *I* need 'em aft."

Inns floated by Buchanan in compliance, joining the others. The starman held back, saying, "Really, sir, we've got some panicky ones."

Several more crew members joined them at the intersection. The commander recounted his numbers, then nodded at Buchanan. "All right, you stay. Stand by your boat, Ensign!"

"Aye, sir," Dubois sang out. It felt like a drill.

Buchanan went farther into the staging room as Inns glared at his back. The team moved out, Inns swept away with them.

"Nice," Dubois said. "What panicky ones?"

"Her, for one," he said, gesturing towards Sims, "and I noted others. You'd've had your hands full alone, Ensign."

"Agreed. Thanks. Poor Inns, I think he hates your guts."

"Shoulda spoke faster than me. Orders, ma'am?"

She smiled. "Stand to your post."

He flashed her a mock salute. "Aye, aye."

Buchanan started to turn and stopped. The bulkhead beyond the entrance groaned. A pronounced hissing erupted from it, kicking off a minor dust storm.

"Hull break," he whispered.

Dubois looked startled. Ahead of them was the core of the ship. If there was a leak, then the ship was splitting apart. She

thumbed her communicator to life and waved Buchanan back
to her side.

"Lifeboat 2-2-7 to Damage Control. We have an atmospheric leak here, minor so far." She paused, listening.
"Affirmative, it—"

Something metallic tore, and the hiss became a tug. She
relayed the new information, turning to Buchanan. "Get them
into the boat. We're blowing free."

He didn't wait to be told twice. People began herding
through the access tube. Dubois went to the door, looking both
ways down the corridor, then swung around to her console.
She slapped a switch. A thick door slid into place, sealing the
room.

She turned to Buchanan. "Hurry it up!"

Buchanan followed the last of the passengers into the boat.
Dubois gave her station a final once-over, suddenly aware that
this was real, that the *Goddess* was dying, and that *she* was
now in command.

She suppressed a flutter of panic and dove into the tube. As
she reached the boat's hatchway there was a ripping sound
behind her. The corridor bulkhead tore open, the rush of
decompression clawing at her. Buchanan braced himself and
grabbed one of her flailing hands, yanking her in. He punched
the hatch controls. The doors hissed into place, locking toggles
ramming home.

"Get them into their seats," she ordered. "Everyone up
front."

She flew over their heads, along the nine-meter length of the
boat's interior. She stopped herself at the flight-deck separation
panel. Her thumbprint worked the lock, opening the doors.
Before entering, she looked back over her shoulder and saw
Buchanan snarled in a knot of people.

She grabbed the nearest person, an Asian gentleman who
seemed to handle himself well in freefall. "Sir, could you give
us a hand?"

Almond eyes blinked at her, mouth forming a confused
"oh." He looked and nodded. "Yes, yes, of course."

"Thanks. Get them seated in these front rows."

He moved to the rear as she slipped into the left-hand
command seat. She could feel the vessel tremble as she
strapped in. The *Goddess* was breaking apart.

Four buttons in quick succession brought the lifeboat's

power plant to life. She looked the instruments over. Vertical strip indicators came to life, digital readouts flickering. She waited while the instruments climbed into the green.

Buchanan came onto the flight deck and into the right-hand chair. As he strapped in he said, "All seated."

"Belted in?" she asked, releasing the jettison safeties.

He looked back. "Yeah."

Without turning, she pointed to a panel near his right thigh. "That's a seating display. If you've got ten green lights, then they're strapped in properly."

He looked and announced, "Ten big green, Cap'n."

Dubois accepted her new rank without comment. She armed the explosive bolts and unlocked the boat's engines.

"I'm not activating our null-field yet," she said. "I don't want to bug-up someone's work back on board."

"Whatever you say. I'm not cleared on these things."

She was surprised, but only for a moment. Of course he wouldn't know; he wasn't Inns. She said, "I'll handle her well enough alone." She keyed the communicator to life. "Lifeboat 2-2-7 to bridge, ready to disengage."

The voice that replied was not the measured tones of the captain or the usual evacuation-control officer. It was hurried, panicked, snapping out, "For God's sake, get free. The field room is going berserk. Get clear, *get clear!*"

Dubois needed no second urging. She shouted over her shoulder, "Brace yourselves!" and hit the launch key.

Nothing happened.

Explosive bolts should have fired, and the boat's launch tube should have pivoted at the stern until they were pointing perpendicular to the ship. The final braces should have sheered and the lifeboat launched, an accelerating cannon shell.

Instead, nothing.

Dubois hesitated only long enough for the computer to buzz her that the sequence had failed, the hull distorted enough to jam the pivot shaft. She hit two more buttons, plus a third marked in red EMER-LAUNCH.

This is going to be rou—

The exterior retention panels blew away. An array of rocket bottles fired, pushing the entire launch tube out and away from the *Goddess*. Dubois and the others lunged to one side with the sudden lateral acceleration. She sighed with relief, thankful this sequence had worked. There was a third, but that involved blowing the outer wall of the tube itself, with the possibility of damage to the lifeboat.

A proximity sensor calculated they were far enough from the ship, and the lifeboat's maneuvering jets flared, shoving against tube baffles. The boat shrugged off its launch tube. Dubois looked over the readouts as the secondary thrusters fired, pushing them back into their seats. She said, "We're free and clear."

She brought the main viewer to life. To their left was the tumbling and distorted wreck of the *Goddess*, her stern blasted open. An odd lightning storm was beginning to arc around the ship.

"My Lord," Buchanan muttered.

Goddess was in her death throes. Her field generators, fully charged from her recent transition, shorted and discharged. Long streamers of energy came to life, leaping through the anomaly that allowed the ship to transit light-years in an instant. An eye-rending violet-amber *something* flared into existence. *Goddess* flickered on its edge, then was gone. She reappeared a moment later, shattered into a thousand fragments.

Dubois felt a familiar sensation, a growing nausea, only worse. Something tickled her intestines. She hissed in shock and pain. Through hazy vision she saw the *thing* coming at them. No, they were moving towards it, accelerating through a curve. The gee-forces multiplied, shoving her into her seat.

Dubois's stomach lurched and the world exploded yellow-white. Someone screamed, a terrible sound, like all the demons of your mind. She felt herself whirling apart, spinning down into darkness, into darkness, into—

2

". . . *never properly introduced.*"

Someone touched her shoulder.

Dubois's mind swam out of its own hell and back into the world. She looked about, dazed and nauseous, trying to organize things around her. The feeling of vertigo faded, and in a few moments she was able to concentrate. She coughed lightly and sat up, pushing against her restraints.

"Back among the living, eh?" Buchanan asked. He hovered half in, half out of the flight deck. She turned and nodded as he continued, "We took a nasty ride there, Cap'n. You okay?"

"Yeah, I think so. How long was I out?"

"'Bout fifteen minutes. I've been spending the time checkin' ev'rybody out." He nodded to the displays. "They all went dead when we fell into whatever it was."

She looked at the screens and readouts. Everything had shut down.

"Life-support seems okay," Buchanan said.

Dubois nodded. "They're on a different circuit. We must have gotten a surge through the sensor array."

She unhooked her restraint harness and looked at her passengers. There were eight, evenly split between men and women. Two of the women and one of the men were pale and haggard-looking, apparently recovering from shock. They all stared at her, waiting for her to speak.

Buchanan whispered in her ear, "I told 'em you were in charge and would fill 'em in when you woke up."

She nodded again and said, "I am Ensign Pamela Dubois. This is—" She stopped, forgetting his name.

"Starman First Class Kevin Buchanan," he said, smiling. "She and I were never properly introduced."

There were several nervous chuckles, and Dubois resumed. "We suffered a major explosion back on *Goddess*, as I'm sure you're aware."

"We certainly are!" a flamboyantly dressed man said. A corpulent woman seated next to him slapped his thigh, frowning in annoyance.

Dubois ignored him. "All I can tell you is that the field generators were going wild as we launched. Evidently they caused a distortion of some sort which we passed through. As soon as I check over the lifeboat's photronic circuits, I'll get us a navigational fix and see where we are. In any case, a system patrol boat should pick us up within an hour. The anomaly's traffic-control drone would have notified the authorities immediately of the . . . accident." She thought, *Choose your words carefully.*

Most nodded, if for no other reason than to believe the worst was past. Holding her smile, she floated by them, Buchanan in tow.

She stopped at the end of the passenger area. Two wrapped forms were tied to one side, by the hatchway. Buchanan followed her eyes and whispered. "Dead, and don't ask me how. Both were women, one of 'em Inns's girl. I put 'em back here first, and fast, before the others recovered enough to—"

"Dead?" she mumbled. *Ten came aboard, not just the eight you counted. Is this how you take care of your responsibilities?* Aloud, she asked, "You don't know how?"

"No. One thing, though: it wasn't pleasant. It shows in their faces."

"What happened?"

"There was that thing we dove through, then a flash. The screens went dead. I felt kinda dizzy, and when I turned around, you had two dead, three out, plus you."

Dubois bit her upper lip. "We've got to watch our

step . . . Kevin. Chances are most of these people have never spaced. All they know is all hell's broken loose."

"Sure, sure. *That's* obvious. What do we do about . . ." He eyed the bodies.

"Nothing. They'll be taken care of when we're picked up. Right now, get back up front and put on your best PR face. I'll be back in a minute."

Buchanan smiled. "I was a maintenance jobber, Cap'n, but I'm willin' to try public relations."

She smiled back and turned to the stern bulkhead. A press of her thumb worked the door lock, and she stepped into the small storage room.

The boat's main circuit panel was wedged between boxed supplies and a small toilet. She stepped up to the covering shield, pulling it off with a moderate tug. It drifted to the end of its short tether and slowly recoiled back. She ignored it, checking the breakers. Several had opened, all the flight circuits. She carefully ran through the checklist before resetting them. They held in place, and she ran the check once more. Everything was green and normal.

I wonder what made them open. A temporary surge?

After replacing the cover and resealing the compartment, she turned to the two bodies. They were side by side, tethered to a bulkhead handhold. Curiosity got the better of her, and she unwrapped the crude bond Buchanan had thrown around them.

She drew back in shock. Miss Carolina Sims had looked terrified when hustled aboard the lifeboat. That had been an infinitely calmer expression than the one that distorted her face in death. The eyes bulged from their sockets, all the veins ruptured. Lips were drawn back in a primordial scream, baring clenched teeth and white gums. The face's complexion was mottled, alternating pale and purple, the latter from broken blood vessels. Dubois tried to close the eyelids but they were frozen open, as the jaw was locked closed, as if welded. With relief she resecured the wrapping and headed forward. She ignored Buchanan's "I told you so" expression and entered the flight deck.

She touched the controls. The display screens lit one by one, showing all secure within and without the boat. She looked at the information on the navigational readout and frowned. Clearing it, she tried again, receiving the same display. With obvious reluctance she activated the main viewer.

Someone spoke up immediately. "That's not Sol!"

Dubois saw no reason to comment on the obvious. Earth's sun had never looked like this.

Some one billion kilometers distant was a blazing blue-white inferno, blindingly bright. It was surrounded by a luminescent cloud that shifted continuously, growing, shrinking, elongating and contracting. Thin streams drifted off, fading away. Dubois punched a program into the computer and waited for a reply.

"Like a hole into hell," Buchanan muttered. "Let's get a temperature reading."

"Working on it," Dubois said. The scans were completed a moment later. The answer appeared on the main screen, framing the star. Size, temperature, number of planets, all appeared one by one, including a spectral classification.

Buchanan read, "Class WN-8. WN? What's that?"

"A Wolf-Rayet, Starman Buchanan," the Asian said. His almond eyes danced with delight, the expression of a child with a new toy. He was thin, slightly shorter than Dubois, but with a wired intensity to his movements. His tone was just short of lecturing. "Class W. The N denotes a predominance of nitrogen in the spectral reading, as opposed to carbon for a WC Wolf-Rayet. The nitrogen variety is much more violent."

Buchanan grimaced at the condescending tone while Dubois nodded. "Wolf-Rayet, the hottest class of stars. Look at the surface temperature reading—nearly fifty K on the Kelvin scale."

"Fifty thousand degrees," Buchanan said. "Bright and hot."

"We've plotted over three hundred Wolf-Rayets," the passenger said. "No one's ever been in a Wolf system, though. No anomaly vector has been found to take us there."

"Till now," Buchanan said. "Which leads to the question, how did we get here? And where is here?"

"No planets at all," the passenger said, reading the displays. "Amazing."

Dubois looked at the navigation screen. "There may be a planet or two on the star's other side. Solar interference is preventing a complete scan from here. As for where we are, I don't know. The astral scan can't get a fix." She frowned at a jump in a graph and touched a control. The viewer image reversed, showing the stars behind the lifeboat.

And a violet-amber something. Dubois felt that crawling sensation in her guts and said, "*That's* how we got here."

It just hung there, seemingly throbbing and pulsing with a

life of its own. Occasionally bits of flaming matter would shoot out, cooling rapidly as they flew past.

"What're those?" Buchanan asked.

"Debris. Either rocks or . . . or from the *Goddess*."

"An anomaly," the Asian said. "When the *Goddess*'s fields failed, they formed a visible anomaly. That's a portal home, Ensign."

"No," she said. "That's a death hole. It killed two of us coming through this way. It nearly got me and three others. I'm not about to chance that it won't kill us all going back the other way."

"We're receding from it," Buchanan said. "We should be stationary, but we're not."

Dubois checked the boat's readouts. "That thing's got a negative gravity well. It's pushing us away."

"And it's probably pulling from the other side, assuming that it's become stable and there *is* another side," Buchanan said grimly.

"And why shouldn't there be?" the Asian asked. "It's there, isn't it?"

"This apparition, yes, but as far as we know, it's temporary and the other side is already sealed."

"Shouldn't we check?" asked a new voice. They turned, and a tall, buxom blonde waved her hand. "I think we should check."

Buchanan smiled and shrugged. "The only way to do that would be try and drive through it." He turned to the Asian. "What is your name, sir?"

"John Marito, chemical biologist and amateur astronomer, and I can assure you—"

"Of nothing," Buchanan said. "Mr. Marito, would you please return to your seat."

"You can't—"

"On this boat, I can. Please, sir."

Marito surrendered and strapped back into his seat.

"I'm going to boost us away from that thing," Dubois said, "and set us up in a fast orbit around this star, just to make sure there's nowhere to set down."

"Why set down at all?" the blonde asked. "If that thing's the way home, shouldn't we go?"

"Because it may not be. Transiting an anomaly isn't like using a teleportal. You don't always end up in the same place.

If we didn't hit the anomaly at the precise vector required to return us to the Sol star system, we'd only become worse off."

"Why?" Buchanan asked.

"Because any search party wouldn't know where to find us. The traffic-control drone should have tracked our entrance into the anomaly, this thing notwithstanding. That gives them a course and speed to follow. If we leave here, they'd never find us."

"So S.O.P. is to find a planet."

"Right. Set down and wait. Rescue will arrive, sooner or later, *if* we're patient." She touched several controls. "I'm activating our null-field. Normal gravity, coming up."

The lights flickered for a moment, then weight returned. There was a mass sigh of relief. Few, it seemed, enjoyed freefall.

Dubois rubbed her hands together. "Now," she muttered, "let's get this thing ready for travel." She touched another stud. The deck under their feet vibrated softly, followed by the solid thunk of something locking into place.

From underneath the windowless lifeboat huge, triangular wings slid out. As they locked into position winglets popped out of their underwing recesses and pivoted up and around until they locked into the vertical.

"What's going on?" Buchanan asked.

"Atmospheric control wings. Not needed for deep space, of course, but this boat was built on the dunce principle. Anyone of reasonable intelligence can scan the instruction tape and control her. To go anywhere the wings automatically deploy. They also serve triple duty, padded on top with solar cells and the forward edges serving as the free-hydrogen scoops. The winglets hold the primary communication arrays."

Buchanan looked impressed. "Who designs all this?"

"This is a General Life Design. Tyler Instrumentals helped outfit it, as well as building their own." She pushed down a button, initiating her orbit program. A rumble came from the stern. "Those are the secondary engines. We'll be up to primary drive speed in around twelve hours. The scoop-fields will deploy then, feeding the ram engine. Our acceleration will go from 2.5 to seven gravities."

He looked numb from the explanations. "You enjoy reciting all this? What's our range?"

"With the primary drive you say 'endurance,' and theoreti-

cally that means unlimited. The scoops work down to seven
hundred klick-seconds but are best at over a thousand.
Considering the output of that star, there's a lot of free fuel for
conversion."

He smiled. "So power's no problem."

"None at all." She turned to Marito. "You're in luck. As an
astronomer you'll be the first to study a Wolf-Rayet up close."

Marito grunted a semblance of pleasure, apparently still
upset with Buchanan's dismissal of him from the flight deck.

The starman tapped the star's informational display. "Have
you seen the spectral reading on this thing? All in the lethal
range. Only our hull and safety fields will protect us."

"I've seen. Extreme ultraviolet, too."

Marito overheard and could not be contained. "The atmosphere of a Wolf-Rayet is extremely turbulent. You'll note the
broad emission lines. Those are caused by streams of matter
being hurled off its surface at thousands of kilometers per
second. That is also what causes that luminescent cloud
formation. The energy of the star ionizes the nitrogen and
carbon in its atmosphere and—"

"*Thank* you, Mr. Marito," Buchanan said. "If we need to
know more, we'll ask." He whispered to Dubois, "I bet he's
an instructor."

"A rated professor," Marito said.

Dubois smiled. "And he's got a professor's ears too."

When she was satisfied that the lifeboat was in a satisfactory
orbit, Dubois locked the controls and stepped into the main
compartment. Buchanan followed, staying near the separation
panel. Dubois looked at her passengers and thought, *My turn
again, my time to command. I hate being on stage.*

"This is our new home," she said, "for a while, anyway.
We'll all grow to know it intimately before we get out of this
star system." *Lord knows when that'll be.* "I think we can save
time and bother if we get to know each other right away. We'll
start with—"

"Where do we sleep?" The flamboyant gentleman spoke
again, voice and manner agitated. "And what food do we
have? I could—" His wife elbowed him again.

Dubois looked him over. He must have been one of the
"panicky ones" Buchanan had spotted. She sighed. *Nothing
ever goes smoothly.* "All right, the facts of life first. You're

sitting on your bed. The chairs disassemble into two components, frame and padding. 'Frame' isn't exactly the correct term. You'll find that the base and the backrest are actually solid sheets. That's our paneling. If you'll look here," she pointed to the ceiling compartments, "and here, along the deck, you'll see small slots. By using them, and the panels, we can compartmentalize the boat into several sleeping areas. The design was meant to be used as a base camp if the boat landed on a planet. There's not a lot of room. It was assumed that most people would sleep outside, in pressurized tents. Obviously we can't use them. When we're done with the interior, we'll have five semiprivate bunk spaces. I say 'semiprivate' because they won't be soundproof.

"I plan on leaving the front two rows of seats, the eight you're in, intact. That gives you all somewhere to sit for any extraneous maneuvering I may have to perform."

Marito said, "Is it possible for you to set up some sort of observation equipment. I wish to study this star as much as possible."

"We'll see what can be rigged." She licked her lips and pointed to the rear section. "That area will remain clear. That is our combination rec room and dining area. Beyond that bulkhead is the storage compartment, with miscellaneous equipment, toilet facilities, our 'kitchen,' as well as the food. I can assure you of its bland, uninspired, and inoffensive nature." *Just like flavored, soggy cardboard.* "Our water is recycled, as is our air. It can last indefinitely. The food can supply thirty-four, the boat's capacity, for six months; obviously it will last longer for us. We're very lucky there're only ten of us."

She put her hands on her hips. "Questions?"

"We can't keep wearing these clothes," the blonde said. "What else can we wear?"

"As little as you want, dear," the old man next to her muttered. She gave him an affectionate smile.

"Good question," Dubois said. "As an answer, we have . . ." She reached up and tugged open one of the overhead storage compartments. From it she removed an orange packet. "This is an adjust-for-all jumpsuit. We also have the necessary items to alter it beyond its normal capacity." She saw the annoyed look the overweight woman gave her, and mentally winced at her indiscretion. *Watch what you say, watch what you say.* "And, for those with more imagination, we have straight fabric so you can make whatever you wish. There is also a supply of slip-on shoes, durable and comfortable."

There were no more questions, and she resealed the compartment. "Now, as to introductions. I suggest we introduce ourselves in turn, giving a bit of your background and where you were headed or returning from." She pointed. "Care to start us off, Mr. Marito?"

He stood and bowed formally at her. "Very well." Turning to the others, he said, "I am John Marito. My chief profession is in chemical biology, working at the Berkeley Genetics Research Lab. I hold teaching credentials in my field, specializing in genetic mutations and alterations. I am also an amateur astronomer, president of my association. I was on Golden on business. I chose to return aboard the *Goddess* because I needed the time to compile my notes." He smiled sadly. "All of which were, of course, lost."

He sat down abruptly, catching them all by surprise. Dubois looked at the blonde who had spoken earlier. The woman picked up the silent cue and stood. She was the tallest of the women, over a hundred eighty centimeters. Her body was muscular, though not overly so. She moved with a sure grace, her blue eyes laughing at some unheard joke. She was beautiful, with high cheekbones, and a gently rounded chin. Dubois felt a moment's rush of envy. The woman obviously worked on her appearance and succeeded.

"My name is Hilary Kahn. I'm thirty-seven and work as secretary to this ancient gentleman seated next to me—"

"Ancient?" he grunted in amusement.

"—Benjamin Daggit."

"And she's more than a secretary," Daggit said. "*She* runs the business. *I* go along for the ride."

Dubois didn't believe that. Daggit was old, perhaps approaching a hundred, but that meant little anymore. He appeared to be an active man, his body trim yet filled out, not sunken with age and neglect. He still had a full head of hair, though mostly gray, and his brown eyes glistened with intelligence, not a trace of senility.

Still, she marked him as a possible problem. If he was careful, Daggit could see another twenty years or more. His present situation, however, could place him under a great deal of stress. She had to be careful not to make it any worse.

"What business are you in?" Buchanan asked.

"Interstellar Caterers, Incorporated, son," Daggit replied. "Ever hear of us?"

"No."

"You should have. Who do you think supplied the feed back aboard the *Goddess*?"

"You were on business, then?" Dubois asked.

Kahn sighed. "Unfortunately. I'm still waiting for the vacation Ben promised me." She grinned, a mischievous gleam in her eye. "And if this is his idea of a vacation . . ."

There was a scattering of laughter. Dubois silently thanked Kahn. If she could keep them laughing, she could keep their morale up.

The introductions went on. The dapper gentleman was Roger Bonay, the woman his wife Lisa. She was almost laughingly overweight, her clothes too tight in all the wrong places. The couple bothered Dubois; Lisa, because she didn't seem comfortable with her size, as though it had been recently acquired, yet was too large for it to have been gained all of a sudden. It could be, though, that Dubois sympathized. She felt her own uniform constrict her form, and thought, *Damn designers*.

The couple had been on a second honeymoon to Earth. Bonay dealt in cut crystals, an importer/exporter. Dubois couldn't quite believe it. Bonay was too smooth, even to be some sort of fancy salesman. She found him sexually attractive on a subtle level, as if he were playing her as a trick. She broke her attention from him with an effort, turning to the others.

Kelly So, teenager, traveling to Earth to visit relatives. He looked like a body builder, around Dubois's height, in excellent shape. He could be no less. When he returned to Golden, it was expected that he would enter the Collective Forces Academy of the planet, as his father had. He was aiming for a career in deep space. Dubois felt a slight thrill of closeness with the boy, someone who shared her goal. She doubted, however, if he would go far with the CF. There was a hint of the rebel in So, perhaps nothing more than his young age. If he could hold on to it, he could do well as an explorer.

Clinging to his upper arm was Jeanine Quont, tiny and

petite. She was a year younger than So, and they had met aboard the starship. It was obvious they had become more than friends. It could mean trouble for Quont, as her Earth parents probably would not approve of her romance with a soldier-to-be.

The strain of the last few hours showed worse on Quont. She reminded Dubois of a trapped, lost kitten, eyes darting from side to side in fear, unsure what was safe or who was friendly. Fortunately she had found an anchor in So. If they were as close as they appeared, he could comfort her and free Dubois of the immediate responsibility.

Last was Nan Poullard, a strange and quiet woman from the east coast of Eurasia, Earth. She was an enigma, from her bright white hair to her pale blue eyes and even paler complexion. She spoke with a frightening frankness, as though deceit were a word she had never heard and would never understand.

"You see," she concluded, "I'm dying. I was returning from Golden, where I had undergone the last possible tests. It is a rare thing, relatively new and unknown to medicine. I am incurable. So you see, Ensign Dubois, I have little to fear about this voyage. Indeed, I rather prefer it this way."

Dubois nodded and said nothing. Poullard had a point, one she did not approve of. That frame of mind might be all well and good for her, but such a fatalistic attitude was contagious. She made a note to speak with Poullard later and ask her to keep such "there's nothing we can do" thoughts to herself.

She looked at the assortment of people that had been thrown under her charge. There were no special talents among them. They represented a slice of life from the upper crust. If they had one thing in common, with the exceptions of Jeanine Quont and Nan Poullard—and possibly Kevin Buchanan—it was that they were successful, resourceful. Pamela Dubois found herself in command at last.

Welcome to the big time, she told herself.

The orbit she had plotted for the boat was days in length. The boat kept to it automatically, its computers finding the task hardly worth their effort. When a velocity of one thousand kilometers per second had been reached, a net of fine, rigid feelers extended from the front of each wing. They were charged and began drawing in free hydrogen to feed the

lifeboat's nuclear ramjet drive. Their acceleration increased to
sixty-eight meters per second per second, an increase as unfelt
by those within as the original acceleration had been.

Long before then Dubois held her first service for the dead.
The two women were wrapped more securely than Buchanan's
original handiwork, and the temporary airlock was rigged
around the main hatchway. She consigned the souls of Miss
Carolina Sims and Mrs. Anna Welt to an eternal orbit around
the violent star, purging the airlock to launch them on their
way. For not the first, or last, time she wondered if Mr. Welt
had been left aboard the *Goddess* or was waiting for his wife to
arrive on Earth. The enormity of the disaster they had escaped
came home to her again and again as she thought about its
human toll.

The interior was converted as she had described. They
divided themselves into shifts—half awake, half asleep—for
the use of the five compartments.

She learned more about Kevin Buchanan. Son of a factory
foreman, he had resolved not to be stuck in the same position,
watching CRTs and overseeing computer operations. He had
few ambitions beyond never settling down. *Goddess* was the
second luxury liner he had worked aboard, and he performed
his duties with just enough precision to maintain his rating. His
ultimate goal was to be in charge of maintenance aboard one of
the large freetraders, traveling from star system to star system
and leaving home far behind.

She made Buchanan scan the boat's instruction tape and
drilled him in the use of the controls and computer systems.
His phobia of a computer job wasn't caused by his inability to
work them. He probably could have taught her more about the
system's inner workings. He learned quickly the boat's operations, and when she felt he was good enough, they split into
shifts. One would always be on duty, awake with that shift's
passengers. The automatic alarms would call either of them if
something was wrong or if someone tried to contact them.

Their "rec room/dining area" was the single largest open
space on board, three meters square. The lack of overhead
racks at the stern gave it a clear two-and-a-half meters of
ceiling as well. Those awake gathered there, enjoying the
moderate amount of elbow room. It appeared huge in comparison to any other station, and all too soon it began to shrink,
mentally if not physically.

The kitchen was in the aft compartment. Storage cases were moved out and dispersed throughout the boat. In addition to the kitchen, the compartment also held the toilet and shower. No two actions could be performed simultaneously, necessitating a great deal of forethought for some basic human functions.

John Marito got his observation setup. Electrical hardware had been provided in a series of underfloor compartments for energency boat repairs. Mixed in with tents, work tools, breathing masks, and the like, were spare circuit boards, screens, photronic connectors, et cetera. Dubois, Buchanan, and Marito struggled to rig a secondary viewscreen at his seat, and found that Lisa Bonay knew more than the three of them together. The jury-rig was working by the end of the boat's day, much to Marito's delight and Dubois's puzzlement. There was more to Mrs. Bonay than size.

Time passed. The lifeboat went into primary drive smoothly, conserving its limited supply of reaction mass for the secondary engines. They fell around the Wolf-Rayet star, a self-contained universe, going nowhere.

3

"That's a ship."

At the end of the fifth day Dubois and Buchanan were alone on the flight deck. Dubois was coming on duty and was checking the boat's status board. Buchanan slipped into his right-hand chair and, to her surprise, closed the separation doors, shutting them off from the rest of the boat.

"What are you doing?" she asked.

"Reviewin' our situation here, Cap'n. May I?"

She had already grown accustomed to the rank, now semiofficial. The others had agreed that the boat needed a captain, and she was the ranking officer. She didn't need their approval, but it helped. She nodded for him to continue.

"We've plenty o' power. The ramjet's workin' beautifully, operatin' with flawless precision. We can literally go on forever, just like you said. As long as we have engine power, we have air, gravity, light, and water. The last, however, along with the food, can only last twenty months. Beyond that we eat and drink recycled garbage. But who wants to? Can you imagine livin' in this can for more than a month, let alone twenty?"

Dubois resumed her check while replying, "No, I can't. We don't have any choice. We have to wait." She turned to him.

"You've known this for days, Kevin. Even the others know. What are you driving at?"

"This: What are we doin' to change that fact of death? We assume that someone is comin' to find us. What if we're wrong?"

She sighed. "The automatic distress beacon sends out a clear signal. Anyone entering this system can't help but—"

"You're not listenin'. What if there is *no one comin'*? What if we're on our own, period?"

"We aren't. Someone will come through that anomaly and find—"

He cut in again, viciously. "You mean that hellhole? How do we know that it even is an anomaly anymore? Or that someone can come through this way? You know your theories better than I do, Cap'n, but isn't it true that an anomaly vector can dump you into a star system that has no return vector? What if that's the case here?"

Her gaze was cool. "In which case our rescuers would find themselves trapped here, with us. At least there'd be more of us."

"And what if the hellhole scrambled all the transit courses? You're assumin' the anomaly drone tracked our entry course and speed. When ev'rything went to hell back there, it may have dumped us somewhere that entry vector shouldn't have."

"You're saying no one can follow us."

"Exactly." He paused and took the plunge. "Captain, I think we should try and drive back through the hole."

Dubois's eyebrows shifted upwards. The thought of their first, involuntary transition made her skin crawl. "No. It could kill us all."

"You don't know that. *I* don't think it will. Those of us here *lived*. We can survive it 'cause we already have."

"Assuming it works the same both ways. Besides, we don't know where it would dump us. As you said, I know anomaly-theory better than you. What if the entire matrix has shifted, as you're suggesting? We wouldn't know where we'd end up, and no one would ever find us."

"Anywhere's better than here. There's no place to land, no planet to even *try* and live on. What chance do we have here? None."

"We've over a year before we have to make that decision."

"Wrong. You just admitted yourself we'll be goin' crazy at

the end of a month. Hell, I'll give us six months before we try tearin' our way through the hull. And you can check your psych-text theories on that.''

"To hell with theory," she snapped.

He drove on. "Then consider this: that hole may collapse at any time. Marito has suggested it may be temporary. In which case the longer we stay, the less our chances of ever gettin' outta here.''

"And it may collapse if we try and drive through. It could tear us apart.'' She was red-faced and breathing far too hard, even for an argument.

Buchanan looked at her with a curious expression for a moment. When he spoke again, his voice was softer, gentler. "You're afraid to go back through, aren't you? I don't mean you're afraid of anything on the other side. You're terrified of the transition itself.''

She kept silent and he continued. "The others who blacked out—Nan, Jeanine, Roger—seem the same. I don't know what happened when we fell through the first time, but I can imagine.''

"I doubt it," she hissed, blinking rapidly at the memory. The scream, the vertigo, the sensation of her body flying apart; the memory alone was enough to make her pale. To go through it all again was unthinkable.

"You know I'm right," Buchanan whispered. "Staying here is suicide. We'll kill each other if we don't go crazy first, and I think that's a worse fate than chancin' the hellhole.''

Dubois swore silently to herself. *He's right, he's right. If we stay here we're dead—and I'll have given up.*

"Okay, Kevin," she finally said. "We'll take a shot at it as soon as we finish this orbit. We'll follow it around till the scanners can get a fix on our hole, then we'll correct for shortest-distance.'' She tried a smile. "Hell, even if it kills us, we'll go trying.''

He nodded. "Right. Want me to tell the others?''

"No. Command has its secrets, and we must keep ours. We'll let them know just before we transit. That way there'll be no arguments.''

"Agreed. We'll—''

The forward scanner bleated for attention. Both heads looked to the display as it flashed, cleared, and began printing information.

"Something blocked the star," Buchanan mumbled. "Just a flicker."

More figures appeared, this time with different explanatory terms. Buchanan shifted his eyebrows.

"Size, approximate shape. Way too small to be a planet. Maybe an asteroid or something."

Dubois checked the readings and slaved the viewer to the scanner. The star filled the screen, and she dialed up maximum magnification, automatic filters knocking down the glare. Their target showed on the screen, framed by a computer-imaged rectangle. The object's shape was barely visible.

She studied the readouts for a moment, orbit and speed, then leaned back, face carefully blank. Its orbit was all wrong; it was too close for its orbital velocity. She felt a numb chill spread through her.

Buchanan looked up from the readouts and turned to her. "If it's an asteroid we can—"

Dubois shook her head. "That's no asteroid, Kevin."

"Then whatever. We—"

She cut him off with a blank look. "No 'whatever.' *That's a ship*."

"My . . . God. I think you're right."

Buchanan reread the displays a third time, squinted at the main screen, and repeated himself. "You're right, you're right. Lord, oh Lord, what we've found!"

Dubois's fingers played on the controls. She killed the drive, allowing them to coast. They had built up enough velocity so that they would slingshot around the star at a safe distance. With the constant acceleration gone, their orbit would be tighter than originally planned, but still well outside safety limits.

"What are you doin'?" Buchanan asked.

"Not jumping to any conclusions. The computer says it's in a synchronous orbit but that it's too close to hold that orbit naturally. Ergo, it's under power. Ergo, it's a ship—of some sort. What sort? Not human. Alien! Are they friendly? I'm not jumping into anything without first considering all angles."

"But they might be able to help us."

"They can probably destroy us. This boat doesn't even mount a lighter, let alone a laser battery. What makes you think they're peaceful?"

"What makes you think they're not?"

"Common sense and a will to survive. No, we're going to handle this *very* carefully."

Buchanan was exasperated. "Captain—Pamela—don't you realize what's happening? We're the first humans ever to make contact with another intelligent race, another civilization. You can't throw that away just because of a damn suspicion!"

"I'm not throwing it away. I merely said I want to consider our best approach." Her hands worked the controls carefully. The boat's location beacon went silent. "I think I'll boost us straight out at maximum acceleration. That'll put us into a tight curve which, if I plot it right, will bring us to a dead stop straight out from it. And that'll give us a clear silouette."

"We'd be lit by the star."

"It'll only matter when we get closer. And we can't very well get between it and the star." Her fingers danced while she spoke, programming the computer. She watched it plot a diagram of the orbit and refined it. Satisfied, she prepared to let it run.

"Marito won't like your orbit," Buchanan said.

"Marito isn't in command here."

"And you are?"

She initiated her program before looking at him, locking the board as she turned. "Are you questioning that?"

"I don't know. You might be altogether too timid for the job now."

"I'm in command of this lifeboat because it's my responsibility. If Captain Newhurst himself was aboard, I'd still be in command. This is my vessel, and you'll do as you're told, Starman."

He regarded her with a cool stare. "And how will you enforce your orders . . . Captain?"

Dubois's left hand brushed a panel. It popped open and dropped something into her palm. Before he could blink, Buchanan found himself staring at the muzzle of a stub-laser. "Other than the arms locker in the rear," she explained calmly, "this is the only weapon aboard. It's the only weapon on the flight deck, and it is only accessible to me, by *my* touch. Any questions, Starman?"

He shook his head, surrendering easily. "No. You're in command."

She resecured the weapon and nodded. She pointed to the

console. "I've locked this course into the computer. It can only be changed if you know the access code. Only I do. It won't unlock the boat until we're dead still, by which time it won't matter."

Attitude jets pulsed and the main drive reengaged with a low throb. Buchanan frowned, his voice sounding slightly hurt. "You didn't tell me ev'rything about this boat, Cap'n."

"Even Inns didn't know everything, Kevin." Her tone was softer than before, and she gestured upwards with a thumb, joking, "And if you don't like it, get out and walk."

He looked up at the emergency escape hatch and shook his head.

Further conversation was interrupted by an insistent rapping at the door. They could hear Marito's muffled voice demanding entrance.

She motioned towards the bulkhead. "Open it up. Time for show-and-tell."

Marito argued, but Dubois pulled rank. Buchanan, to her surprise, backed her up. The others fell in line and remained silent. The lifeboat accelerated away from the Wolf-Rayet star at nearly ten gravities, shunning off speed faster than it had been gained. They came to a halt right on the money and began the gradual approach towards the alien vessel.

It took two days to complete the maneuver. During the last twelve hours they began attempting communication, with no success. Either the alien craft was ignoring their signals or they communicated by a different process.

"Either is possible," Marito said as they drew closer. "They may not consider us important. Or perhaps ship-to-ship communications are foreign to them."

"Or perhaps they're waiting for us to get within range of their weapons," Dubois said.

Daggit stood behind them and coughed lightly. "I don't think so, Captain. I would imagine they could have bracketed us with long-range missiles long ago. Assuming they are hostile, that is."

She shrugged. "You could be right. I'm just being cautious."

"The sign of a good leader."

His tone was fatherly, and Dubois, to her dismay, found

herself responding. She smiled inwardly. *He's a good man. Hilary's lucky.*

The main viewer displayed a filtered image of the star, the vessel still within a computer-drawn bow. The latest scanning information appeared alongside it and Dubois gasped.

Buchanan picked up on her reaction and said, "We knew it was *close* to the star, but this . . ."

"What?" Daggit asked.

"That thing's just outside the star's halo," Dubois said. *"What?"*

Unlike the relatively tame actions of Sol, the Wolf-Rayet threw off stellar matter at a rate of several thousand kilometers per second, as opposed to mere hundreds. The ejecta formed a luminescent cloud, or "halo," around the star. It extended outwards for millions of kilometers, cooling as it grew farther from the star, running through all the colors of the heat spectrum. The core was a violent blue-white, the outer fringes a wavering red-orange. The alien ship hovered just beyond that outer fringe.

"What would the temperature be like there?" Kahn asked.

Dubois checked the readings. "Just under a thousand degrees Kelvin; cooler than Sol's surface temperature."

"So the boat can take it?" Daggit asked.

"If it were just radiant or frictional heat, I'd say yes. The hull's a third of a meter thick, and we've heavy heat- and radiation-shield fields. But that ship is within some stellar matter. It may make no difference; it may melt the hull. It's not just a matter of temperature, but where to dissipate it."

"So approach is impossible?" Buchanan asked.

Dubois was about to suggest just that when Marito pushed his way forward. "There is a way. You should approach via the alien vessel's *shadow*, keeping it between us and the star. Relieved of the radiant heat input, the shields should be able to handle the rest. Satisfactory? Bear in mind that the halo matter is thin, not compacted like the actual star. That greatly improves the heat-dissipation problem."

She bridled under Marito's smug tone, but it did seem as though he had a solution. She nodded. "We'll give it a go, but if the computer says *run*, I'm punching out of there at full power."

Marito smiled and went back to his cubicle for more study.

Dubois watched him go and said, "He reminds me of a kid at
Christmas. I hope he gets a pleasant surprise."

Buchanan nodded fervently. "Especially since if he doesn't,
neither do we."

Dubois instructed the flight computer and sat watching its
progress. The lifeboat moved ahead with precise deliberation,
altering course with gentle curves under the steady thrust of its
main engines. After hours of steady deceleration, they fell
below the ram engine's operational level. The scoops retracted
neatly and their conventional rockets ignited to take over the
load.

When they were slowed enough for bow and belly jets,
Dubois flipped the boat again. Once more bow on, they
approached the alien vessel, now less than a thousand kilometers away.

"We're entering the fringe," Buchanan said. "Shields firm,
hull holding nicely. Temperature's well below the redline."

She nodded. The last, they both knew, would change with
terrifying speed if the heat shields failed.

The shadow of the alien vessel enveloped them, forming a
dark tube which they traveled down. It was too much like
falling into a pit for Dubois's peace of mind.

The gentle mutterings of the passengers filled the space
between instrument chirps. Marito, seated next to Poullard,
looked annoyed, then snapped, "Would you all please be
silent." He glared around, meeting with calm aloofness even
the angry stare of Benjamin Daggit.

Dubois looked back at her passengers. "Let's stay calm,
shall we?"

Marito broke eye contact with Daggit and turned back to his
own screen. Daggit nodded acknowledgment and turned back
to Kahn.

The ensign looked the others over. Kelly So was busy
soothing Jeanine Quont. The young woman was almost pale
with fright, but wasn't making a sound. Her eyes just stared
back.

Roger Bonay fidgeted in his chair. His wife appeared angry,
as though she were about to strangle him. Once again Dubois
was struck with the oddness of the couple.

Last was Nan Poullard, her eyes cool and emotionless.
Dubois was convinced that Poullard would face Armageddon
with the same sense of detachment.

Marito looked at her. "Still nothing from the aliens, Ensign?"

He's the only one who still calls me that, she thought. *A constant reminder.*

Buchanan replied for her. "Nothing. No response to any've our signals. Maybe I should flash the forward floodlights."

"Not yet," Dubois said, turning back around. "Hit the strobe and attitude lights. We'll use the floods when we get closer." After a few minutes she said, "Still no indication that they know we're here."

The alien vessel was only a handful of kilometers away, and they slowed steadily. They were down to a crawl when they were within several hundred meters. Dubois had programmed a half-dozen escape orbits, all on display, ready to choose the one that best suited the situation. Buchanan's eyes hurt from staring at the scanning screens, and not for the last time, he was glad he had failed to take command.

Marito was not tired of staring at the alien ship, and he fervently wished he could take command and get closer, faster. He kept his desires to himself, however, watching as the starman tried again and again all conventional means of communication.

The alien vessel did nothing. The closer they came, the truer an indication of its size they got. It was two-and-a-half kilometers long, a kilometer wide. The basic shape was like the letter I, with the ends swelling into flattened barbell-like forms, one larger than the other. Dubois mentally tagged the smaller one "bow," the other "stern."

The bow came together at an edge, neatly curving into a hook reminiscent of a bird-of-prey's beak. The stern was blunt, no openings, no features. No engines were in evidence; no means of propulsion could be seen. There was a maze of assemblies jutting from the main hull, partially distorting the smooth lines, yet it all held a symmetry of design, a unity. The ship looked as though it belonged as one, each part flowing into the next with graceful, if vaguely menacing, beauty. Curves seemed to be the dominant theme of its design.

They passed under the ship bow to stern. The vessel was cocked at an off angle, where they were in deep shadow. The hull was blank, featureless, with no openings.

"I think we'll risk a sunside pass-over," Dubois said. Marito clucked his approval and Buchanan remained silent. He held his mouth shut as they came out of the vessel's shadow and into the star's full fury. The ambient temperature went up slightly while the radiant heat on the hull shot into the caution zone.

"I don't recommend much of this," he said.

"I'll make it fast," she said, goosing the stern-maneuvering jets. The lifeboat surged ahead. "Look while you can, Mr. Marito."

The Asian cursed the boat for lacking any recording ability. "We'll miss so much. Can we make another pass?"

"No." Her voice was firm. The temperature level was approaching the upper half of the caution zone. She didn't want it to rise farther.

They passed into the shadow again and Dubois slowed the boat to a crawl. She spun the boat so they were stern-on with the alien vessel, the rear cameras feeding them images. It was tricky, unnatural maneuvering, but she wanted to be able to boost straight away from the ship if necessary. Also, the engines were the nearest thing to a weapon they had.

After fifteen minutes of study it was Buchanan who made the assumption first. He said, "I think it's abandoned, empty."

Dubois spared him a glance. "A derelict?"

"Looks like it. No response to us, no lights, nothing. I've never seen a deader-looking ship."

"Young man," Marito said, "you haven't seen much. Why should they respond? Perhaps we haven't stumbled onto how they communicate. Why should there be light? Perhaps they see via infrared."

"We've tried infrared, sir," Buchanan said. "No answer. Nobody's home."

"I still say there's—"

"Put a lid on it," Dubois said. "I'm taking us in closer."

She brought them to within fifty meters of the ship. They stayed on the dark side, not risking the temperatures on the sun side again. Several times they saw what might have been portholes, but all were dark. Nothing else looked familiar, and Dubois was beginning to agree with Buchanan.

"What's that?" Daggit asked. He had been leaning over and staring at Marito's screen. Now he pointed to the lower-right corner.

Whatever had been there had already drifted out of the

camera's field of vision. Daggit gave instructions, and Dubois slowed the boat neatly to a halt, adjusting the angle. They saw a dark shadow, coming down from amidships.

"A flat space," Dubois said. "Looks like it leads to an opening."

"Was that there before?" Buchanan asked, a trace of trepidation in his voice.

Dubois shook her head. "I . . . I'm not sure."

"We might not have seen it the first time," Marito said. "We were farther away, going faster. And since we're using the stern cameras, we're seeing what the boat has already passed over, not what's coming—a different angle." He paused, staring at the screen in fascination, and whispered, "Move us closer."

"Forward floods on full," Dubois said, turning the boat. A battery of floodlights snapped on around the nose, illuminating the hull above them. It was dead black, seeming to absorb the light. It was flat, devoid of detail. The cavern beyond hung down from the ship, foreboding, a shadow-slit in the darkness. Something occasionally glinted from within.

Dubois moved the lifeboat closer and said, "Switch to spots, two and three."

The center pair of four lights shifted, changing from wide angle to narrow beam. They pierced into the cavern.

"Damnit!" Dubois yelled.

Eyes, mouths, legs—

"It's okay," Buchanan shouted, his own heart pounding. "It's okay!"

Dubois took a deep breath and fought to calm her racing pulse. What she had first perceived as some hideous monster now resolved into individual shapes—smaller vessels within the cavern, each with bulbulous windows, gaping intakes, and landing gear. She swallowed hard and said, "It . . . it's a hangar."

"Good-sized too," Buchanan said, trying to eliminate a faint tremor in his voice. "Radar scan says it goes back at least a hundred meters. It's some twenty meters high."

"Two hundred wide," finished Dubois. "The next question is, do we go in?"

"Of course we do," Marito said. "To not do so would be—"

"You're crazy," Buchanan said. "Any other time and I might agree with you, Professor, but now . . . This thing's got me spooked. Let's get the hell away from this ship and outta this system, *fast*."

Dubois's basic instincts agreed with Buchanan. She fought down her feeling of dread, whether to overcome her obvious fright of a moment before or because of her legitimate curiosity, she didn't know. And Buchanan's attitude towards the alien ship had changed very suddenly. It was apparent he was a good deal more apprehensive about it than he had let on.

The sheer jolt of their surprise, however, was spurring her on, to see what else lay ahead, if this was a derelict or not. It was a challenge and Marito's reverent enthusiasm was contagious. She could smell the fear in the lifeboat's air but there was something else as well—curiosity and a desire to *know*.

"New scan on the hangar," she said. "At least two hundred deep. Ah, a wall at 210 meters."

"Damn good-sized hangar," Daggit muttered.

Dubois brought the lifeboat to a hover not a dozen meters from the opening. Her inner conflict needed very little to resolve itself one way or the other.

Marito provided the push. "We could just go inside for a look-see. We don't have to land."

Dubois looked at the computer simulation of the hangar's interior. There was more than enough vertical clearance; the lifeboat was only four meters tall. The wings could be a problem. The widest path through the parked alien craft was not quite twenty meters. That gave two meters to a side as clearance. *Hell*, she thought, *I could fly* over *some of them*.

She decided. "Okay. A fly in, fly out."

"You're nuts," Buchanan said. "We—"

It was too late. Dubois keyed the thrusters and watched the computer move the lifeboat forward. It entered the dark a moment later.

Buchanan's fingers flew. Two secondary screens displayed the view port and starboard. All the boat's exterior lighting came on. They were a pool of radiance heading into ink.

Dubois left the main screen on forward, projecting onto it the computer display of the radar scans. Green-outlined shapes would appear on the screen before they came into the light, alien craft of a bewildering variety. The computer carefully steered around them all.

A buzzer sounded, the computer calling out in alarm. Dubois looked startled. The boat was fighting something. It fed in a touch on the nose jets, to bring the bow up, only to have it settle back down again. The stern began sinking as well. Dubois looked at the flickering readout.

"Gravity!" she said. "We're entering an external gravity field."

Automatic systems reacted faster than human hands. The ground-proximity radar triggered the landing jets while deploying the landing gear. The outside pull went from less than one percent Earth-normal to ninety-six in three seconds. The tricycle gear locked into place just in time, the lifeboat settling by the stern. The main gear hit, shocks compressing, nose coming down. The suspension sank to the limit of its travel, then relaxed, the shock of landing absorbed.

Dubois shut down the jets and sighed. "We're down, like it or not."

"Can we lift off?" Daggit asked. Kahn sat stiff at his side, apprehension on her face for the first time.

"Yes," Dubois said. "We've more than enough fuel, and the belly engines were designed for takeoffs and landings in heavier gravity fields. The thing that bothers me is—"

"Sure," Buchanan snapped. "Who the hell turned on the gravity? Satisfied, *Captain*? Just what the hell is goin' on?"

"Watch your language," she rebuked, turning to Marito. "I'd say we've just encountered an automatic system, wouldn't you, Professor?"

"I'd be inclined to agree. A logical assumption for why it came on so suddenly."

"And I don't mind touching down for a moment. Maneuvering a twenty-meter craft in tight quarters isn't exactly fun time."

"When do we get out of here?" Buchanan asked.

"In due time. It'll be tricky backing out."

Buchanan tapped fingers on controls. "Well, let me save you some time, Captain. I'll—"

The main screen image shifted as he changed from forward to rear scan, the computer-enhanced figures reappearing. They all watched in mute horror as the radar showed the opening shrinking, growing smaller, smaller . . .

My mistake! Dubois's mind screamed. *My damn curiosity.* The flat area outside bulged, the roof of the "hangar" coming down as the floor rose. The two met, like lips, and flowed together as one. A seamless seal formed, no evidence that an opening ever existed.

And Ensign Pamela Dubois raged at herself while panic fought to gain control of her passengers.

My mistake!

4

First Probe

Buchanan looked at the display and calmly said, "I think I'll scream."

Marito was cool and detached. "Please, don't."

Dubois said nothing, recalibrating the scans to confirm that the entrance was completely sealed. The entire two hundred meter width was solid, not a crack anywhere.

There was one short scream from Jeanine Quont, quickly hushed by So. Roger Bonay took it as a cue, standing and yelling, "You got us trapped in here." He pointed at Dubois. "It's your fault! If you—"

Daggit stood, turned, and backhanded Bonay back down into his seat. He sat back down as a completion of the motion, somehow maintaining an air of dignity. Hilary Kahn bit her upper lip and managed to flash Dubois a thumbs-up.

Dubois ignored the short ruckus and asked, "What now?"

Buchanan managed to keep most of the bitterness out of his voice. "You're asking? As the man said, this was your idea. Why don't you *tell* us?"

Dubois suppressed a flash of anger and nodded. She unfastened her harness and stood, looking them over. "Stay in your seats. I don't want anybody moving around."

She walked by them, towards the boat's stern. Buchanan and Marito ignored her order and followed.

"What're you doin'?" Buchanan asked.

She ignored him. At the stern she worked the storeroom hatch control and the panel slid aside. She stepped in, closing and locking the door in Buchanan's face.

Dubois looked the compartment over. More room had been created by shifting crates out into the boat's main area. The sink had been rigged, and she could see the attachments for shower and toilet nearby. She paid them little attention, reaching instead for a T-shaped handle that hung on the wall.

The hook end went into a floor slot, and she pulled. The panel opened easily, pneumatic arms hissing and pushing it out of the way. Revealed were five boxes of three different sizes. She pulled out one of the triplicates, a meter long and half that high and wide, and laid it on the remaining deck space. She opened a fourth box where it lay and inspected its contents: six basic hand lasers.

"I hate these things," she muttered. Like any spacefarer, though, she could handle one with deadly familiarity. She removed one from the locker and clipped it to a wall. She closed the box and merely glanced at the fifth box before resealing the floor. Its label was plain, bold red letters screaming, WARNING! EXPLOSIVES!

I hope we won't need those. The panel locked back into place.

Opening the crate revealed a folded and compacted service pressure suit. There was no room to provide suits for everyone, so the designers had equipped the boat with three, two for the crew members and one extra. It was lightweight, not at all like a regular working spacesuit. Lacking the armor supports, it was a multilayer jumpsuit, complete with twist-lock boots, gloves, and hardhat. A life-support backpack, chest radio and control box, and a hip tool kit, completed the suit.

Wishing for combat armor, she began stripping off her bright orange boat's suit. Finished, she began checking out the pressure suit and the tedious task of sizing it for herself.

The door opened again twenty minutes later. Buchanan stared at the suited figure and shook his head. "You're nuts. What're you gonna do out there?"

The faceplate was open and conversation was easy. Dubois

was still running the internal safety checks, and spoke
absentmindedly. "I'm going to check the entranceway first, see
if there aren't some controls to reopen it. If so, *you*, Buchanan,
are going to back this boat out of here. I'll join you outside."

"And what if there aren't any, or what if they don't work?"

"Then I go the other direction, to the wall in front of us now,
and see what I can see. Hopefully I'll provoke some sort of
reaction from whoever's operating this ship."

"Sure," he sneered. "Like a laser through the face plate."

She regarded him with cool, green eyes. "Perhaps."

"I concur with your course of action, Captain Dubois,"
Marito said, a slight emphasis on the rank. "I wish to come
along."

She shook her head, twisting her entire body for emphasis.
"No. I appreciate your concurrence but don't need it. Nor do I
need you along to slow me up in case of anything sudden."

"I assure you that I—"

"*No*. Starman, let's set up the lock."

Their dining table was next to the main hatchway and had to
be moved. Then they began assembling the temporary struc-
ture. It had last been used for the disposal of their dead.

Prefab panels slipped into place, toggles squeezing them
together. Their edges molded to each other under the pressure,
forming a crude but effective seal. It was improvisation of the
rankest sort, meant only for emergency use.

Halfway through, Buchanan told Dubois to step aside and let
the others finish. She was too clumsy in the pressure suit and
was only slowing matters.

She watched them work, and noted for the first time how
silly they tended to look, all wearing identical orange jump-
suits. Mrs. Bonay's paunch was almost embarrassingly empha-
sized, while Hilary Kahn's breasts were made even more
prominent. Despite each of them having their own individuali-
ty in the suits, they still appeared to be stamped from the same
mold.

An assortment of clowns. She smiled to herself. Every suit in
the boat was the same bright orange, visibility being the
overriding factor in their design. They looked like a Day-Glo
party.

The lock was finished in short order. Buchanan closed the
hinged inner door and pressurized the container to twice
normal capacity. He looked at the readouts and was satisfied,

depressurizing it to normal and opening the door. He stepped aside.

"I still think you're nuts," he said.

"So do I," she agreed.

She opened one of the overhead racks and pulled out one last piece of equipment. It was forty-five centimeters long, a tube joining a ten-centimeter ball and a thirteen-centimeter box. The front of the ball held a wide-angle lens, the rear of the box a seven-by-ten screen. The front-bottom of the box sloped to provide an easy handhold on the connecting tube. A short thong acted as a wrist strap.

She turned on the scanwand and made a quick check. It was a combination light and scanner, capable of reading over a large portion of the spectrum, from infrared to ultraviolet. It was also an environmental monitor, complete with a "bad air" warning and a radio tracer. It was easily the most sophisticated piece of portable equipment they had, and the lifeboat carried six. Dubois had once been told that, given nothing else, a person stood a very good chance of surviving on an unknown world with the scanwand alone.

She clipped the wand to her left thigh, then reached back into the storeroom, pulling out the laser and attaching it to her right thigh.

Marito looked aghast at the weapon. "You can't—"

Dubois was in no mood for a moral debate and snapped, "I can."

Buchanan handed her a short, folded ladder as she stepped into the airlock. He patted her on the shoulder and, when she looked, mouthed silently, "Good luck." She managed a feeble smile in return.

She pulled the door closed and sealed it. Her heart pounded harder than ever as she flipped down her faceplate and started cycling the lock.

Most of the air was pumped back into the boat, but the system was not wholly efficient. When she opened the outer doors, she felt a minor tugging as the last traces of atmosphere were swept out into the hangar's vacuum.

She looked about her, into the darkness beyond the pool of the boat's lights. The strangeness of where she was hit her for the first time, her mouth suddenly dry. This was no remote image; this was a reality separated from her only by a centimeter's thickness of Duraglas.

She knew she should leave the lock immediately. The

makeshift panels around the door formed an airlock only in the strictest sense. They could hold out the vacuum for a while, but within seconds leaks would begin to form, allowing the boat's atmosphere to bleed off. She looked around her, at the floor and corner cracks, and could see a few wisps of vapor already drifting by.

Licking her lips, Dubois stepped out onto the port wing storage pod. It had a slip-proof cover and was fitted with small steps. She stepped down twice and was on the port wing. Reaching back, she hit the lock controls, the doors sliding shut without a sound.

Her first duty was to the boat. She noted that the huge triangular wing had deployed perfectly, forming a smooth seal with the round, faired pod. The main hull width was not enough to contain the wings, one laying on top of the other, so the pods had been added to make up the difference. They flowed smoothly into the leading edge strakes near the bow, adding more lift surface. It typified the boat's design: simple and efficient.

Dubois followed the wing's marked walkway to its trailing edge. Two slots were there for the ladder. It was a two-meter drop to the alien deck. Extended, the ladder was not quite three meters in length, providing a slant of sorts for ease of use. She unfolded it and locked it into place and . . .

. . . hesitated. *C'mon*, she told herself, *you can't stall forever.*

"Hello, hello. Radio check, Cap'n."

She nearly jumped out of her suit. Calming down, she replied, "The radio works, *Starman*. Keep off the channel!"

"Aye, ma'am."

She went down the ladder quickly, hesitating again at the bottom rung. *Now or never!*

She stepped down. The sensation through the insulated boot was disconcerting. The floor sagged away from her, unsupportive. She looked down, expecting to see depressions in the decking where her feet were. She was surprised to see flat, solid flooring. Still, the sensation persisted.

She squatted, grabbing her scanwand. Flicking on the light, she studied the floor. It seemed to be made up of a fine grid, full of holes, even and symmetrical in size and shape. She pushed a gloved finger against it. The sensation of yielding was there, yet the finger bent, as if meeting a solid.

"Bizarre," she muttered. Her suit's tool kit held an

assortment of items, and she pulled out a long screwdriver. The end was thin enough to fit through the grid, and she used it as a probe. It stopped after only a few millimeters, and she shined the light for a closer look. The tool hit nothing visible.

"Bizarre and bizarre."

Straightening, she replaced the tool and looked up at the lifeboat. The lights were bright and glaring but she could still see that the hull itself was as clean and intact as the day it had left the assembly line. The light glare caused her faceplate to polarize, dimming her vision, and she looked away.

Dead astern was her destination, and she began walking in that direction. She looked back at the assortment of drive nozzles, from conventional fuel to free-hydrogen, and they all appeared okay. She walked slowly, waving her light from side to side. She kept her right hand free and loose by the laser.

She had 170 meters to go, avoiding strange, alien craft. She stopped to study only one. It looked like a bulged, bug-eyed fish of the greater depths. The shape was unsettling, and she moved on.

Her radio bleeped for attention. She said, "Damn," and switched it on. "Yeah?"

"Buchanan and company here. Where are you?"

"About fifty meters astern. Can't you see me?"

"Negative. We're getting lens flare from our lights."

"Kill the stern array. I'll wave my torch."

She watched as the rear floodlights faded out, then waved her scanwand's light at the boat. Buchanan yelled in her ears, "Cap'n, above you!"

Dubois reacted in a convulsion, knees collapsing, laser coming up, light tracking to show a target—

—which wasn't there. She frowned and looked closer, turning her light away. A patch of yellow illuminance was hanging an indeterminable distance above her. She slowly straightened, holding her laser's aim steady, and activated the scanner.

"What is it?" Buchanan demanded.

"Nothing. As far as I can tell, it's a grid of some sort crisscrossing above me. No apparent wires. Where it intersects, it glows. It's a lighting system." She stepped to one side. "It follows me."

"So we can see. We can see it move. And barely see you."

A thought struck her, and she looked at the lifeboat. "Kevin, kill all external lighting."

The lights vanished without a sound, leaving the boat illuminated by a patch of yellow light from above, one slightly larger than the boat itself. She smiled. "You've got lights too. Our floods drown the yellow light out."

Buchanan laughed nervously. "Okay. Take it easy now."

"Sure." Dubois turned her torch back on as the boat's lights returned to life. She resumed her walk towards the sealed entrance.

She arrived there several minutes later. Where the gaping entrance had been was now a smooth wall. It climbed away from her, up to an unseen ceiling overhead, curving down into the floor, forming a graceful shape and showing not a seam, not a crack, not a sharp line. She looked from left to right. Any search here was useless.

She had brought the lifeboat into the hangar just left of its centerline. Therefore the left wall was marginally closer and her next destination.

She almost missed it. It curved gently into the vanished entrance. There was no break, no corner. Only that damnable, continuing curve. Dubois flashed her light on high ahead of her and along the wall to the right. It almost totally absorbed the beam. Enough was reflected to show it was there. Radar scans beyond thirty meters were distorted, possibly also absorbed by the metal.

"Dead end, Kevin," she reported. "No controls here." She described how thoroughly the entrance was sealed.

"I don't see much point in your going to the forward wall," he said. "C'mon back."

"Negative. I'll finish the mission."

"You make it sound like something that has to be done. Get back here. Let *them* make the next move."

She ignored him, walking swiftly. The lifeboat was her orientation. She kept the wall to her left, and when she had completed enough of a circle to put her in front of the boat, she knew she had arrived.

"I'm at the forward bulkhead," she said. "Totally feature-less. I'm going to walk to the other side."

"I've got you on radar, Cap'n. Take it easy."

The lights from the boat provided some illumination, being

less than thirty meters away. She waved her light once and
started walking. Almost immediately she found the first
marking.

It was a broad stripe on the wall, extending from floor to
ceiling. It was half a meter wide and a rich shade of brown.
Dubois shrugged and dismissed it as nothing important.

Half a meter away was another one, this one a third thinner.
And another, and so on.

Strobe striping, she thought.

She stepped away from the wall, torch shining towards it.
The stripes grew very thin, the gap between each shrinking in
proportion. They were barely several millimeters thick for a
while, then began to grow broad once more, ending with one
identical to the first.

"Something strange here," she said, describing the striping
and finishing, "I think they mark something. I'm going to
where they're thinnest."

"Keep clear, Cap'n. Don't take stupid chances."

She was at the wall, annoyed with Buchanan's mother hen
attitude. "What chances?" she asked, reaching out and
touching the wall. "What can—"

They should have had her on visual, only the cameras
weren't equipped with hoods and were picking up too much
flare. Buchanan was watching the main screen, the computer
image from the radar.

And from that screen she vanished. There was a flicker, then
she seemed to fall away, fading out as she went. Buchanan
stiffened, and shouted over the radio. No one answered.

"She's found a door," Marito said, maddeningly calm.

Buchanan whirled towards him. "A *door*? Who opened it?
What got her?"

He looked at the others, his own fear reflected in their eyes
as they looked at him for some sort of leadership. *Oh, hell*—

He jumped away from the console and jogged towards the
stern. There were two more suits. . . .

"Wait, Starman," Marito said. "You can't—"

Buchanan wasn't listening. All he knew was that Dubois, a
fellow crew member and the boat's captain, was gone. His
terror of what the alien ship held in store was matched by the
terror that, with her gone, *he* would be in command.

He had to find her.

• • •

Dubois picked herself up off the floor and made sure her suit was still intact. The last she remembered was touching the striped wall and pushing to see if it, too, felt yielding to the touch. It turned out to be more than that. Her arm had gone through the wall. Balance gone, the rest of her had tumbled after.

She flashed her torch around. The room was an oval ten meters long. The ceiling was three meters overhead, with the same yellow lights. Ceiling and walls all curved together and into the floor, a grid identical to the hangar's. Striping that matched that on the other side covered the wall she had fallen through.

"An entrance," she muttered. More cautious this time, she touched the wall. Her finger went through, then her arm. She pulled back out and smiled. A closer look showed that there was a wall but that it retreated from her touch. It flowed around her finger, forming a seal yet allowing it through. She was willing to bet it was airtight.

She looked at her scanwand, checking it for anything new, and her eyebrows arched in surprise. She was no longer in a vacuum. The pressure around her was fifty percent Earth-normal, a steady five hundred millibars. She had no idea what sort of atmosphere made up that pressure, breathable or deadly, but it confirmed one thing: the seal *was* airtight.

An airlock without the wait.

The other side of the room held three gaping openings, and she held her curiosity in check. Buchanan and the others were probably in hysterics. The wall must cut off radio signals or she would have heard from him by now.

"Kevin?" she tested. "Do you read me?"

She got what she expected: nothing. Swallowing an irrational fear, she pushed through the "wall" and back into the hangar. Everything seemed the same there. She smiled at the striping, then radioed, "Kevin, this is Dubois. I'm okay."

Another voice replied, "Daggit here, Captain. I'm afraid Starman Buchanan and Mr. Marito are in a bit of a row at the moment. Kevin went to suit up when you fell off our screens. Oh, here he—"

Buchanan's voice cut through, biting. "What the hell happened?"

"I found a door," she said. "The room beyond is obviously

a staging area for shuttle pilots and personnel. There are probably lockers and such hidden away somewhere. There are three doorways. I'm going back to try one."

"*No!*"

The sheer insistence in his voice stopped her. "What was that?"

"I said no. You don't go. You *can't* go."

"Are you going to stop me?"

"No, you're going to stop yourself, once you start thinking properly. You're alone. That was fine as long as you were on our screens. On the other side of that wall, though, you're gone. Remember your basic survival guide, Cap'n. Don't wander around alone. Either myself or one of the others goes with you. We'll move the boat closer to the wall and a third person will stay in that room as liaison. Evidently radio is cut off by the wall, so we'll have to rig something. If we're lucky, those on the other side of the bulkhead will be able to communicate well enough."

Dubois hesitated and found herself nodding. "All right, Kevin. I'm coming in."

She turned to the boat and began walking, her suit rustling about her. She—

—stopped. She raised a hand and slapped her thigh. She heard the fabric crinkle inside her suit, but she also heard the meaty "slap" from outside, through the helmet sound disks.

Dubois brought her scanwand's readouts up to eye level in a hurry. A light was flashing and she could *hear* the alert tone. That should have been impossible. Sound does not travel in a vacuum.

Except that she was no longer in a vacuum. The scanwand was reading an atmosphere. The hangar was being pressurized.

"Kevin," she said softly, sounds around her becoming clearer as the pressure increased. "Kevin?"

His response was hesitant. He was watching the same thing occur on his instruments. "Y-yes?"

"I'm getting a positive pressure reading out here. Do you confirm?" A silly question, but she had to ask.

"Affirmative. Get back in here!"

This time she didn't argue. She hurried for the lifeboat, the alien ship coming to life around her.

5

Opinions and Debates

Dubois stretched out over one of their cots, the privacy panels removed, and sighed with relief. After the time in the pressure suit, wearing nothing but her underwear felt indecently good. Her body itched at contact with free air, and she luxuriated in the sensation.

"How's the pressure?" she asked, accepting a cup of broth from Poullard.

"Steady at 920 millibars," Buchanan said. "If we can breathe it, the pressure's fine."

"Have you got an air sample yet?"

"In the can now. Should have an answer in five minutes."

"Even if we can't breathe it," Dubois said, "we might be able to get by with just breather masks. We've lot of those."

Buchanan grunted agreement. If the air was unfit to breathe, he doubted if he would trust it rubbing against his skin.

Sensing she had loafed just enough, Dubois pulled herself around and up to her feet. She went forward and slipped into the command chair, looking at the center-pedestal computer screen. Buchanan followed and took the right-hand seat. Marito squatted in the doorway. Dubois looked at the Asian, smiling at the anxious expression on his face.

Buchanan saw it, too, and said, "You look ecstatic, Professor. May I ask why?"

"Certainly. If this atmosphere appears to be nonlethal, I can step out of this cylinder and explore. Astronomy is my hobby, the possibility of extraterrestrials my passion. And to actually *meet* one . . ." His voice trailed off.

Dubois shook her head. "Don't get your hopes up too high. Everything that's occurred so far could be still-functioning automatic systems."

"Even so, this is a once in a lifetime opportunity. I shall not waste it."

"What if all this isn't automatic?" Buchanan asked. "What then?"

"If it's not, then we say, 'Take us to your leader.'" She smiled at her own joke and went on, "Acutally, if this *isn't* all on automatic, I'd like to know why our 'hosts' haven't shown themselves yet."

Marito seemed posed to give an explanation when the computer chimed and the atmospheric analysis flowed onto the screen. He mumbled to himself, reading the figures, and leaned backwards, oval face round with astonishment. "Oh, my. This is . . . is a little . . ." He was unable to finish.

Buchanan said it for him. "This is flat-out impossible. Too much of a coincidence. Impossible."

Dubois read the figures, then again. There was no mistake, the computer responding to the double-check with the same display. The air outside the boat was breathable. More than that, it was perfectly so. Nothing was out of place, the proportions in exact balance for human life.

"I think your statement is unwarranted, Starman Buchanan," she said, seeking a moment's distraction in officialdom. "It is, therefore it is possible."

"Can you just stick to callin' me Kevin?" he complained, adding, "But even . . . sure, their air is our air. Naw, no, the odds are too great."

"I concur," Marito said. "When I said if the air was nonlethal, I meant that it would not kill on contact with our skin. But this . . . This ship is occupied. They've analyzed our air somehow and mixed an atmosphere that is appropriate."

"More than just 'appropriate,'" Buchanan muttered.

"How did they do that?" Dubois asked. "Where would they get a sample?"

There was a moment's pause, then she answered her own question. "Of course, when I went outside. The air that couldn't be pumped back into the boat, plus leaks."

Buchanan nodded. "Yeah, but that isn't much, especially in all that volume."

Marito mumbled, "It only indicates fantastic equipment."

"Pressure," Dubois said. "That was the clue. The pressure on the other side of that wall was only fifty percent normal. In here it's now nearly a hundred percent. When I went through their 'door,' they must have gotten a pressure reading somehow."

"Through a suit?" Buchanan asked, doubtful.

"The wall squeezes around the suit and measures the resistance." She pulled on her lower lip. "And it could be automated."

Dubois stood and went to the rear of the lifeboat, calling back, "What's the temperature outside, Kevin?"

He read the scale. "It's a warm twenty-four degrees Celsius out there and still goin' up."

She stepped into the airlock and closed the inner door, sealing it. She didn't bother to cycle the lock. One motion and the outer door slid aside. A swift shift in pressure and the hanger lay revealed before her.

The air was warm, several degrees hotter than the lifeboat's standard twenty degrees. She realized she was holding her breath, and forced herself to exhale. A long pause, then a deep breath in . . .

"It smells wonderful," she said.

"Good," Buchanan said. The inner door was open and he stood behind her, the others clumped behind.

Bloody fool, she thought, but kept the reprimand to herself. She smiled. "I was going to put my uniform back on, but if the temperature keeps going up—"

"Over thirty now and seems to be leveling out."

"—that would be suicidal," she finished. "I suggest that everyone gets comfortable."

Buchanan was already down to shorts and undershirt. He had clipped on a utility belt with scanwand and laser. He jumped down to the wing, then slipped off the leading edge, bouncing onto the alien deck. Dubois watched his reaction, amused.

"Damn strange," he said, bouncing on the balls of his feet.

"That's what I thought, but it doesn't seem to yield visibly, and that makes it stranger still."

He made a scan around them. "This thing hasn't the range for clear resolution in here. Temperature is steady at three-one degrees. Hot, but livable." He looked at the boat. "You inspect the hull?"

"Only peripherally. Let me get a belt and I'll join you."

"Isn't this a bit dangerous, exposing ourselves to whatever's on board?" Roger Bonay asked. "I mean, they may be hostile."

"*If* there's anyone here," his wife said. "I agree with the captain. I think this is all automated."

"A trifle beyond our technology," Daggit said.

"Not as far as you might imagine. And who says we're the best?"

"Not I. I think we're the worst."

Mr. Bonay sniffed loudly and returned to the boat's interior. Marito pushed by those at the lock and jumped down, landing awkwardly on the deck and falling. Lisa Bonay didn't hesitate, and was down immediately to help him up.

"Thank you. I shouldn't have been so anxious."

"Think nothing of it," she said. "You okay?"

"Fine, fine."

Buchanan walked around the stern, frowning. "Don't play athlete. Use the ladder." He turned and walked towards the bow.

Dubois came out of the boat and down the ladder. She was wearing a jumpsuit, sleeves pushed up, all too aware that she should have dressed immediately. She was in command and appearances were everything.

Roll with it, she thought. Scanwand in hand, she circled the stern, looking the engines over again.

Kelly So and Jeanine Quont climbed out of the lifeboat and stood out on the wing, careful to stay within the marked walkway. They looked about the dark interior in wonderment. They held hands, So not about to let her go, as much for his own comfort as for hers.

"Do you think we'll meet anyone?" she asked, voice low and soft.

"I don't know whether to hope so or not," he said. He hoped he sounded confident enough. "This is a trifle beyond me."

"Beyond him," Kahn said quietly, standing in the hatchway with Daggit. "Imagine how it is for us, eh, Ben?"

The old man smiled, eyes twinkling. "Nothing's beyond us, Hilary. Nothing, that is, except some unseen aliens."

"If there are any."

"Yes, there is that."

She looked thoughtful. "You know, I'm not as afraid as I was."

And he looked surprised. "*You* were afraid?"

"Please! Seriously, if there's air to breathe here and light, there must be power. If we can explore this ship, we might be able to use it to get home. And if there's a crew, they might be willing to lend a hand."

Daggit shrugged. "I only cater meals, ma'am, but if you find me a garden, I can grow you some vegetables."

She dimpled. "It's a deal."

Marito looked up at Daggit. "A garden? I don't—" He stopped, squinting to cut down the glare from the boat's lights. Mrs. Bonay noted the gesture.

"What is it?" she asked.

"The . . . lights . . ."

She looked. "They looked okay to me. Is a bulb burning out?"

"No," he whispered. "Not ours. *The ship's.*"

She could barely see the illumination grid above them. "What about them?"

"Ensign Dubois would notice. They've shifted spectrum, less yellow and more white, like our own."

Mrs. Bonay stepped away from the boat several paces and looked up again, a pattern of yellow-white light above her. "You're right, and it's glowing brighter too; larger."

Dubois and Buchanan came jogging around the boat's stern. Dubois waved at Marito and Bonay. "Come on. Back aboard."

Marito came, but protesting. "Why? What's the problem?"

"Like everything else here. We don't know what's going on."

She watched Buchanan scurry up the ladder and hustle So and Quont into the boat. She motioned Bonay up first, then Marito, following him after a brief pause for a last look around.

As Bonay went by Buchanan and through the hatch, he

pointed to a far corner. "We noticed the lights changing color and brightening. Something glowed over there, so—"

Marito stopped and turned. As the three of them looked towards the corner, it pulsed into glowing life. There was a soft and silent explosion of light, rippling out from the corner to all sides of the hangar. The ceiling was awash with soft, white light, destroying the shadows and overpowering their flood-lights.

Dubois looked about in silent amazement, and Marito fairly cooed with delight. Buchanan automatically held his laser at the ready, scanwand shifted towards the near wall. The striped "doorway" was now plainly visible, brown bands on an ebony wall.

The floor was black, the walls were black, the hulls of the alien ships around them black. The only light came from above. It hit the walls and vanished, never reflected. Only those brown bands clearly defined the wall. The other dimensions could be seen where the ceiling light ended.

"I don't think we need the boat lights now," Marito quietly commented. "The energy grid lights will be enough."

"The what?" asked Buchanan.

"Lines of energy, of current, crisscross overhead. When they meet, they cause an incandescence in the air. A light bulb not requiring a vacuum bulb around the filament, nor any metal as a filament."

Dubois stepped farther out onto the wing, laser still on her hip. She aimed her scanwand at the striping, taking a reading, and said, "I want to know who turned on the lights."

"Automated?" Marito sneered. "I thought you were con-vinced there was no one on board."

"I'm not convinced of anything, Mr. Marito. Nor do I want to assume anything." She looked at him oddly, with a tilted grin. "Unlike you."

Marito looked puzzled by her tone. She continued, "You know the old adage. When you *assume* something you make an 'ass' out of 'u' and 'me.'" Her expression froze. "Don't *assume*, Mr. Marito."

Marito's face contorted. Buchanan stepped between them and asked, "What's our next move, Cap'n?"

"As I outlined before. We organize an exploration team, plus a relay comunications team in the room on the other side of that wall."

"Er, *my* idea, Cap'n," he gently reminded.

She smiled at him. "Not any more."

"Who goes?" Marito asked, all too eager.

"I should go with the exploration team," he protested. "Some other fool can tend the boat."

Dubois shook her head. "No, Mr. Marito. Between all of us, only you, Kevin, and myself can successfully pilot and navigate this lifeboat. As Kevin is in charge of the radio team, and I'm leading the exploration, that leaves you back here. Is that clear?"

"Appallingly."

She left him, disgruntled, at the control consoles. The others stood in the dining area, waiting for her. Dubois modestly pulled up the zipper of her jumpsuit. *On stage, on stage, forever up for review.* She had never fully comprehended what it meant to command. She wasn't enjoying the experience. She was leading the exploration as much as to get away from their stares as to find out who, or what, was aboard. *Maybe I'll go alone.*

She checked over her supplies a third time. A small backpack would carry some food concentrates, a water tank (with a feed tube attached to her shoulder), plus a radio set. A utility belt with tools, scanwand, and the inevitable laser, would complete the outfit. Another, duplicate set was waiting for whomever she chose to bring along.

"I still think I should be the one wandering around," Buchanan said.

RHIP, she thought. *Rank Has Its Privileges, and this is* my *escape.* She said, "Don't play hero, Kevin. You've got a cautious streak that can get this boat out of here, if need be."

"Naw, I'm just a coward."

She grinned and looked at the others. So and Quont were too young, despite the boy's academy training; forget them. Daggit was too old and Kahn appeared to have no intention of leaving him alone. Nan Poullard had been shy and quiet the entire journey, keeping much (too much) to herself. Dubois couldn't count on her.

That left Roger and Lisa Bonay. She looked at the husband and said, "I assume you're in good shape."

"You go to hell," he said. "I'm not going anywhere out there!"

Before Dubois could say anything, Lisa Bonay spoke up, voice and tone biting. "That's *it*, you sonuvabitch. The party's over. You're fired!" She turned to the uncomprehending Dubois and said, "I'm your helper, Cap'n."

Dubois shook her head. "I can't—"

"You can. My name's not Lisa Bonay and this is *not* my husband. His real name is Roger Forsythe and mine's Frances Tyler."

Buchanan's face lit up with understanding. "So *that's* why you worked so well on the instrument panels with us. Tyler, of Tyler Instrumentals. You make most of the equipment for this boat."

"Damn right, and I test it all personally." She turned to Dubois. "The charade allows me to move about more freely than I otherwise could. As it was, a rival contractor recognized me back aboard the *Goddess*. I would have been stymied on Earth when we arrived."

Dubois nodded and smiled. "Well, I can't argue with your credentials, but this makes you even less eligible. I can't risk someone as—"

"Can it! I'm not dead yet, and I'm already out of contact with my company, which no doubt assumes that I *am* dead." She grabbed the suit. "Now, where can I change?"

It was a nonsensical question as all of them knew the interior layout, her especially. It succeeded in gaining a grin from Buchanan.

But Dubois was not amused. She waved a hand at Tyler's paunch. "I don't think it will fi—"

The engineer thumped the "fat" and proudly said, "The best padding money can buy."

Dubois yielded to the inevitable and nodded. Tyler looked about theatrically, then pointed at the storeroom. "Ah, that will do nicely."

Suit in hand, she went to change.

6

Explorations

The four of them stood near the striped wall. Dubois poked the probe end of her scanwand through and looked at the readout.

"Ninety-two percent normal," she said. "Same pressure as here."

"But is it breathable?" Tyler asked. She shifted her backpack to a more comfortable position. With the padding removed, she had shed fifteen years of age. She was Dubois's height, just a shade heavier, and very muscular. Frances Tyler was known as one of the most cutthroat corporate executives alive, with an equal reputation for fairness and honesty. She simply had no compunction about putting a competitor out of business.

While Dubois was happy to have her along, she was also worried that the engineer might try and take over. Tyler had more experience with the unknown; as she had said, she tested her company's equipment personally. So far, however, she seemed content to let Dubois lead. The ensign almost wished she would take over.

She blinked, remembering Tyler's question, and said, "Only a sample will tell."

Buchanan said, "It should be. Whoever, whatever, pressurized this hangar knew how to mix an atmosphere for us."

"Yes, *here*, but there was an atmosphere on the other side of this wall before there was here. Would they flood their entire ship with *our* air?"

Buchanan had no quick reply. Dubois pulled on a breather mask, an addition to their equipment Tyler had recommended, and adjusted the gas-tight goggles. She took several experimental breaths, confirming that the regulator functioned properly. Tyler did the same, and everybody checked everybody else's equipment.

Kahn, who had volunteered to stay with Buchanan, said, "What do we do if . . . if something happens to you?"

"Simple," Dubois said, voice muffled by the mask. "Do nothing except run like hell for the boat. Kevin, it'll be up to you to get out of here any way you can. Ram that door or cut through with a laser. Just get them out of here."

He gave a mock salute. "Aye, aye, Cap'n."

Dubois nodded curtly, then pushed through the wall. The sensation was much clearer without the padding of a pressure suit. The wall material clung to her as she crossed its boundary, caressing and just short of clawing. It did not impede her movement, just . . . fondled.

Tyler followed her through. She looked back at the wall, then at Dubois. "*That* was . . . odd."

"To say the least. I didn't feel it so clearly before."

Tyler activated the test kit they had brought along and watched it cycle through its function. She looked frustrated. "This will only tell us oxygen content, not if there's something fatal in the air. It'll be a risk one way or another."

The box winked green. Dubois said, "So the oxygen content's okay."

She reached up and cracked her mask off a bit, taking one deep breath before slipping it back into place. She looked at Tyler. "Seems okay, like the air in the hangar."

"As far as my earlier question is concerned, it seems that our 'hosts' have indeed filled their entire ship with *our* air."

Dubois nodded and pulled her mask off completely. "I think it's okay."

Tyler watched for a few moments, then followed form and breathed deeply. "*Smells* fine."

Dubois laughed. "I'll trust your nose more than mine." She turned and pushed her upper torso back through the wall. "Hello, Kevin."

Buchanan blanched at the head and chest poking from the wall. "That, er, looks a bit, uh, strange, Cap'n."

She smiled. "You and Hilary can come through now."

A small base was set up in the staging room. It was as well lit as the hangar, and Buchanan and Kahn had brought along chairs for comfort. The radio set was placed near the wall; an antenna poked back into the hangar. For further orientation, the radio also mounted a homing beacon.

Dubois and Tyler each carried a half-dozen transceiver relays, four-centimeter balls with adhesive on one side. They would drop one at each intersection if they changed course. The balls would relay their signals, maintaining a continuous line-of-sight communications chain. They were their electronic version of bread crumbs.

"We'll try and keep this walk to an hour," Dubois said. "That should let us explore a healthy bit. Let me repeat myself: under no circumstances will you come in after us, unless it's because one of us was fool enough to break a leg. And even then get someone else to come in with you, so that there is always someone by the radio here. Understood?"

Buchanan restrained an argument and nodded. Dubois turned to Tyler. "I think we're ready."

Tyler made sure her air mask was secured to one side, and said, "I think so. Which one?"

Dubois looked at the three entrances. "We're facing the bow now. It seems logical that the center way would go the farthest forward. We'll take that one."

The duo stepped into the corridor. It was pitch-black, not continuously lit. Dubois flashed her torch ahead, the beam mostly swallowed by the walls. She controlled a nervous shudder and stepped forward. Above her a patch of soft white light appeared, acting like those earlier in the hangar. Tyler followed her in and they moved ahead, the light flowing with them.

Hilary watched them go and shuddered, remembering the crawling sensation coming through the wall had given her. "I think they're nuts," she said.

Buchanan nodded. "Sure they are. So am I." He turned to her and smiled. "You play cards?"

• • •

The corridor would have driven a claustrophobic insane. It was not quite two meters high and perfectly circular. Even the floor was curved. It was smooth, featureless, and dead black. The spot of light, the room behind them, grew steadily smaller.

Dubois subconsciously counted her steps. After the fiftieth one they came to a striped section. She looked at Tyler. "Another door?"

"Probably, assuming the owners of this ship have any sense of logic."

Dubois faced the section. It was much smaller than the one in the hangar, the stripes starting thinner and shrinking to a single millimeter. She reached out and pushed at the center. Her hand went through smoothly. Just as quickly she jerked it out, disgust and fear on her face.

"What?" Tyler asked.

"Cold, freezing cold." She rubbed her fingers, restoring warmth, then carefully poked the scanning end of her wand through. An instant later the screen flashed answers.

"Perfect vacuum, no air at all," she said. "I think this is a warning. Always probe first."

Tyler nodded and the two went on. They passed other "doors," all having a cold, hard vacuum on the other side. Every few minutes they made a radio and beacon check. Both signals came in strong. Dubois ignored all intersections they came to, preferring to stay on a straight course as long as possible.

The dark remained constant ahead and behind them. Just as the monotony began to sink in, they came to another striped section, this one on both sides of the corridor and pointing upwards. The stripes appeared to join on the ceiling, above the lights.

Dubois pushed against the wall. It was solid. "I don't understand."

Tyler pointed upwards and performed the honors, slowly reaching up with her scanwand. It went through the light grid with no interference, cutting off some of the light. It probed through the ceiling.

Digits danced on the readout. It showed a positive pressure, right on the expected ninety-two percent level.

She turned to Dubois. "Well, it—"

The wand was jerked through the ceiling. It broke from Tyler's grasp almost immediately, but by then her forearm had gone through. Whatever had grabbed the scanner now had her. In one convulsion she was gone.

"Tyler!" Dubois yelled, forgetting the open radio circuit.

Buchanan hissed painfully and asked, "What happened?"

"Unknown. Tyler made a check through the ceiling here and something yanked her through."

"Get out of there, Cap'n!"

Dubois shook her head. "I can't leave her—"

"Your own orders, Cap'n. Get out of there!"

"She could be alive. She got a positive pressure reading just before . . . just before . . ."

"Get back here."

"No can do," Dubois said, suddenly calm. She pulled her laser. Taking a firm grasp, she slowly pushed her scanwand up and through. The screen flashed positive air pressure, then there was a yank and she was through, climbing upwards at a bewildering rate.

"Kevin?" she called. "Kevin, do you read me?"

Silence. The walls were blocking her transmission. She looked above her, lights racing on all sides to keep up with her. She shined the torch ahead but it didn't get very far. She shifted to radar and looked in horror as, on screen, a wall appeared and she was going towards it at—

She eased to a stop and stepped out onto an open area, the "wall" the ceiling overhead. Tyler was there, pale and breathing hard. She looked up at the ensign and said, "That beats the hell out of any amusement ride I've ever even *seen*."

Trying to calm her own pounding heart, Dubois only nodded. "Must be some kind of elevator." The exit was an open hole in the floor. She noticed Tyler's scanwand hovering in midair and grabbed it.

"How do we get down?" Tyler asked.

A few meters away was another hole. Dubois took out a relay and tossed it in. It vanished swiftly. She very carefully leaned over and watched the tiny patch of light follow it down.

"Maybe we'll get radio contact with Buchanan now," Tyler said.

Dubois took another look down the shaft. The ball was gone. "I hope so."

"What'll we do?" Hilary asked. She was dancing from foot to foot, glancing now and again towards the middle doorway, half expecting something bug-eyed and horrible to come slithering out. "What'll we do?"

Buchanan was at the corridor and frowning. "Pamela, do you read me? Captain, just click the circuit if I'm getting through. Hellohello."

"It's no use," Hilary said. "They're . . . they're gone."

Buchanan didn't argue with her. Now he had to make a decision: obey Dubois's last order or go in after her. He felt that same sinking sensation. *I can't command!*

"Dubois to Buchanan, Dubois to Buchanan, do you copy?"

The starman sighed, openly relieved. "Roger on that, Cap'n. What happened?"

"We, uh, found the elevator."

"You what?"

"Call it a lift tube. We're at least a hundred meters above your level now. Don't worry. We've confirmed a way down. We're continuing our exploration."

John Marito sat on the flight deck and fumed. Everything was happening away from him, out of his view, beyond his control.

Marito was thirty-six years old. For the last ten years of his life he had lived the researcher's dream, hoping to discover the major breakthrough that would make him immortal. The odds were against him, not because he was incompetent but because of the laboratory's system. An individual's genius was quietly bent to the company's glory, not the person's. Frustrated at work, Marito had thrown himself into his off-hours hobby: astronomy.

And astronomy had led him to one of its more obscure branches, SETI. The search for extra-terrestrial intelligence had been going on for over a century without success. Man's expansion to other planets had increased his coverage but had not improved his success rate. Marito had not been on Golden for biological research; he had been to a SETI conference.

He looked at the lifeboat's main viewer and tuned in the image of the hangar around them. *Here is the proof*, he thought, *the fabled first contact. And what am I doing? I'm sitting by the phone, waiting for a call.*

Dubois would find them first, if E.T.'s existed on this ship. Tyler would hog the glory, as she always did on any of her test exploits. It was as if she achieved everything personally.

Marito knew the system; he understood how many people were
pushed aside to make Frances Tyler's reputation.

Dubois would take his glory from him. She was like the rest,
seeking reward at the expense of others. She had no right to
force him to remain here, not when there was so much around
to be explored. She had no right.

"None at all," he mumbled, standing.

He looked at the others still in the lifeboat. Daggit was
snoring lightly, just behind the cockpit wall, oblivious to the
world and his secretary's potential danger.

Callous oaf, Marito thought.

That imposter, Roger . . . what was his *real* last name?
Roger Forsythe sat talking quietly with that silent woman, the
shy one, Nan Poullard. She spoke very little to Forsythe and
never let her eyes meet his. It was obvious, though, that they
were infatuated with each other.

All fools. To bother with them is a waste. I have work to do.
He moved towards the hatch.

He had taken four steps when Daggit's voice came from
behind. "Where're you going, Mr. Marito? You're assigned
radio watch here."

He turned. "If it's that important, *you* do it."

Daggit sat up and stared at him. "Mr. Marito, you'll get
your chance for wandering sooner or later. For now, you're to
stay here and act as comm man for the boat. I think it would be
wise for you to remember that."

Marito glared his response. Without another word he turned
and stepped through the hatchway. Daggit watched him go and
scowled. *Never trust that SOB*, he thought. *Never*.

Forsythe and Poullard watched the short argument, then
turned back to each other. Poullard said, "This is not good. We
should all work together."

"Mr. Marito is getting tired of Dubois's leash. Aren't you?"

"No. I have no ego involved here, nothing personally to
gain. If I did, perhaps I would understand."

Forsythe tried not to frown. As a professional escort, he was
used to dealing with shy women and even fatalistic women.
Poullard's complete lack of self, however, was disconcerting.
She's given up on herself, he thought. *She's going to die, so
there's no point in doing anything special for herself.*

"Miss Tyler is not your first employer, is she?" Poullard
asked.

The abruptness of the question caught Forsythe off guard. She read it in his eyes and quickly apologized. "Forgive my forwardness, Mr. Forsythe. I am afraid my upbringing did not include subtlety."

"Neither did mine," he said, smiling. "And, no, Miss Tyler is not my first employer."

"Do you enjoy your work?"

"As a matter of fact . . ." He was about to say yes, but when he thought about it, he shook his head. "No, not recently. I'm getting old, I suppose."

"We all do. You are searching for something, and you are unsure if you will ever find it."

He felt vaguely defensive. "And you? What are you searching for?"

"On Golden, life. Of course, I did not find it. I knew I would not." She barely sighed. "I have resigned myself to fate, Mr. Forsythe."

"My name is Roger."

Poullard smiled at his tone and at his offer. "And mine is Nan, Roger. You know, I believe you and I are much alike." His eyes widened in a question. She said, "Yes, we are. We are both searching for something, for someone, and we are both very much alone, from choice rather than chance. Our differences are few except in one great respect. You have not accepted our situation here; you rebel against it. I, on the other hand, see no reason for struggle. It is . . . inevitable, for me." Her smile turned distant. "You may win your struggle. I . . . I will fade away."

Something inside Forsythe yelled that she was wrong. The silent shout brought the chill of fear, and he knew why. For the first time in his adult life he found himself caring for another.

"I hope you won't just 'fade away,' Nan," he said.

And something long dormant stirred inside Nan Poullard. For all her life she had worked for others, forsaking herself for their good. Could she now accept something for herself?

Her smile grew warm once more, and she locked eyes with him, feeling a thrill of fright at so bold a move. "Perhaps . . . perhaps I won't."

Marito walked away from the lifeboat at a furious pace. So and Quont were cuddled by the starboard landing strut. The couple and he ignored each other. He wanted away from his

fellow humans for a while, to learn more about their alien
enclosure.

The obvious destinations were the objects that Dubois had
all but ignored: the alien shuttle craft. The nearest was some
twenty meters distant, and he reached it quickly.

Its main hull was egg-shaped, four meters in length. At the
tapering end were two bulging clear areas, showing the
cockpit. The rear was mottled with various bulges and creases.
Its only means of support was a single meter-thick landing leg.
Marito marveled at its balance.

Walking around showed nothing new. He peered into the
interior. He assumed a forward wall was the control panel and
that a simple bench was the pilot's seat. There were no
provisions for anyone else.

"Get inside," he muttered to himself, searching for a
handle, a control. He began touching the hull at the edge of one
glass bulge.

There was a burping sound and the bulge dissolved away,
revealing the interior. Marito looked round-eyed, then swallowed his fear.

"It's what you wanted," he said aloud. After a pause, he
climbed in.

He adjusted himself on the bench, facing forward, and
sighed. It was incredible.

There was a louder sigh and the bulge reformed, sealing him
in. He impulsively pounded on the "glass," causing a dull
booming sound. Regaining control over himself, he stopped.
He had found the exterior control easily enough. He would find
the interior one when he was ready to get out. For a fleeting
moment he wondered about air, then told himself he'd get out
in plenty of time.

The panel before him was shaped like an upside-down U, his
feet slipping beneath it. He noted that the bench was soft and
warm, comfortable even without a backrest. He surmised *they*
hadn't need of the extra support.

Everything seemed a little tight for him, indicating the aliens
were small. The panels were blank. No knobs, no bulges, no
slots, no indicators. Dark and nothing at all. Looking about
revealed the same blank interior. He felt disappointment well
up inside him, and ran his fingers lightly over the panel's top.

Light glittered under his fingertips and the shuttle hummed.
He stopped, and so did the lights and humming.

"Oh, my," he whispered. *The entire panel is touch sensitive!*

No doubt the readouts were geared for eyes seeing a different range of the spectrum, yet the overhead lights in the hangar had been yellow before adapting. There was some overlap.

"And you just saw the panel lights," he said. He touched his finger to the panel's center and held it there.

It sounded like a heartbeat, then a circle lit. He had no idea what it was for. Carefully he began running his hands over the rest of the panel, this time letting his touch linger for a moment. In short order it was all aglow and not the least bit comprehensible.

"Oh, my my my," he muttered, eyes as glowing as the panels. He felt ecstatic.

He reached out in both directions, easily touching the side walls. More lights, and the shuttle throbbed with unseen power. It was coming to life.

He couldn't drop his arms. He looked in horror to his left, then his right. The walling was flowing around his hands, binding them at the wrists. He felt a surge of uncontrollable panic. He tried to push with his legs, but the bench had curled up over his lap, around his buttocks, sealing him to it. More connections were made with his legs. He would have screamed if not for the mitt-shaped section of roof that came down and delicately engulfed his head. It was dark, sound fading. Marito gasped for breath and felt something icy stab into his lungs. There was a flash of vertigo, then nothing.

Dubois and Tyler came back into the staging room all smiles, relieved to be back in the light.

"This damn thing is empty," Dubois said. "Not a soul aboard. We've been on what seems to be the bridge, not that I recognized half the things we called 'controls.' Marito's going to have a field day."

"We'll still have to take it slow," Tyler said. "This ship's not fully pressurized, and for all we know, the crew could be in hibernation. Anything we do can trigger something we don't know about."

Dubois nodded. "Sure. Any exploring will still be done in pairs."

Buchanan nodded and smiled at it all. "I'm gettin' more

curious myself. Let's get back to the boat for supper. We can lay out plans for tomorrow."

They came out into the hangar and nearly slammed into So. His face was white, eyes panicky.

"What's wrong?" Buchanan asked.

"It's . . . it's Mr. Marito. He's in one of the shuttles, one of the alien shuttles, sealed in."

Dubois cursed. "That fool. He was supposed to stay with the boat. I hope he likes his confinement." She added to herself, *I should let him rot there.*

But So was shaking his head, obviously frightened. "No, no, it's more than that. He's collapsed. We—I . . . can't tell if he's alive or . . ."

Dubois, Tyler, and Buchanan exchanged glances, then broke into a run, leaving Kahn and So to bring up the rear.

7

"He's breathing."

"He's more than a fool," Dubois said, squinting for a better look into the shuttle, "but I can't think of a more accurate word."

Marito was slumped against the inner wall, hands hanging loosely at his sides. His face was bone white, eyes open in flaccid slits. He looked dead, but an occasional twitch betrayed some life. Dubois recognized the obvious signs of a deep coma. The appearance must have terrified So.

"Curious cat," Buchanan said. He was busy adjusting his laser for narrow beam. "Ev'ryone, back outta the way."

"Have you tried to find a control mechanism yet?" Tyler asked. "I've only tried the one side."

"No, but there's no time. Look at 'im. He's slippin' under, and fast."

Tyler looked at the single leg. "It could be tied into the ship's main system, providing him with air."

Buchanan pointed to Marito. "I doubt it, not lookin' at him."

"You don't know what he did to—"

Buchanan brought the laser up, narrowing his eyes to reduce the glare.

"Wait!" Dubois ordered. "She's right. We can't just go

around blasting things apart. Marito found the way in; so can
we. Frances, give me a hand."

They ran their hands around the bulge, hoping for a grip to
pry it open. One of them hit the right spot. The glass burped
and was gone. Dubois jumped in and grabbed Marito.

"Low respiration," she said. "Get him out onto the deck."

She handed him out and they laid him on his back. Tyler
turned and ran for the boat, shouting, "I'll get the medikit."

Buchanan pressed his fingers to Marito's throat. He
frowned, probed around, and snapped, "No pulse!"

Dubois slapped her airmask over the unconscious man's
face, overriding the regulator and turning the flow on full.
Buchanan was already tearing open Marito's tunic, getting
ready for manual heart compression. There was a tug on his
shoulder, and he turned to see Nan Poullard motioning him out
of the way. The others from the lifeboat were close behind.
Kahn had thought of the medikit immediately and had diverted
towards the boat to get it. Everyone had come along with her.

It became obvious that Poullard knew more about emergency first aid than any of them, surprising Dubois with her skill.
She placed the kit next to Marito and opened it, handing
Dubois the pneumatic intravenous tube. Dubois cut open
Marito's suit leg and attached the IV. Poullard slapped the
cardiocup over his chest. The kit sensed the lack of heartbeat
and applied the proper jolt of current.

"Pulse," Buchanan said, watching the scale. "Growing
strong."

Poullard pulled off Dubois's airmask and replaced it with the
kit's respirator. She made a series of yes/no decisions with the
kit as it adjusted the airflow, nutrient feed, and prescribed a
drug and narcotic mixture. She did this with a minimum of
fuss, almost by rote. She monitored Marito's vital signs for a
moment, then turned to Dubois.

"We will have to leave him hooked up to the kit for now,"
she said. "He is on maintenance, and the kit will give us a
rundown on follow-up procedures." She motioned for Forsythe to step forward, unfolding the collapsing pallet she had
ordered him to bring.

Dubois said, "You seem to know quite a bit about these sort
of problems."

Poullard shrugged. "I was First Nurse at a senility sanitari-
um for eight years. It becomes a reflex after a while."

Dubois understood, and watched as the others carefully picked Marito up and carried him away, the medikit on his chest. She turned and looked at the alien shuttle, where Kelly was sticking an inquisitive nose.

"Get the goddamn hell away from that thing!"

He jerked back as if stung.

Marito was placed in the stern-most cubicle, the privacy panel left off. Poullard rechecked the kit hook-ups and set the emergency alarm.

"I think this makes things clearer," Dubois said quietly. *Why do people talk softly around the sick?* "No one goes *any*where alone. No one touches or fools with *anything* unless we at least have some glimmering of an idea what it is."

They all nodded agreement. After a pause, Buchanan said, "So, Cap'n, tell us what you and Frances found."

Dubois appreciated the change in topic and tried to accommodate it. "The control room, the bridge, as near as we could tell. It's the biggest compartment we've found, next to the hangar and staging room, with one massive blank wall. We think it might be some sort of viewscreen, but we couldn't figure out how to activate it. We fooled with a few of the controls—"

"And she tells *us* not to fool around," Forsythe muttered.

"—but only got blinking lights in return. Every station looks like the shuttle's cockpit, and damnit all, what the hell was Marito doing out there anyway?" Dubois hoped she wasn't shaking as much as it felt. *You came damn close to losing one of your passengers—another mistake!*

"I wonder what happened to him?" Kahn asked. "He obviously figured out how to get in. Why did he seal the door behind him?"

"I wouldn't have believed a man could suffocate so fast," Daggit said. "He couldn't have been trapped more than half an hour. There should have been plenty of air, plenty of time for him to worry the door open again."

"Unless he fooled with the controls instead," Buchanan said. "He probably pressurized the interior with normal *alien* air."

"Makes sense," Dubois said. "I should have taken him with me. That would have satisfied his curiosity."

Tyler flopped into a chair and sighed. "And he probably

would have killed you both. He calls himself a scientist, but his curiosity has no discipline. Look at what it got him. He could have taken you with him."

"Perhaps. Still—"

"No more recriminations, Cap'n," Buchanan said. After a pause he asked, "What do we do now?"

"Nothing. We call it a day, and then Frances and I will go out again tomorrow, this time a little better prepared, mentally at least. We'll also take the tracer and see if we can't get some kind of visual layout of this ship."

"Back to the bridge?" Tyler asked.

"The logical starting point. Kevin, you'll take Hilary or someone else and come with us. You'll set up on the bridge this time. Then Frances and I will explore while you two wait."

"Again?"

"Again."

8

Gone

The control room was a crescent ten meters across. Despite the size, there were provisions for only four crewmembers, if the upside-down U panels were any indication.

They established themselves as before, confirming that they had positive communications with the lifeboat. They had left the radio set in the staging room on automatic and, through it and a series of relays, had a solid line to Daggit and the others.

Buchanan looked at a point far down the corridor that led to the bridge. "Love that, er, elevator."

Tyler said, "Wait till you try the drop."

Buchanan grimaced.

"We'll work our way to the bow," Dubois said, "then circle back underneath you. Hopefully, we'll be able to stay above the level of the hangar and head towards the stern."

"Don't bite off too much, Cap'n," Buchanan said. "Just stick with the bow for now. We'll try the stern later, maybe from one of the other doors."

She considered, then nodded. "Okay. Today, the bow."

They walked as before, Dubois in the lead. Tyler carried the one main addition to their supplies. The tracer was an inertial recorder, recording their movements, how far they went, what turns were made, in relation to a starting point. It had been set

72

at the lifeboat and was now storing their progress through a corridor leading forward off the bridge. When they returned to the boat, they would drain the device into the main computer and get back a series of maps.

The corridor was like the others, except that it branched more often, an intersection every several meters. Dubois resisted the urge to head down one, wanting to go as far forward as possible.

"I'm getting tired of small, dark hallways," Tyler said, voice low, eyes apprehensive. "It seems—"

"*Shh*," Dubois hissed, stopping. She tilted her head to one side, listening. Tyler heard it too.

The corridor was throbbing, but to no regular beat. It would rise, fall, hold; rise again, hold, then drop off.

Dubois put her hand to one wall and could feel it move under her touch. She jerked back, repulsed.

"It . . . it feels alive," she said.

Tyler touched it also, keeping her hand there and fighting back a wave of nausea. "Like a cold snake. I wonder if we should go on, Captain."

Dubois nodded. "Yes. We already know there's a lot of automatic systems on board. We may be near a power plant of some sort, a pumping station."

"I don't like it."

"Neither do I. Still . . ."

They moved on, not bothering to radio Buchanan about the wall. Marito's accident and condition lay heavy on their minds, increasing their apprehension as their eyes darted from side to side at the walls. A short time later they realized they had not passed another intersection. Neither commented on the change, but their pace slowed.

The corridor ended. It emptied into a dark space, and as they stepped forward, the lights overhead vanished, replaced by darkness. It shocked them for a moment. They had grown used to the ship's ever-present tag-along lights, and neglected their own torches. Hands fumbled for scanwands.

"Don't hit your torch yet," Tyler cautioned. "They may have had a reason for keeping it dark here."

Both of them made radar scans ahead. There were no return echos. The readouts remained blank.

"I can't see you, Frances," Dubois whispered. "Where are you?"

She felt a hand on her shoulder and a disembodied voice asked, "Is this you?"

"Yes."

"Then here I am. Shall we hit the lights?"

As an answer, Dubois turned her torch on full flood. The darkness around them vanished.

There was no room before them, and half a meter ahead there was no floor. Dubois stepped forward and adjusted her light for narrow beam, hoping for range. It didn't shine on anything below, above, or in front of them.

"What is this?" she asked.

"I have no idea. It seems useless, just an empty space."

"It's at least thirty meters to the other side, the same up and down. We'd get a return echo if there was anything closer."

Tyler took out a relay. "I'll set this for squawk. We'll get a depth reading, if nothing else."

"Set it for one minute. No sense screwing up our communications longer than that. I'll alert Kevin."

While she passed the warning on to Buchanan, Tyler adjusted the tiny ball. When both were done, she tossed it out into the dark. A steady tone came over their radios.

It kept floating away, straight up and out.

"A zero-gravity field," Dubois said. "There's no gravity out there."

"Obviously. But why?"

She shrugged. "I can only speculate. This may have been a recreation area. What better way to relax in space than to float in nothingness? They may even have projected stars around them, a planetarium. We had similar arrangements aboard the *Goddess*."

"There could be some special equipment in there," Tyler said, looking down.

Dubois shrugged again. The ball kept squawking for the full minute, then stopped, out of sight and gone. A range check showed it had never reached the other side. They turned back to the pulsing corridor.

Once inside again, the lights came back on. Dubois elected to take the first corridor to the right on the way back. Tyler said, "I thought you told Kevin we'd only check the bow today. Well, we've found the bow."

"Too soon. It's too close to the bridge."

"Then why *this* corridor?"

Dubois smiled. "Because I'm right-handed."

The abandoned condition of the ship was becoming more and more apparent. Every "door" they found led only to a vacuum-filled enclosure, closed off to their exploration. A more obvious sign was the complete lack of intelligent reaction to their presence. Internal systems reacted to direct stimulus, but there was no initiation of systems, nothing to tell them that someone was in control.

"Except in one respect," Tyler said to Dubois's assertion. "The ship's adapting to us. The atmosphere, the lights, the temperature, and so on. They've all adjusted to us rather than showing what the aliens must have been like." She paused, then speculated, "Perhaps they had shifting metabolisms. The ship kept pace with them. Or maybe the ship was designed for survival as much as the crew was trained for it. Maybe the ship itself is alive."

Dubois grimaced. "I prefer the first theory. I don't want to think of this as being 'alive.'"

"It could be. An advanced enough computer system, adjusting to changing conditions. Perhaps even a level of artificial intelligence. The crew died, for whatever reasons, and the ship simply went on, on its own. It got trapped in orbit here, with just enough power to maintain the interior and hold orbit, not enough to escape. Or perhaps it's 'recharging its batteries,' which is why it's so close to the star."

"So I'd still like to know what happened to the crew."

"Wouldn't we all."

They came to another striped doorway, and Dubois looked at it. She did what was becoming the norm, sticking the probe end of her scanwand through. What surprised her was the positive pressure reading, the first since they had discovered the bridge. She pulled the wand out and said, "An atmosphere. That's new."

Tyler nodded. "Shall we go through?"

On the other side was a broad corridor. It was no higher but three times wider. They went down it slowly, finding to their dismay that the ceiling lights had abandoned them again. They turned their own torches back on.

The corridor curved gently to the left, then straightened once more. Tyler said, "I think we're heading towards the stern again."

Dubois nodded. The corridor slanted downwards, and she said, "Along the belly."

The corridor emptied out into a huge room. It registered as a square on the scans they made, again out of the norm. It was the first sharp-edged shape they had found. They walked slowly into the room, lights fanning from side to side. Dubois pointed her stick to the right and got a wall reading on the edge of the unit's range, just under thirty meters.

She squinted at the readout. "I'm getting an odd reading here."

Tyler scanned to the left. "Here too. The walls aren't flat. They're lumpy."

The ship's throbbing, for so long merely a background noise, leaped to the fore of their minds. Dubois motioned in her direction. "Let's check mine."

They moved cautiously. Dubois scanned the floor beyond their light. "It's not smooth. Watch your step."

Tyler nodded. The blood pounded in her temples, and she fought a rising fear of being trapped. *I'm not used to this. It's been years since I've done any field work. Why did I have to—*

Her toe brushed something and she hissed in surprise. She jumped to one side, shining her light down.

"Oh, damn!"

Dubois spun, then looked. Her throat felt constricted and a cold sweat broke out along her back.

It was a body.

"It's dead," Tyler whispered, breathing ragged.

It was short, hardly a meter and a half tall; squat and almost circular. Little could be seen of its features. It lay in a depression, the bulge of the body just rising above floor level.

"We . . ." Dubois licked her lips and tried again. "We've found the crew."

Tyler controlled her first reactions and stepped around Dubois, getting closer to the wall. Light on full, she flashed it ahead. Alien shapes were lined up neatly, the wall holding them firmly.

"A mortuary," she said. "A bloody mortuary. We're in the morgue."

Dubois nodded, kneeling besides the alien shape. She frowned in puzzlement. She had thought that the body lay in a depression. A closer look showed that to be wrong, or an understatement. There was no clear line where the body ended and the floor began. The two were fused together.

"Cap'n?" Tyler said. "Pamela, did you hear me? This is a morgue, nothing but dead bodies."

Dubois stood, nodding again. She looked around once more and said, "Let's get out of here. I've seen enough for now."

"I won't argue. Lead on."

They tried not to run from the room.

Buchanan broke open a ration bar and ate it in three bites. He had grown tired of playing gin with Hilary as soon as it became clear she was well above his playing level. One thing he couldn't stand was being a consistent loser. He had some satisfaction, however, in knowing that she would not play poker with him for exactly the same reason.

He lounged against the forward wall, enjoying the way it seemed to mold to his back. Very comfortable. It appeared to pulse gently, lulling him. He yawned, thoughts wandering.

Kahn walked slowly about. She resisted touching any of the panels, remembering what had happened to Marito. She looked back at Buchanan, sexual innuendo playing briefly in her mind. He *was* handsome, and it might be interesting being half of the first couple to make love within an alien spaceship. Perhaps . . .

But then there was Benjamin. They weren't married, and technically she was only his secretary; a business relationship. It wasn't that simple. Occasional partners in bed, they were an excellent business team. He followed his sense for success and she provided the logical controls. She was a master of business law and knew all the necessary legal "doors." Daggit provided the more subtle paralegal "in's."

She was happy with the arrangement. Daggit was never confining, demanding only when it came to business, always providing. A life contract would only solidify things, and that could ruin everything.

She looked again at Buchanan. His eyes were closed and he appeared to be dozing. The radio was close at hand, though, and she knew he would be wide awake at the first squawk.

Kahn stepped by the sleeping starman and went around the curving crescent of the bridge. She didn't notice when the curve blocked her line of sight to Buchanan, concentrating instead on the architecture around her.

The ship gently throbbed, slipping into a regular beat as she came nearer to the corner. The end was a blunted point. Ever so gently she felt herself relax as the pulsing seemed to match her own heartbeat. And slowed. She smiled, feeling at ease.

The inner wall was striped in an odd pattern. She looked closer, frowning. Instead of the stripes going either horizontal (for a door) or vertical (for an "elevator"), this one was both, forming a cross. Dimmer stripes came from the corners, forming an X across it. She didn't think the pattern had ever been seen before. She stepped closer.

Her frown deepened. The throbbing was taking on an impatient tone. Nearer the stripes it grew deeper, reaching into the subsonic. She sensed it in her bones, insisting. Her frown slackened, eyes glazing slightly as she felt herself being lulled; at ease, apprehension fading.

Everything's fine, she thought. *Is something wrong?*

Ever so faintly she placed her hands on the center of the pattern. She felt the substance of the wall yielding, just like a normal door.

Everything's fine. Nothing's wrong. She started to pull away.

The wall wasn't having any of that.

It flowed smoothly and cupped her wrists as four tendrils formed and projected out. She watched in shock, calm shattered, as they lashed out with a delicate swiftness, crisscrossing her body. She was too stunned to cry out as they tightened, holding her immobile. She drew in a breath to scream when a fifth tendril came out, whipping around her neck. It tightened, straightening her throat so her head was forced back. Its end flattened into a large circle, and she barely got out a squeal before it engulfed her head. Her struggles useless, she felt the breath robbed from her lungs. She never noticed when she was lifted from the floor, muscles twitching in futile efforts. The tendrils retracted, collapsing once more into the wall.

Hilary Kahn was gone.

9

"Nothing remains the same."

Dubois and Tyler came back onto the bridge looking drawn and haggard. They flashed nervous smiles at each other, their expressions the same: *We made it*. Neither looked forward to returning to the ship's lower areas.

Dubois looked at the lightly snoring Buchanan and shook her head. She smiled, suddenly feeling mischievous. After being oppressed for so long in the ship's corridors, she couldn't resist the impulse. She quietly unhooked her airmask, made sure the feed valve was closed, and held it over Buchanan's face.

He tried to take one breath, then snapped full awake, terror in his eyes. The starman understood what was happening in the next moment and threw the mask aside, shouting, "What the hell were you tryin' to—"

Dubois and Tyler staggered back, laughing loudly, and his anger vanished. Somewhat quieter, he said, "I've been had. Sorry I fell asleep."

"Don't worry about it," Dubois said. "If we'd've shouted, I'm sure you would've come a'running."

"Natch."

Tyler looked around. "Where's Hilary?"

"She was poking around the room last I saw," Buchanan said. Then: "Hilary?"

There was no answer to the call. Dubois frowned, all the tensions from her explorations returning. "Hilary?"

Nothing.

The little noises of the ship took on a sinister note. Dubois glared at Buchanan, ready to verbally rip his head off. One look at his face was more than enough to tell her he was already screaming at himself. Anything she could add would be pointless.

Tyler walked from one side of the bridge to the other, seeing nothing in the first corner, then stopped at the second. She unclipped her laser and slowly moved forward. Dubois pulled her own weapon and came up behind her.

One lifeboat-issue boot lay on the deck, upside down and discarded. Tyler bent over and picked it up, examining the crepe sole to confirm its identity. They all knew, however. It was Hilary's.

They looked at the two walls that converged less than two meters ahead of them. They were blank, featureless, unmarked.

"Same as yesterday," Dubois said.

Tyler shook her head. "No it isn't. There was a doorway marked here, remember? Vertical stripes instead of horizontal, so we assumed it was another elevator. Cold vacuum on the other side. We wondered why it didn't pull us through."

"There's nothing here now," Buchanan said.

Tyler was adamant. "There *was*."

Dubois slowly stepped forward. "Which wall?"

"The left."

"If Hilary had been here, she would have been out of Kevin's sight."

Buchanan looked back. "You're right."

Dubois unclipped her scanwand and moved it slowly towards the wall. She touched it gently, then pushed. The wall held, not allowing the probe through.

Licking her lips, she moved down and tried again. And again. Then in the corner. The walls were solid.

"You're sure about the stripes?" Buchanan asked Tyler.

"Yes, damnit, they were here."

"Yes, they were," Dubois said. She stepped away from the

corner, the others retreating to give her room. "They were here. I remember." She looked at them. "What do we do now?"

"Get back to the others," Buchanan said.

Dubois's laugh was harsh. "You trust the corridors?"

"What do you mean?"

"There was a doorway here yesterday. Now it's gone. What does that tell you?"

Tyler said, "Things are changing, and not for our convenience, not anymore."

"Exactly. This ship's been adapting for humans all along. Now it's evident it adapts for other reasons as well. *Nothing* remains the same."

"You don't know that for sure," Buchanan said. "There may—"

"There may be a logical explanation, but right now I'm assuming that nothing stays the same. Do you agree with me, Frances?"

"I have a choice?"

"Then how do we get back?"

Dubois looked at Buchanan. "Maybe we don't. Do you want to ride down the elevator and have a wall grab you?"

"Don't try an' scare me, Cap'n; I already am. 'Wall grab you.' Very poetic, but not necessarily accurate. How do you know she fell through a door, or that a *wall* grabbed her? Maybe there *is* something alive aboard this ship. *It* may have her."

"*It* does," Tyler said. "'It' is the ship. Hilary's fallen through a doorway that no longer exists. How do we find her? How does she find her way out? She's lost, Kevin."

"Which is what I meant," Dubois said. "Of course nothing 'grabbed' her. She got curious and got sucked in like Frances did when we first explored. Only this time the way back has shifted. And if it's shifted, how do we follow any trail?"

"If she's alive."

Dubois turned to Tyler. The engineer went on in the same quiet voice. "There was a vacuum on the other side of that door. Airmask or not, she wouldn't have survived."

"We have to assume she's alive, at least for the moment."

Buchanan looked down then back up, face brightening. "Her radio! She's got it on."

Dubois cursed herself for not thinking of the obvious and turned her own set on. "Hello, hello. Hilary? Hilary, can you hear me?"

"What's up?" asked Daggit.

Dubois swore again. She had forgotten that the lifeboat was automatically patched in through the transceivers. She briefed him swiftly, finishing, "Get everyone back into the boat. Leave the gear in the staging room on automatic. We're on our way back."

"You're sure her radio was on?" Tyler asked Buchanan.

"Sure. We were both monitoring for any calls from you two."

"Come on," Dubois said. "We're going back."

She led off. Tyler gave the bridge one last look and mumbled, "Assuming we can find our way."

The corridors and elevators were still there. All had an unspoken belief that they would wander the ship's interior forever. It didn't happen, and they made good time back to the hangar.

The others were standing outside the boat, looking nervous. Forsythe, in particular, was clearly shaken, hopping from one foot to the other.

Dubois looked at them all, thinking, *What can I say? Marito's accident was one thing, but this . . .*

Daggit spoke first. "All right, Captain, she's lost. When do we start looking for her?"

The question was not unexpected, especially from him. She hesitated. Daggit was looking at her with a frown, as if to say, *I'm worried like hell and you had better come up with a plan to find her.* Swallowing lightly, she said, "Do you know where to start, Mr. Daggit?"

"That's not the point. You've got to—"

"It's precisely the point," Buchanan said. "This ship's two-and-a-half kilometers long, one klick wide, and around five hundred meters tall. Do you know how much cubic meterage that is? If we don't know at least what part of the ship to search, we'll *never* find Hilary."

"We've already begun taking some steps," Dubois continued, tone softer than his. "We dropped transponders every twenty meters or so. Our communications will be a little jumbled but they'll give out a continuous signal, combining to form a pretty strong transmission. If she's moving, she can home on it with her radio. We've also left transceivers on the bridge and in the staging room, and with everything else, she'll be able to contact us if she gets within range of any one radio ball."

" 'Be able to contact us'?" Forsythe snapped. "What do you mean? Something's got her, for Christ's sake. Let's get out of here!"

"What's got her, Forsythe?" asked Tyler. "She's lost, damnit, not captured. If she keeps walking and doesn't fool with anything, there's a good chance we'll hear from her. Once that's done, we can begin triangulating on her position. So, to your worries, Mr. Daggit, the best thing we can do for Hilary is to sit tight, except to fan our radio net out farther."

"Or we can scout and see if *we* can pick up *her* radio signal," Buchanan said. "Either way, it's only a matter of time."

Daggit's frown slowly loosened, finally changing to an optimistic smile. "Okay, you've got it pretty well figured out."

Forsythe looked at them and repeated, "We have got to get out of here."

Dubois looked annoyed. "How, Mr. Forsythe? We haven't been able to figure out step one about this ship's controls. You saw what happened to Marito. Shall we just hit all the buttons at once and hope we don't blow ourselves to kingdom come? And please find me the controls in the first place."

"Hey," a weak voice called, "let's keep down the noise."

They all turned, stunned to see John Marito standing on the lifeboat's wing.

". . . so after the door closed I decided there was no need for panic," Marito was saying. Poullard poured him another glass of water, which he accepted silently and sipped from. "I must have triggered the thing to life when I fiddled with the controls. Silly of me. I should have been more cautious."

"Damn right," Tyler muttered.

"Anyway, I touched the opposite sides of the cabin, where I thought there might be more controls, and that's when it happened."

"What?" Dubois asked.

"The shuttle . . . *grabbed* me."

They all looked skeptical. He nodded and repeated, "It grabbed me. I must have activated the life-support system. The cabin walls flowed out and cupped my hands while the bench curved around my lap and legs. Then . . ." He took a shuddering breath. "Then this . . . this *paw* came down and grabbed my face. I was unconscious immediately."

" 'Paw'?"

He looked at Dubois. "Paw, mitt, face mask, call it what you will. The shuttle is a psycholink vessel. The pilot controls it through thought. When I made the final contact, it tried to integrate me into its controls. The thing that covered my head was probably part of the life-support system and brain-link. The alien atmosphere knocked me out. And my mind was of the wrong pattern for shuttle linkage, so it shut down, releasing me."

"That's a guess," Buchanan said.

"Sounds like a good one," Tyler said. "It makes sense." She frowned in concern. "If it was a thought-link, I hope it hasn't done any damage to your brain."

Marito's left eye twitched at the thought, but he shook his head. "I . . . I don't think so."

Daggit asked, "How come it didn't recreate our own air for you, Mr. Marito? The rest of the ship has."

"Because it is only a small shuttlecraft. It probably doesn't have the ability for such broad deviations."

Buchanan leaned back and looked thoughtful. He said, "It *grabbed* you."

"Well, yes, but I may have misinterpreted. Why?"

In short order Marito learned of Hilary's disappearance. The Asian frowned in dismay and said, "This is terrible. She must have bumbled about, activating some control or another. Why did you let her play with such things? You don't know—"

Dubois's voice was hard. "If she *played*, Mr. Marito, I'm sure it was no more harmful than your own misadventure."

"Madam, I am a scientist and what *I* was conducting was research into—"

"You're a little damn professor, Marito," Buchanan said, "and you don't know when you're in over your head."

"Captain Dubois, do I have to listen to—"

"No. Can it, Kevin. Mr. Marito, he has a point. From now on you will limit your 'research' into areas I authorize. No more one-man stunts. Understood?"

He bit his lip, then nodded. "Understood. What are our chances of finding Miss Kahn?"

"We had first thought they were good. If what you say is

accurate, however, she may be lying somewhere in a coma, like you were, and we've no way of finding her. On the other hand, if we're right, if she just fell through a doorway and is lost, it's probable she'll stumble into range of our network and then we'll have her.''

Daggit was looking sick again. He could only picture his beloved Hilary wrapped up in some alien machinery, dying. Dubois and Buchanan looked at him with concern, keenly aware of his age, knowing the strain his fear for Kahn was putting him under.

Dubois stood and went forward, wishing for the moment to be alone. She bent over the radio panel and made an adjustment. Picking up the hand microphone, she said, "Hilary, you are now in range of our radio. Respond immediately." She tapped a button. The unit would repeat the message continuously, sending it out through their series of transceivers until either Kahn replied or one of them turned it off.

A sudden weariness came over her and she slumped into the command chair. *Command*, she thought bitterly. *I wouldn't be here if I didn't want command*.

The book again: "A lifeboat will be your first true taste of command and responsibility . . ."

She grimaced. She was gagging on the taste.

I don't want this! The thought of the eight people, all depending on her for the proper decisions, began to grate. It was growing frightening. What would it be like with several thousand, an entire ship to command?

But you're doing what you want to, a portion of her mind said. *Deep space exploration*. She was *out there*, dealing with the unknown.

She could feel the alien vessel outside throbe. *What are we dealing with?* she thought. *Perhaps Forsythe's right and we should get out, now*.

But there remained the obvious question: *How?*

She remembered the fifth box stored belowdecks in the stern, the one marked EXPLOSIVES. It held six little charges, meant to be used on an alien planet to remove obstacles, either for farming or for emergency takeoffs. They were variable focus, allowing a choice from full-circle destruction to single-direction punch. Could they be used to blow through the hangar door?

She almost laughed at the thought. They were far from being enough for the job. Like so much else, they were added as an afterthought by the boat's design team, an obsession to fill every nook and cranny.

Frustration filled her again. No way out. She blinked rapidly and scanned the instruments to avoid thinking about it. She almost turned back to the others, ready to rejoin the conversation, when something caught her eye. She took a closer look. Frowning, she called, "Kevin, come up here."

He came quickly. "Yeah?"

She tapped the ambient temperature readout. "We're down to twenty-four and holding steady."

His frown matched hers. "I wonder when that happened?"

"I wonder why." She punched a request into the computer. A graph appeared on one of the screens, showing temperature and time. "Just a few minutes ago, a gradual drop-off."

Buchanan looked at the other instruments. "Look here. Pressure's up, now a hundred percent Earth-normal." He punched up another graph. They compared the two, then looked at each other.

The times matched.

They checked the third external monitor and were unsurprised to find that the gravity was now a full gee, with a third time match.

As calmly as possible Dubois walked by the passengers and stood in the rear doorway. Nothing outside seemed to have changed. It was still flooded with alien light, the dark walls unseen. It was noticeably cooler, a more comfortable temperature. Yet there was something about the air . . .

Buchanan stood alongside her and noticed it as well. He said softly, "It almost smells perfumed."

The others stopped their conversation and looked at them in curiosity. Suddenly Daggit sniffed heavily. He stood and bolted for the door, shoving Dubois and Buchanan aside. He walked out onto the wing as though in a trance, heedless of the NO STEP markings on the solar cells. Each step crushed a hundred millicircuits. He took another deep breath, closing his eyes. When he opened them again, tears streaked down his cheeks. He mumbled, "Oh Lord, oh Lord . . ."

Dubois jumped to his side. "What's wrong? What is it?"

"That smell," he whispered. "That odor."

The others were spilling out around them. He looked at them. "Can you smell it? Can you?"

"Fancy perfume," So said.

"You're damn right! The most expensive you can buy!"

Dubois felt something draw tight within her. She knew what was coming, and felt a sudden rush of cold fear rising like a tide.

Daggit said, "That's Hilary's favorite perfume. She's been wearing it this entire trip." His face collapsed into anguish, every carefully erected wall in his mind crumbling as the truth rammed home.

"This ship has her! *What is it doing to her?*"

10

The Search

The lights, hangar, and shuttles were still the same. Nothing had changed—physically.

What had been growing familiar, however, was now once again dark and foreboding. There was the almost-undeniable urge to run, to escape. The derelict had become sinister.

Dubois's face hardened and she said, "I think we've wasted enough time being oblique about this."

"What are you talking about?" Marito asked.

Dubois ignored him. "Kevin, get out the lasers, *all* of the lasers."

He nodded and jumped towards the boat's rear compartment. Marito grabbed Dubois's elbow. "Just what are you going to do?"

"Stay out of my way," she snapped, breaking free. She, Tyler, and Buchanan were already armed. Kahn had had a fourth. That left two more. She looked about her. *Who else to arm?*

Buchanan returned, carrying the weapons. She handed one to So. "You'll stay with the boat. You're our rear guard." One more. Who . . . ? She turned to Daggit. "Mr. Daggit, can I trust you to follow *my* orders where and when to fire?"

There was no hesitation. "As far as it goes, Captain, but I'd be less than frank if I didn't say I'd kill anything that tried to stop me from freeing Hilary."

She could see it in his eyes, still moist but holding an inner rage. The mournful emotion of a moment ago had been joined with another, the drive for vengeance.

"Thank you for your honesty, sir." She turned to Marito, automatically dismissing Forsythe and the others. "I am forced to issue you a weapon, Mr. Marito."

He shook his head. "No, *Ensign* Dubois. I won't take that gun and I won't kill *anything* on this ship. You may call yourself Captain and the others may fall into place, but not I."

"Fine." She grabbed his hand and shoved the laser into it. "Stay with the boat and Kelly. You'll be their pilot out of here. Please don't hesitate to at least cut your way out if need be, or if you can."

He looked at the laser, revolted, then nodded. "Very well. To cut through the hull, but nothing more."

"Good enough. Kevin, Frances, you're with me."

Tyler asked, "Where to?"

"The bridge. I'm going to blast through that wall."

"That's dangerous," Buchanan said. "We don't know what sort of defenses this ship has."

"Are you suggesting we don't even *try* to rescue Hilary?"

"No. There's another way."

Dubois paused. "I'm listening."

"Simple: if she's got her radio, and if it's on, we can go through the ship corridor with our scanwands and get a fix on her. We'll shut off all the relays so we won't get any false signals."

Tyler saw the flaw first. "We'll be out of contact with the boat; no communications."

"We'll find Hilary faster. Even if the signal's not strong enough for voice, we should be able to get a fix."

"It's dangerous."

"It'll work!"

There was a shift in the air, new currents whispering about. Apprehension danced on all their faces as the ship pulsed around them.

"What?" Forsythe whispered.

Dubois walked to the wing's trailing edge and slipped down to the deck, laser drawn. She stepped away from the stern, looking over the wide expanse of hangar to the left.

"What is it?" Buchanan asked.

The ship pulsed again, a throb of louder and longer proportions. They all looked around, up at the ceiling, expecting to see paws reaching for them.

Dubois felt something shift beneath her feet. She jumped to one side, shouting a warning, laser aiming between her legs. She stopped, seeing nothing.

"What the hell is going on?" Buchanan shouted.

Dubois was fascinated with the floor. She pushed on it with a toe. "It . . . it doesn't *give* anymore. It's changed, as solid as our hull."

Marito's voice was a hushed tone. "It's *changing*."

The grid pattern vanished. It started beneath the lifeboat and fanned out across the hangar. Patterns appeared, swirling clockwise, colors shifting , spreading quickly in all directions. When it was still, the lifeboat stood on what appeared to be an elaborate wood floor, half-meter squares of rich tan bordered with dark brown. It was Daggit who identified the pattern.

"My mansion," he said. "The main floor is just like this, walnut and cherry wood."

"They're using Miss Kahn's mind as a model of normal Earth conditions," Marito surmised. "But it's incomplete. No Earth spaceship would have such a floor."

"The air, the scent," Dubois said. "Mr. Daggit, did Hilary have a preferred temperature?"

He hesitated. "Well, no, but she liked it warm. Said the temp here was fine."

Dubois frowned and Daggit continued, "At home, though, she left it wherever I set it."

"And what was that?"

"Twenty-four degrees."

Dubois and Buchanan exchanged glances. Tyler asked, "Is that the temperature now?"

"Yes. And the pressure's up too."

"No doubt the gravity as well," Marito said, adding in exuberant tones, "The ship *does* adapt. Miss Kahn is the model and we are the test subjects." He looked like an ecstatic child.

"I don't think it's that intelligent," Dubois said. "Everything that's happened so far has been in reaction to something we've done. The lights, when we came in. Air, pressure, from a sample released by the boat and me going through the wall.

Your accident because you touched something. Hilary must have done likewise."

"So how about my plan?" Buchanan asked. "Do we go?"

Tyler nodded and Dubois agreed. "Let's get ready. I want to start immediately."

The three of them went through the wall and into Wonderland. They looked about the staging room and gaped.

An assortment of pastel shades—blue, yellow, white, tan— all flowed around them, from one side to the other. There was no set pattern. It was like a blender in reverse, the colors forming out of a common shade, separating, becoming more distinct. As they watched, the room grew, becoming square. When it was done, it had become a low-ceilinged rectangle, four by ten meters. The walls were a soft yellow, the floor's wood tones and pattern matching the hangar's.

"I'll bet Hilary prefers light shades," Tyler said, "her favorite being yellow."

"I have a question," Buchanan said. "Is the ship pickin' Hilary's brain and controllin' her or is she controllin' it, at least partially?"

"Why do you assume it's the ship?" asked Tyler. "What about some *thing*, hidden members of the crew?"

Buchanan shrugged.

"They're good questions," Dubois said. "Ask Hilary when we find her."

They started for the bridge. Every relay on the way was shut off. The only unit left on was the beacon in the staging room, giving them a reference point. Once on the bridge Tyler activated her scanwand and nodded to Dubois. All she got was a weak signal from the beacon.

Dubois turned on her own wand. The beacon's signal had been shifted to a different frequency, leaving the regular communications channel clear. Tyler was set on the former, Dubois the latter.

"If we could have done that to the balls," Buchanan said, "we'd still have contact with the boat."

"You can't," Dubois said, "so we didn't, so forget it."

"Where to?" Tyler asked.

"The morgue."

Buchanan looked uncomprehending. "Where?"

In the rush of the past few hours they hadn't told anyone of their find. They filled him in now, leading the way. Buchanan looked reluctant, but no more than they did.

Nothing had changed. They walked to the room's far side, careful to step around the alien forms in the floor. A search showed four doorways.

"Which do we take?" whispered Buchanan.

"If she disappeared from the bridge's port side," Dubois said, "that would make one of the right-hand doors here closest."

"The second one," Tyler said. "And don't ask why."

A wink's as good as a nod, Dubois thought, and grunted approval. They stepped up to the door.

"Horizontal stripes," Dubois said. "A level corridor, *if* past experience still means anything."

Buchanan reset his scanwand and pushed it through, receiving a positive pressure reading. He went through, the others quickly following.

Ahead of them the entire corridor lit up, the light racing away from them and staying on. As the leading edge rushed by, the corridor changed, from circular to square. The now-flat floor was wood tone, the walls yellow, the light white.

Tyler said, "Hilary's at work again, or this is a new reaction to anyone entering a corridor."

"I'll bet they're changing throughout the ship," Dubois said.

"Just so they don't move," muttered Buchanan.

Dubois glanced at her scanwand, though there was no need. The unit would bleat for attention if it picked up a signal. Looking ahead again, she started off, the others trailing behind single file.

They checked every door they passed. The other side of each showed a vacuum.

"What if she's in a room with a vacuum?" Buchanan mused. "She could be wrapped in some sort of pressure bottle."

"We'll mark the location and come back in pressure suits," Dubois said. "Satisfied?"

"We should have suited up imediately," Tyler said. "Just for safety."

Another mistake I've made, Dubois thought. *Now it's too late to change. We're too committed.*

They walked for an hour, finding only branching corridors

and vacuum-filled rooms. They altered course from time to time, always trying to remain on a sternward course. One corridor slanted downwards for a while, then leveled out again. It was the only variety. Their surroundings did not change, always the same cheery-bright yellow, their boots squeaking on the "wood" floor.

Dubois tensed and slowed. Ahead they could see a bright spot. As they got closer they saw it was an opening into a larger, yellow room. They stepped out into the staging room, their radio gear sitting against the wall. The others slumped in resignation, but Dubois noted the door they had come out of.

"Far left," she said. "We've tried the center, so that leaves the far right. Let's go."

"Where?" Buchanan asked. "Back to the bridge?"

"Yes, via this corridor if we can. Then we'll see if we can get under that null-gravity room up front."

"The what?"

"I'll explain as we go. C'mon!"

The bright surroundings were growing depressive, as was the bland sameness. With very little effort they could imagine they were strolling the halls of Daggit's mansion. The illusion, though, was shattered by the continuing appearance of alien ebony-striped doorways. The reinforced knowledge that it was all a facade only heightened their anxiety, deepening their depression.

"We'd better head back," Tyler said, shoulders slumped. "Get some rest and try again later."

"Once we find the bridge," Dubois replied, equally fatigued, but determined nonetheless. "Then we'll start back."

Buchanan was less optimistic. "*If* we find the bridge. What if we don't?"

"We backtrack this route."

"We've made at least a half-dozen turns already, Cap'n. How can we be sure we'll find our way back?"

"Frances is getting a reasonably clear signal from the beacon. We'll be able to—" She stopped.

Her scanwand was bleating.

Dubois held it before her, transfixed. The strength indicator lit up, a series of dots in the center of the screen, curving to show direction. She turned from left to right and back again, locating the direction by centering the dots.

"Ahead and to the left," she said. "Let's go."

They broke into a run, Dubois's eyes fixed on the indicator. More dots were stacking up, the signal strength increasing.

Some dots vanished, the signal fading. She stopped, the others almost bumping into her. She waved the wand, scanning for a new direction.

They went backwards several meters, stopping before a wall marking unique in their experience. On the yellow wall black stripes went up and down and side to side, with a second set forming an X on the first cross. The X was slightly gray, letting the cross stand out.

"Here," Dubois said. She reset her scanwand for a pressure reading and stepped up to the wall.

"Take it easy, Cap'n," whispered Buchanan, breathing deeply. He unclipped his laser and wiped sweat from his upper lip.

Dubois's jumpsuit clung to her back, wet. She slowed her breathing, arms trembling with exhaustion after their brief but hectic run. She pushed the wand towards the center of the markings.

She stopped less than a centimeter from contact. The corridor was lightly drumming around her, falling into step with her pounding heart. It slowed. Far from relaxing her, it raised her apprehension, a visceral instinct crying for caution.

Buchanan and Tyler seemed unaware of the ship's throbbing. She looked at them, beads of perspiration forming on her forehead. *Something's not right here!*

"Well?" Buchanan said.

"You . . . you don't feel it?" she asked.

They shook their heads. Dubois licked her lips and stood back, forcing her legs to move. The pulsing lessened. She pointed to the marking. "What if . . . what if Hilary had found a marking like this? And touched it. And . . ." She let them finish the thought.

"And she was caught," Tyler said, "by . . . something."

"Exactly. Step closer to it, Frances, but *don't touch anything*."

Tyler did so. Less than a meter from the wall she felt herself relaxing, feeling the pulse match her own. Everything seemed fine, and there was something about the mark that—

Dubois snatched her hand away, yanking Tyler around. She

blinked, eyes refocusing, and realized she had been about to push through the wall.

"Christ Almightly," she whispered. "I . . . I . . ." She couldn't finish.

Buchanan's grip on his laser grew slippery. "I think I'll take your word that something's goin' on here. You've been resistin' whatever pull that mark has because you're suspicious, on guard. Hilary wouldn't've been. She would've touched."

Dubois nodded. "And now no more Hilary."

He stepped back, raising his laser. "Look out. I'll give it a tickle with this."

"No!" Dubois snapped. "Remember what you said? What sort of defenses are there?"

"If there were any, wouldn't they have been used before now?"

Tyler said, "You're still assuming there's someone aboard."

"I'm not assumin' nothing, not anymore."

"Right," Dubois said. "So no shooting. Everything *reacts*, nothing initiates. What sort of reaction would your shot trigger?"

His aim eased. "Quite correct." He motioned towards the "door." "But she's right through there, damnit. We can't just leave her, not when we're so close."

"*If* we're so close," Tyler corrected. "All we know is that she's in that *direction*."

"We'll circle forward," Dubois said after a pause. "See if there's another approach."

Buchanan seemed about to argue, but relented in silence. Tyler marked the spot with a transponder stuck on the opposite wall and they walked off at a brisk pace.

The corridor curved, ending in a conventional doorway. They made a pressure check and pushed through after getting the green. They came out onto the bridge, the starboard end of the crescent. Hilary's signal went out.

When they looked back, the wall was bare, no markings. Dubois shifted an eyebrow. "I suppose that was to be expected."

"No signal, no door," Tyler said. She pushed at the wall. It held. "Nothing. A one-way door."

Buchanan was breathing heavily, frustrated. "What do we do now?"

"Back to the boat," Dubois said. "We try again later, this time suited up for vacuum. I want to be better prepared when we see what's on the other side of that marking."

11

Fusion

Breakfast was a quiet, tense affair. Daggit had withdrawn into himself, waiting for any real news. Forsythe, So, and Quont likewise kept to themselves. Dubois felt partially responsible: the three of them had been excluded from virtually all discussions. She downed the last of her tepid tea, knowing that they were almost worthless for what she had in mind.

Buchanan pulled out a fresh map and showed the route he had accented. "This seems the most direct. We took some wild turns yesterday."

Dubois shrugged. Buchanan asked, "Do you plan on going through that marking?"

"Yes."

"But what about defenses? You said yesterday—"

"I said we needed to be better prepared. I'll be in a pressure suit. It's the best I can do."

"A suit isn't worth a damn against a laser."

She put down her cup. "Look, someone's got to go through that wall if we're going to find out anything. That someone's me."

"The captain of a ship should never—"

"I'm not a captain. I'm an ensign, period." She stood and turned to Tyler. "Ready, Frances?"

"Sure."

"Then let's suit up." She turned back to Buchanan. "For what it's worth, I'm not going in totally unprepared."

"Like hell."

"We're stopping at one of the regular doors." Dubois bent over and began pulling on her pressure suit. "I want to see what's on the other side other than vacuum."

The three of them stood in front of the horizontal striping. Buchanan double-checked Dubois's suit, stepped back and nodded. "If you insist."

She nodded. "I do."

She activated her scanwand and pushed it through, confirming there was still a vacuum on the other side. Satisfied, she went through.

No lights, no sound. She snapped on her scanwand's torch and flashed it around. She was in a small room, a ball three meters in diameter. The floor curved down and away from her before warping up into the other side. Odd shapes were laid around, none recognizable. Yet it all had a familiar feel. She studied her surroundings more closely. There was a bench, similar to the ones on the bridge and in the shuttles, missing only the upside-down U control panel. An assortment of appendages hung from the walls and ceiling, as well as a few sticking up from the floor. She looked for a moment more, comprehension growing, and stepped back out into the corridor.

"Curiosity satisfied yet?" Buchanan asked.

"Not yet," she said. They went to the next door.

The room was like the first in dimensions, but with subtle variations. There weren't as many wall decorations and the bench was on another wall. Dubois nodded to herself, sure now what the rooms were.

"Cabins," she said, standing once more with her companions. "Crew quarters. I'll bet every door with a vacuum on the other side leads to someone's bunk space, or a storage room. The ship only pressurized the corridors and other main areas."

"The morgue is a main area?" Tyler asked.

"It feeds directly off a corridor with no separating wall. Besides, I never said my theory was perfect."

"Okay, so we know what's there," Buchanan said. "Can we get on to that odd door?"

They found it only by stumbling across the transponder they had left behind. The marking opposite it was for a normal door.

"It's changed—again," Tyler said.

"On the bridge it vanished," Buchanan said. "Why shouldn't it change?"

Dubois thought for a moment, then said, "It may no longer lead to the same place."

"You're still getting Hilary's signal here."

She looked at Buchanan. "So what? It's only a direction."

He stepped away, hesitating for a moment before starting to shed his suit. Dubois looked mystified. "What are you doing?"

Naked except for shorts, Buchanan held his laser tightly and stepped up to the door. The pattern shifted before he got there, once more an X-on-cross.

"I thought so," he muttered, face relaxing. The ship pulsed. He blinked several times and stepped away. "*Whew*. That . . . that . . ."

"Exactly," Dubois said.

Buchanan nodded. "As I was saying, I thought so. It shifts at a lifeform's approach. The suits block out whatever it uses for sensors."

"What about on the bridge?" Tyler asked. "We were on the bridge without suits and the corner markings were for an elevator, then were gone. Nothing like this."

"Like the cap'n's, my theory ain't perfect. Maybe the ship's internals weren't on full alert at that time. Maybe that's a one-time-only door."

"Maybe someone baited a trap for Hilary there," Dubois said. She snapped at Buchanan, "Get back into your suit. If it's a normal door now, maybe we can go through with no trouble."

"Maybe," Buchanan mumbled, doubtful. He pulled his suit back on.

Ready again, Dubois stepped forward, scanwand ahead of her, laser drawn. The stripes had become "normal," and there was no reason for fear. If she had never seen the spot before, she would have stuck the wand through without hesitation. As it was . . .

The probe went through easily, reading a vacuum beyond. Steeling herself, Dubois went through. Tyler and Buchanan waited for her to disappear, then stepped forward.

The wall shimmered and the markings vanished. Tyler slammed a gloved fist against the now-solid wall.

Pamela Dubois stood in darkness, oblivious to her companions' absence. She spoke without turning. "No lights. We'll have to use our torches."

Remembering what Tyler had said earlier, she first made a radar sweep of the area ahead. The scan showed she was in a corridor some three meters wide. The ghostly image on the screen emptied out twenty-five meters ahead.

"Seems clear," she said. She turned on her light and turned around—and found herself alone.

A surge of panic swept through her. She jumped to the smooth, unmarked wall, pounding on it uselessly. Controlling herself, her grip on the laser tightening, she flashed her light around. All was dark, the walls absorbing the beam.

Any way out is ahead, she thought. Turning her back to the wall, she began walking down the corridor.

Hilary's signal had surged in strength when she came through the wall. It continued to grow stronger. Dubois shifted to tracer and saw she was getting closer. Near the corridor's end she could see a faint glow. *Something* was there.

The room was a dozen meters across, a circle with a low ceiling. The walls, ceiling, and floor was dead black and nonreflective, like most of the ship had been. Machinery was arrayed around her with no discernible order—balls, eggs, curves, arches of assorted sizes. They all glowed with changing hues and intensities, amber and gold, all apparently functioning perfectly. Dubois frowned and stepped into the room, trying to look all ways at once. For the second time she felt an air of familiarity about the place.

She had once been within the computer core of the *Goddess*. The feel here was much the same, the quiet workings of a million cybernetic synapses. This was the alien equivalent; she felt sure of it. The derelict's "brain," the computer operation and memory banks. This was where it "lived."

There is no one alive on board this ship, she thought. Everything had been controlled, been preordained, from here, by computer. It was reacting along preprogrammed lines, tit for tat.

Dubois walked around slowly, carefully, touching nothing.

She secured her laser in its thigh hooks and began a thorough search. She had to find a door, a way out.

To her right she saw another opening. She went to it and looked through. The room was easily twice as large as the one she was in, also circular, but with a higher ceiling. Long cables hung from the ceiling, ending several meters above the floor.

Spaced evenly around the room's circumference were round containers, each three meters across, two meters apart. The cables were clustered over the containers. The nearest was to her left, little more than two meters away. The line ended ten meters to her right.

The latter seemed active. It glowed with a warm golden light. She went through the doorway, stepping down to the floor.

For a moment it felt as though she were moving through molasses. Then the resistance was gone and sound came through her helmet's sound disks.

Air, she realized. She looked back at the doorway. From this side she could see a faint amber shimmer—a force field. It was opaque to air yet let her through.

She turned her attention back to the container and moved closer. The sounds around her were soft, relaxing. It was the same pulsing she had heard by the strange marking, only this time it wasn't trying to match her heartbeat. It just throbbed in a relaxing manner, steady and constant.

Her foot kicked something and she flashed her torch downwards. She found the tatters of Kahn's jumpsuit, along with her radio and laser.

Dubois felt a chill along her spine and looked up. The cables dangled from the ceiling, still and quiescent. One ended in a mittlike appendage—Marito's paw. Each set around the room was identical.

She moved towards the glowing container, knowing what she would find.

It held Hilary Kahn, relaxed and unmoving. Dubois imagined she was naked, though it was difficult to tell. The light came up from beneath her, silhouetting her in strong contrast. She was spread-eagle, an opening in the container's top conforming to her shape. Her hands and feet disappeared into the metal. Her mouth and eyes were covered, head drawn back and neck straight. Cuplike affairs covered her breasts and a disk lay on her stomach. A probe had been inserted into the urethra, presumably as a catheter.

Dubois looked closer, squinting against the glare. Kahn was not covered by the metal—she was fused to it. Where flesh and metal metal joined was separated only by color.

There was a flash of recognition. *The aliens in the morgue . . .*

She felt bile rising in her throat. Grimacing, she fought it back down.

No doubt the alien computers were taking blood and metabolism readings from Kahn, carefully matching chemistries and, with equal care, keeping her alive. Dubois watched her chest rise and fall with a steady rhythm and wondered if she was conscious.

"Hilary?" she said softly. No response. A little louder, "Hilary?"

A knee jerked and she could see the skin around the eyes twitch, nose flaring slightly. A deep throbbing shook the room.

"Oh," she muttered, grasping the side of the container for support. She fought a growing weakness in her knees. *She can hear!*

"Hilary," she said, controlling herself, "try . . . try and relax. We'll get . . . get you out."

Tall order. How do I get out?

She stepped away from the container, towards the door. A gargling sound came from around her, reverberating in her helmet. A word, not quite clear. The room's throbbing picked up for a moment, then slowed. Hilary became still.

But that one pseudoword stuck in Dubois's mind. It had sounded like *need.*

After several minutes of futile shouting over the radio, Buchanan had finally stopped. He looked at Tyler. "Just what do we do now?"

"I haven't the slightest idea. Try and relax. Pamela's a competent woman. She'll get out."

"Assumin' nothin's got her trapped on the other side. I say we blast our way through."

Tyler shook her head. "Wait first."

Another five minutes dragged by. Buchanan paced back and forth like a caged animal.

The walls suddenly throbbed with a gargle. They swung around, half surprised, half terrified.

"Something's got her!" he yelled. He unclipped his laser, aiming in one smooth motion. "To hell with this."

"*No!*" Tyler shouted.

The beam flared, splashing against the wall. It sizzled, and a meter and a half high gap grew. It puckered inwards and they felt the tug as air was sucked into the vacuum beyond. Abruptly, the flow stopped.

Buchanan ignored it, ecstatic. "There. Let's—"

A grunted sound broke out around them. His look of triumph melted into one of concern. Tyler stepped away from him, drawing her own laser. Anything that came at them would have two spaced targets to grab at.

It only wanted one. The corridor space around Buchanan turned dark blue, lights vanishing as long tendrils formed from the ceiling and lashed out.

He had no time to react. They grabbed him roughly, twisting him off the floor, laser clattering away. He screamed once, the tendrils drawing tight. They pulled, and he vanished through the ceiling.

The lights returned, the corridor once more a bright and cheery yellow with wood floors. Stunned, Tyler looked at Buchanan's laser. It had happened in less than a second, not enough time for her to even consider firing her own weapon.

Dubois appeared at the gap in the wall. She looked at the shaken Tyler. "What the hell happened?"

"You . . . you're all right," Tyler said, dazed.

"*What happened?*"

"Buchanan tried . . . *did* cut through the wall to get you out. Then something . . . something grabbed him."

Dubois grabbed Tyler's sleeve. "Come on! We may still be able to save him."

They went through the cut, its edges bubbling as it began to close. They charged down the corridor, through a door that had formed into place the moment Buchanan had cut through the main wall, presumably to protect the delicate computer arrays. They passed through the machinery, towards where Kahn lay.

Dubois slammed into the amber field, bouncing off. It had stiffened into an impenetrable barrier.

"Force field," Tyler said. "We can't get through."

"I did before. It was just like a doorway, only transparent. There's air on the other side."

Knowing what had happened to Buchanan, there was no

thought of using laser fire. Tyler looked around in puzzlement. "What is this?"

"Welcome to the brain, the computer room. Hilary . . . Hilary's over there." She pointed to the glowing container.

"Did you—"

"She's alive, fused with the metal, somehow. We'll need time to figure out a way to—"

Buchanan came out of the ceiling, his screams sounding over their radios. He hovered over the container next to Hilary's as it came to life, a golden field enveloping him. The cables came to life, working on his suit. His struggles were useless.

The tendrils and the cables are the same, Dubois thought. *They're part of the same system.*

Buchanan's helmet did a half turn and popped off. His cries became weaker as the helmet microphone was pulled away, vanishing altogether as the equipment was tossed into the center of the room.

"Why can't we hear him?" Tyler asked.

Dubois said, "We're in a vacuum here. That door we came through at the corridor's end wasn't there before. When Kevin cut through, it shut automatically, preventing air from reaching here."

They watched Buchanan's silent struggles as he was neatly stripped and placed into the container. Arms and legs were gently stretched out. Metal caught and held, flowing over hands and feet. Attachments like those on Hilary covered his chest, hips, and abdomen. It seemed momentarily confused by his penis but adapted quickly. His knees twitched as he struggled, still yelling. He turned and saw Dubois and Tyler watching and shouted at them, not understanding why they couldn't help.

Cups came out and covered his eyes; a caplike arrangement caught the back of his head and pulled it down. The final attachment appeared out of the container, a tube inserting itself carefully into his mouth as his head was tilted back, neck stretched for a smooth trachea entry. His struggles faded as the alien life-support took over. A moment later they ceased completely.

"Oh, oh damn," muttered Tyler. Her stomach jerked, and she clenched her teeth to prevent vomiting into her helmet.

Dubois tried to focus her attention on something else. Her

breath came in shudders as she said, "We . . . we've got to get out of here, Frances. *Now*." She pulled her gently away from the door.

Beyond, she could see the tendrils retracting to their relaxed position, the glow around Buchanan now matching Kahn's. She blinked back the tears.

Kevin!

She had yet to explore the rest of the compartment. Leaving Tyler sitting on the floor, she went to the room's other side, searching. She almost shouted in relief when she found the markings of a doorway. On the way back to recover Tyler, she saw that the emergency doorway was gone, the end of the corridor dark and healed.

With Tyler she returned to the exit. She made the customary check for pressure on the other side, finding some temporary escape in routine. The readout flashed green. They stepped through together, into another bright yellow hallway.

The wall behind them was blank.

Hit and miss guided them to a familiar corridor, marked with Buchanan's fallen laser and the transponder. Tyler was walking on her own by then, and Dubois picked up the weapon. The wall held the markings of a normal door, no signs of the damage Buchanan had done.

"Where do we go from here?" Tyler asked softly.

Dubois looked at her in concern. Something inside Tyler had jerked upon seeing Kahn and Buchanan's fate. She couldn't help wondering if that was the fate they all faced. Dubois had the same haunting suspicion.

"We'll get back to the boat, Frances," she replied, equally soft. "We'll get back to the others."

"No," Tyler said, shaking her head. "I mean, and then? What will we do?"

Four words, all simple, with no ready answer.

"We'll see, Frances, we'll see."

Tyler jerked away from her. "'We'll see'?" she cried. "Damn you! Don't you realize what's happened? We're not getting out of here, *Captain*, Ensign, whatever the hell you are. This goddamn ship is going to absorb us all, each in turn, until . . . until—" She broke off, fighting for breath.

"Take it easy," Dubois said, stepping up to her side. "We'll get out of here."

"I asked how. If we use lasers, we'll end up like Kevin."

"Not in the hangar. Not there. This is a security area, the computer center. They'd naturally have the best defenses here. But at the hangar we can—"

"Don't humor me, Pamela," Tyler said, voice more under control. The seasoned engineer, used to handling emergencies, was returning. "The hangar is a secure area too. The defenses there are liable to be even tougher."

She has a point, Dubois acknowledged to herself. It was one she didn't wish to dwell on.

She took Tyler by the arm. "Whatever we're going to do, Frances, we've got to get back to the boat and warn the others."

Tyler relented. They began walking when the lights went out. Tyler gasped in panic, the floor shifting under their feet. Dubois froze in a tremble, waiting for the tendrils to lash out, to grab—

The lights came back on, in shifting patterns. The corridor had changed and was now six-sided, the lighting a tube pattern overhead. The colors were warm—rich browns and greens. It locked into the texture of smooth leather, the floor a fine hexagonal grid.

Neither one commented on the change. Both recognized what was happening and moved swiftly towards the boat.

The ship was assimilating Starman Kevin Buchanan.

12

"—need—"

Marito was studying the alien craft that had almost killed him. The change in scenery had occurred within the hangar without any great alarm; change had become the new norm. The type of change, however, had been momentarily disconcerting to Daggit. He couldn't identify it with anything in Hilary's nature.

The lighting overhead now appeared starkly functional, arrayed in long tubes. The decking was the hexagonal grid but with a glow rising up through it. Marito was taking advantage of the added illumination to inspect the craft's underside.

He heard two distinct sighs of relief and turned. Tyler and Dubois stood just inside the hangar, looking around, their faces pale. He frowned. *Where is Starman Buchanan?*

He walked towards them, voicing his question as Tyler walked by, helmet in hand. She didn't answer, heading straight for the lifeboat. Dubois followed, then stopped to scowl at Marito. "What are you doing there? I thought—"

"I wasn't doing a thing. Where is Starman Buchanan?"

Dubois swallowed and said, "With Hilary."

"Eh?"

"The ship has them both. They're sealed inside the computer room and—"

"The what?"

She groaned in frustration. "Will you let me finish?" She opened her mouth to continue, thought better of it, and motioned for him to follow her to the boat. "Come on. I want the others to hear too."

Back aboard, Daggit sat alone, pale and shaking. Tyler had grunted only that they had found Kahn alive. From her refusal to discuss it further, as she headed for the storage room, Daggit had inferred that Hilary's condition was desperate.

Dubois came into the boat and found all eyes pinned on her. She didn't—couldn't—look at Daggit.

Marito, just behind, said, "Well? What did you find?"

She hated him for his abruptness. *How do I tell this?*

"Hilary *is* alive, is she not?" Poullard asked. "And where is Kevin?"

"They're both alive," Dubois said, "but they're both . . ." She paused. *Begin again . . .*

"There's no one left of the original crew. We've found their morgue and their bodies. Ev—"

"What?" Marito interrupted. "Where?"

"Forward, near the bow." He seemed ready to ask another question, but she cut him off with a gesture. "Everything that's happened so far has been controlled by the ship's computers. They appear to be functioning normally, though your guess is as good as mine as to what 'normal' is. Hilary and Kevin . . . Hilary and Kevin are there, trapped within some sort of containers. I don't know why they're there, what they're doing, or how to get them out."

"Cut them open!" Daggit snapped, eyes wide. "Cut them open!"

"No." Tyler came out of the storage room, her pressure suit draped over one arm. "Kevin tried cutting through one of the ship's walls to get to Pamela. That's how he was caught. The ship has an automatic defense system, long tentacles. They are very fast and very effective."

"They caught him," Dubois finished, "and put him in a container next to Hilary's."

"But we can't just leave them there," So said. "There must be *something* we can do."

"Unfortunately," Tyler said, "that might not be true. It's not as if they were inside some sort of jar we could crack open."

Daggit's eyebrows shifted. "What do you mean?"

Dubois described the containers, the connections, and how

the flesh had merged with the alien material. Daggit's face lost
all color, his eyes wide and glazed as the full impact of what
had become of Hilary Kahn hit home.

Dubois shot a glance towards Poullard. She was already
prepared, moving quietly closer to the old man. She placed a
reassuring arm around his shoulders and muttered something
calming. He never noticed the tiny injector, and faded quickly
into a deep sleep.

"Captain Dubois," Marito said, "I must see this room. Can
you find that side door?"

"It doesn't exist—" she began, then stopped. His emotionless comment touched a raw nerve. She whirled towards him,
fury dancing in her eyes. "That room holds two of our people,
Marito, literally fused with them. I don't think we'll ever be
able to get them out and you want to go study them like insects
on exhibition—*if* you want to see *them* at all."

His face darkened in anger. "Listen to me, Dubois, I can
imagine you think that I am nothing more than a callous
bastard, but the plain truth of the matter is that I am the closest
you have to a research scientist. You have as much as admitted
that you know of no way to free either Miss Kahn or Starman
Buchanan. Do you mind so very much if I at least see what I
can learn?"

The flash of anger vanished and she slowly nodded. "All
right, Mr. Marito. I'm sorry for what I said. You could be
right." She turned to Tyler. "Give him your suit, Frances.
Let's get him sized in."

The two of them went alone, there being only two pressure
suits now. Beside that, Dubois wanted no one else outside the
lifeboat. The walk through the ship was slow and easy. She
watched things with even more caution than before. They kept
their face plates open, breathing the ship's air, conserving their
own, limited supply. There had been no time to recharge the
suit air tanks and both were down to less than an hour.

"Smells musky," Marito commented, sniffing.

Dubois nodded. "Like a locker room. Kevin sweated like
crazy."

"Curious, how the computers react to body odors and mix it
in with the atmosphere. Perhaps the aliens communicated with
smell, at least partially."

Dubois grunted, only half listening.

"And have you noticed the temperature? It's down to eighteen degrees."

"Kevin liked it cool. Always complained about the heat."

"I know." He chuckled slightly. "We must be giving the ship fits, trying to assimilate our various likes and dislikes, our physical differences, our size and shape."

The entrance was as Dubois and Tyler had left it. The two of them snapped shut their face plates, and the wall shimmered into the tranquil pattern of a normal door.

"We'll push through together," Dubois said. "When I went through alone, it sealed up behind me."

Marito nodded. They stood to the wall and went through. Nothing had changed. The room was still in vacuum. Marito looked about quickly, the arrays of alien circuitry flickering for attention. Dubois tapped his shoulder and led him towards the room that held his fascination.

"This doorway has an energy field," she said. "It works like a normal doorway but with no solid barrier."

He nodded, studying the pale shimmer. "I imagine it's a sterilization field, maintaining the room beyond in an antiseptic condition."

"Sounds reasonable." She turned and walked through, the field no longer stiff enough to stop them.

The containers with Kahn and Buchanan still gave off their golden radiance. Marito stared at them, incredulous. Looking at Hilary's pale and still form, he remembered Daggit's reaction to this news. He was glad the man could not see the reality of that description; the shock would kill him.

Dubois stood off to one side, unwilling to look closer. She was still reeling from watching Buchanan's subjugation. She had no desire to dispassionately study him.

Marito leaned over Hilary's container and extended a hand. He half expected the glow to stop him, but nothing happened. His hand went through and lightly touched her thigh.

The skin twitched and a grunting sounded over his earphones. He turned to Dubois.

"You said Hilary tried to say something?"

She nodded. "Yes. It was only a grunt, like just now."

He shook his head. "No, not like just now. *That* came over the radio. I'll bet what you heard did as well."

Dubois frowned. It was possible. There was so little carrier interference that a radio signal was nearly as clear as an ambient sound coming through the sound disks. With a grunt like she had heard, there was even less to differentiate.

"Radio?" she muttered. Her eyes widened. "That means they're tied into the ship's systems somehow. They're not being used just for samplers."

"It appears so. Remember my experience in the shuttle."

"Brain-link."

He nodded. "Direct cortex connection."

He carefully cracked his face plate open and sniffed, wrinkling his nose. He resealed his helmet.

"What?" Dubois asked.

"The air. It's not like the rest of the ship. Oh, it's breathable, but with disinfectant overtones, like a well-scrubbed hospital. I was right. That field is a decontamination procedure and this room is kept sterile. And that sound; look at them. I'll bet that throbbing is an audible pacekeeper maintaining them in a calm, relaxed state. And the tank glow is some sort of irradiation field, maintaining a healthy appearance."

He returned to his examination of Kahn, now speaking softly in the hope it would calm her. It did nothing. Knees and arms jerked, obviously trying to fight their way out.

Dubois frowned and, overcoming her trepidation, stepped closer. She looked at Kahn and said, "Her restraints have changed."

"How so?"

The metal holding Kahn now looked like a cross, the horizontal bar going across her chest. Her legs were spread in a V and the vertical bar started there, going up and over her abdomen, past her chest, crawling up her chin and covering her mouth. It split and passed on both sides of her nose, then covered her eyes, finally rejoining with a cap that covered the back of her head before merging back with the container. Buchanan's was identical.

Dubois explained the differences and said, "I don't understand. Why the change?"

"Bisexual. It's adjusting to the variety in the human form. Buchanan was its second . . . specimen. It has discovered the differences between men and women."

"It seems to be aware of modesty," she said, hoping for levity.

Marito took it seriously. "No, it makes a kind of sense. It may know about sexual stimulation, and in studying Hilary—"

"It knows *what?*"

"About sex, Dubois. You know, boys and girls, birds and bees. It may intend, or plan, on holding Hilary and Buchanan for a long time, perhaps until they die. Don't look faint like that. *Think*. If we assume that the race that built this vessel had a sexual process even remotely similar to ours, if in just being bipolar and enjoyable, then can't we also assume that they recognized the need for sexual stimulation, not only for enjoyment but for peace of mind and good health as well?"

Dubois fought her twisting stomach, managing to win. "I don't like this conversation."

Marito drove on relentlessly, either out of enjoyment at her discomfort or because he was oblivious to it. "If we assume that, then let us imagine this: this center *needs* living beings to complete its computer link-up with the rest of the ship. It's the only reason for this room to exist, this equipment. The beings chosen will be here until they die. The computer recognizes the need to keep them comfortable. No doubt machinery will fondle and—"

"I get the picture," she shouted. *"Enough!* Let's get back to why we're here."

"What I'm talking about *is* why I'm here. If you're too squeamish, then—"

Dubois grabbed him by the shoulders, thankful she couldn't get her hands around his throat. She would kill him, or worse . . .

"Listen, Marito, why don't we go find one of those odd patterns and push you against it. I've got my own theory brewing and it says that if I do, then *you'll* end up in one of these tanks. Would you enjoy that? Someone jacking you off for the rest of your life? 'Sex on schedule, *sir!*' "

Marito looked at the fury in Dubois's eyes and chose his words carefully. "I . . . I meant no disrespect, Captain. I was merely trying to outline why I think they are here and the seeming display of modesty by their coverings. I . . . I'm sorry if I offended you."

Dubois's anger vanished like a deflated balloon. She released him, taking a step back. "All . . . all right, John, if I may call you that. I'm sorry for popping off like I did."

"It's okay . . . Pamela. I've often been told I'm oblivious to others' feelings."

They each managed a weak smile. Marito turned back to where Kahn lay. "I'm afraid we'll never get her out. We don't know anything about how it fused with her, and the join is too complete. Let's look at Starman Buchanan."

A few minutes later he leaned back and said, "No good here either. The process works too swiftly. Look. Even the hair has been fused, too, each individual strand."

Dubois nodded. "Okay. What now?"

His answered surprised her. "I think we must get off this ship, Pamela. The longer we stay, the greater the chance of never getting off."

"All right. How?"

"The question of the hour. I don't know." He looked at the containers with a curious expression, mind dancing on possibilities. To Dubois it didn't look as though he *really* wanted to leave.

They stepped out into the main computer room, the throbbing cut off by the lack of air. Dubois looked around, sensing the smooth workings of the room. The computers were obviously highly advanced.

Wait a minute!

"John," she said, "were you serious a moment ago, that Hilary and Kevin are now part of the ship's computer system?"

"Yes, it would appear so. That's how you heard them over the radio. They're linked in with the system."

Dubois spat a curse. "Why didn't I think of this before?"

"What?"

"The clue as to how to get Hilary and Kevin out of there, as well as getting us all out of this derelict."

His eyebrows twitched. "Yes?"

"Radio. They heard us, we heard them. *We can communicate* with them. They've got access to the ship's computers. They can give us the answers."

"That's farfetched. You heard how garbled Hilary was."

"Sure. All we have to do is find a closer wavelength and we can *talk* to Hilary and Kevin through the computer link."

"Why didn't they react to our earlier conversation?"

That stumped her, but only for a moment. "One, the suit radios don't have enough power. Two, we weren't addressing them directly, and the system didn't cue them in."

"I wouldn't get your hopes up too high, Pamela. We might not be able to tune in the proper wavelength. Besides—"

"What would the effort cost us?"

"Well, nothing but time. And that may be enough to get us all trapped here. You tell me, what does this ship want with us, *from* us? Why take Hilary or Kevin at all?"

Dubois shrugged. "I don't know, and I don't think that's important right now. What *is* important is to start searching for that frequency and *try*."

"And if we succeed?"

"Possibilities unlimited."

"And if we fail?"

He was beginning to annoy her again, now with his fatalistic attitude. "So what if we fail?" She turned her back on him, walking towards the exit. "We'll need more power, and I know where to get it."

The transceiver Kahn and Buchanan had used on the bridge was still there. Dubois squatted next to the unit as Marito stood by impatiently.

"What are we doing here?" he asked.

"This unit's as good as anything we could take off the lifeboat." She opened an access panel and reviewed the adjustment procedure. "If it doesn't work from here, I'll take it to the computer room itself. Now, I'll adjust it to the lower end of our suit frequency and . . ." She keyed the transmitter. "Testing, testing."

Her voice, badly garbled and barely audible, came over their suit earphones. She smiled and said, "Hilary, Kevin, can you hear me?"

Nothing. She adjusted further down. Nothing came over the suit radioes when she repeated the message, nor did anything reply.

"Try going up the band," suggested Marito.

She did so, just on the edge at first. After getting nothing, she tuned it beyond their suits' range once more.

A gurgling grunt came from the transceiver, then a stream of bubbling gibberish. She looked at Marito, his face a careful blank.

"I think you've succeeded," he whispered.

She keyed the transmitter again and said, "Hilary, Kevin, can you reply?"

More nonsense. Then: "—ou."

"Concentrate, one of you. Hilary, don't try to verbalize. *Think*. You're linked with the alien computer. It may—"

"—ou."

"That doesn't sound like a woman," Marito said.

Dubois nodded. "All right, Kevin, you try and—"

"—g . . . e . . . ou."

"That's it," she encouraged. "You can—"

"—*need*—"

It was the first clear word, and sounded oddly asexual. She missed the peculiarity, turning to Marito in frustration. "I can't finish a sentence."

"He's too anxious. Tell him to relax."

"Relax, Kevin, take it slowly. We're here. Just stay calm and *try*."

"—*am*."

"Good, good. More."

The voice this time was clearly inhuman, without gender, and cold: "Integration incomplete nonpriority interface negative clearance access deny deny cancel—"

Marito looked stunned. "What . . . was . . . that?"

Dubois was white, awestruck. She whispered, "The ship. The ship's computer is interfering." She keyed the transmitter. "Kevin, fight it. *Fight it!*"

The ship growled around them. Tendrils grew out from the corner where Kahn had vanished, unnoticed by either of them. They stretched to their limit, swinging at the humans just out of reach. They stopped, pulled back, and surged forward again, but only halfway. They began to retract, only to extend, the mechanism confused by conflicting commands.

Abruptly the lights went out. There was a hissing sound, then a roar. Dubois shouted, "Decompression. Seal your suit!"

The roar became a hurricane, pinning them to one side of the doorway. It stopped just as abruptly as it had started, the lights coming back on. They swirled in a dazzle for a moment before becoming tubelike once more. Dubois automatically checked her oxygen readout, feeling her suit expand. The pressure around them was down to less than one percent, an effective vacuum, and they had only ten minutes of air left.

She turned to patch into the transceiver. She could use a wire connection and—

It was gone. Looking down and about, she could find no trace.

"Damn," Marito gasped.

Dubois spun and saw what he was staring at. The tendrils from the far corner were just disappearing. They had caught the transceiver as it was flung about in the hurricane. They hadn't tried to take it back through the wall, slashing it to pieces and leaving the fragments behind.

Marito looked at his own air readout. "We haven't enough air to make it back to the boat. Can you tune our suit radios close enough to make contact, get them to repressurize the ship?"

She shook her head. "I . . . I don't know." Her fingers were already at work, though, opening the chest access panel. It pivoted downwards, allowing her to see what she was doing. Her gloved fingers were clumsy, moving the tuning knob without delicacy.

"Kevin, Kevin, can you hear me?"

An incredibly loud grunting sounded in her ears. She winced and said, "Kevin, you're going to have to repressurize the ship. Do it *now.*"

"Negative negative identify unauthorized interface overlap security negative security security."

"The ship again," Marito said. "It's using them as translators, interfaces. But its use is imperfect, hence the incomplete sentences."

She looked at her suit readout again. Marito had been right; neither of them could make it back to the boat. If the computer didn't repressurize the interior soon, they were dead.

Her face hardened, as did her voice. She snapped, "Command input: pressurize *immediately.*"

Buchanan had been in the service. He understood orders. If enough of him had been interfaced with the computer, he could be a translator, as Marito suggested. Output may be imperfect, but perhaps input . . .

The indicator on her scanwand wavered, then climbed quickly. Fifty percent, sixty, seventy, until it was once more at one hundred percent. She cracked open her faceplate a bit, took one breath, and found it breathable.

Marito opened his own and gasped, breathing deeply. "How did you know to do that?"

"Kevin always obeyed a command if you gave it to him hard

enough. I gave him an order and he relayed it into the alien computer.''

"Which means I was correct, that they are now part of the ship's 'brain,' living computers.''

"Yes. I—''

He interrupted. "I wouldn't try it too often, though. No doubt what we're doing is contrary to the ship's programming.''

She nodded. "Should I try again now?''

"I'm not sure. It nearly killed us once. It obviously does not appreciate your trying to communicate.''

"Radio contact must be forbidden, to prevent crewmembers from tampering with the computer core. If anyone could gain access, then anyone could take command.''

"The system must not be complete, or the security program would have functioned immediately.''

"In that case . . .'' She thumbed her radio. "Hilary, can you try this time? We'll—''

"—deny!''

"That wasn't Hilary,'' Marito said. "It was Buchanan. He's blocking her.''

Dubois frowned. "Why?''

"I don't know. That voice was masculine.''

"The computer is neuter. Don't—''

An all-too-feminine cry came over her earphones, causing her to hiss in surprise. She looked at Marito. "I take that back.''

"Adjust my radio and let me try,'' he said. "We might not have much time. You've been appealing to the people. Let me try and talk to the machine.''

She made the adjustment quickly and he said, "Interrogative. Function identify. Execute.'' He looked at Dubois. "I'm hoping either Hilary or Kevin has had enough experience working with computers to interpret the terms for the alien system. It seemed to work for your simple commands. If they work for this, we may be able to—''

"Function incomplete. Programming incomplete. Systems incomplete.'' The voice was hard, cold, and precise, neither Buchanan's nor Kahn's; asexual.

Dubois was breathing heavily when she said, "I think you have succeeded.''

He nodded. "Interrogative, priority. State data needs. Execute."

Both waited for the reply. There was a garbled tone, a few snatches of words, then a dual-toned cry, a mixture of Buchanan and Kahn. Dubois winced at the sound, knowing that the security program must be going into effect. It was clamping down on its living components, isolating them, forbidding this outside communication. She knew this would never work again.

There were more tones, scratches, a groan. Another scream. And one clear word.

"—*need*—"

13

Sacrifices

"Need?" Daggit asked, a slight tremor in his voice. "What could this ship *need*?"

Dubois shrugged. "I don't know, but the desire was clear. It *needs* something."

The others in the lifeboat looked confused, uncertain. Marito said, "Its programming is incomplete. That much is clear. I believe the question is, what does it need to complete its programming?"

Forsythe slammed a fist into his chair's arm. "Why don't we blast our way out of here and be done with this ghost ship? I see no reason why—"

"Shut up, Forsythe," ordered Tyler. "You weren't hired to think. I, for one, don't wish to hear your opinions."

"I no longer work for you, Miss Tyler, so I may speak as I please."

"But *I* don't please," Dubois said, "so shut up just the same. I am not leaving this ship until I'm certain we can't rescue Kevin and Hilary."

"What more proof do you need?" Forsythe asked. "You said yourself that the metal of the ship has absorbed them. The process is irreversible."

Daggit's face flushed and he looked at him from the corner

of one blazing eye. "How do you know that? You seem to be better informed than we are."

Forsythe drew himself up. "It's only common sense."

"Meaning we don't have any?"

Forsythe caught the clear tone of menace in Daggit's voice. He deflated quickly. "Uh, look, we *can't* save them. The ship has . . . assimilated them too far. They're goners."

"I think I know what the ship wants," Tyler said, talking to everyone but looking narrowly at Forsythe. "The ship wants a third body. Let's give it Forsythe."

The man paled at the threat, and backed into one corner of his seat, silent.

Nan Poullard said, "Perhaps you are right, Miss Tyler. Maybe all the ship wants, all it needs, is another body, another brain."

"But why?" Marito asked. "Assuming that is the case, why does it need another?"

"It needs twelve," Dubois said. "There are twelve containers. There are now ten empty spaces." Her smile was tight. "If it wants another body, it's going to be badly disappointed."

Poullard spoke again, quietly. "Mr. Marito, how long would one live under the conditions in those containers?"

He shrugged. "Unknown. No doubt the ship has gotten an excellent understanding of our physiology by now. Aside from their, er, condition, both Miss Kahn and Starman Buchanan seemed in good health. There is no reason to believe that condition would deteriorate."

"I wonder what the ship would do if one of them took ill."

"Probably diagnose the illness and treat it. We've only scratched the surface of the ship's computer functions. Look how quickly it determined our proper air mixture, and from a mere wisp of vapor."

Poullard looked thoughtful and leaned back. Only Forsythe caught the odd expression on her face and felt a moment's chill of apprehension.

Kelly said, "I'm not sure I'd like to use a laser against the hangar doors anyway." His military heritage was beginning to show as he frowned and concentrated on the tactical situation. "From what happened to Kevin, the punishment seems pretty severe."

"I don't think what happened to the Starman would occur

here," Marito said. "After all, he blasted his way into a high-security area. Such is not the case here."

"I'm not so sure about that," Tyler mumbled. She added, voice firmer, "Have any of you wondered about those shuttles, or what we've called 'shuttles.'" To their shaking heads she said, "I have, and it seems funny that all of them have only *one* seat and no apparent room for anyone else. *One* person per shuttle? That seems a trifle wasteful to me."

"What are you getting at?" Dubois asked.

"What sort of craft is perfectly efficient with only a one-man crew?"

A myriad of suggestions, more than she expected. "Work bug." "One-man cargo." "Inspection shuttle." "Assault fighter." "Scoutship."

She held up a hand. "Whoa. The last two will do."

Marito looked surprised. "What? A fighter or a scoutship? What are you suggesting, Miss Tyler?"

"I'm suggesting what the purpose of this vessel might be."

Her pauses for suspense were maddening. Dubois snapped, "Well, what?"

"A warship, one whose crew was killed. In which case the computer would be starved for its 'biological units,' the twelve empty containers. Now we stumbled along and it's making due with an alien lifeform. It's a warship, designed for battle conditions, to adapt to any condition. That explains why the interior can change. A corridor gets blown out and the ship rearranges to compensate."

"Or it could be an idiosyncracy," Marito snapped, angry that anyone would suggest that *his* alien derelict was an abandoned man-o-war. "We're dealing with an entirely alien culture here."

"Let her finish," Dubois said.

Tyler nodded thanks and went on. "The only problem with this ship is that it cannot involuntarily recruit minds for the biological computer link. That's why you have the shifting symbols. If one of the links dies in the tank it's disposed of, placed in the morgue we found for other uses, or some alien burial rite, or whatever. The computer alerts the rest of the crew that there is a *need*, perhaps as simply as allowing the doorway striping to change. The best one for the job is selected. He goes to the x symbol, and touches the wall, the ship soothing him for his transition from normal crew-membership to the vessel's true command elite. He touches the wall and from then on the process is automatic.''

She took a breath, then a sip of water from a nearby glass. "But the *mechanical* computer sometimes needs servicing. The sensors around the symbol are set to activate the assimilation process only where there's a need and a *naked* volunteer is there. A double-check for safety. A worker wears a spacesuit, and only one is allowed in at a time. Security purposes and all that.''

"A pat theory," Marito said, "but you missed a point. If that area is so secure, why did the computer use Buchanan as a biological link, as you named them? Why didn't it simply kill him?''

"Two possible answers. One, that if all twelve containers had been full, it would have. It *needs* bodies, brains. Without them it is only partially 'alive,' a dog responding to random inputs. Two, perhaps it doesn't kill at all. If the containers had been filled, perhaps any act of insanity—and an attack on the ship's nerve center would surely be viewed as such—would only have the attacker, the 'victim,' whisked off to an examination room. Or broken down into spare parts for wounded personnel.''

"That last is a bit macabre," Dubois said.

"And is purely my imagination. I, like Marito, would like to think that the builders of this ship were peaceful. And I'd like to make one more point.

"Twelve bodies, twelve brains, are needed to fully activate this ship. Assuming that, how many are needed to bring it up to the point where it can blast out of orbit and head for home?''

Dubois looked thoughtful. "Perhaps it only needs two, in which case we could soon find ourselves bound for—''

"Where?" Daggit asked.

"This is insane," Marito said. "I don't see your proof for this being a warship. Those shuttles may really be scoutships for inspecting planets from long range, and/or for inspecting the vessel's exterior. The role of explorer could be served equally well by an 'adapting vessel' design. Why do you assume they were hostile?''

Tyler shrugged. "I don't. You may be right, Mr. Marito, but doesn't it strike you as odd that this ship hasn't *any* multiseat shuttles, if what you say is correct?''

"Nor does it seem right for *your* theory," he said. "Besides, we haven't checked them all."

"I've checked most of them," So said. To Dubois's sharp glance, he added, "Jeanine and I went together. We kept in short-range communications with Mr. Daggit all the while. Every shuttle we saw was a single-seater."

There was a short pause, then Daggit spoke, low and soft. "I still don't understand *why*." He looked at Dubois, then Marito. "Why does this ship need . . . people? The normal computer seems perfectly adequate. Why *living* people?"

Marito pursed his lips and replied, "Look at our own history of computers. For over a century the quest in computronics has been to create a mechanical/electrical computer that duplicates human thought processes. It has been suggested that we could use living matter to do this. The beings who made this ship have taken a shortcut towards that end. They may not be as advanced in computronic research, but they understood how to tap into the living brain. And it's much easier to maintain a healthy body, letting it maintain a healthy brain, than it is to maintain the brain by itself."

"The . . . biological units do all the *real* thinking," Dubois said. "The mechanical units can only react to their programming, with no extraneous options. The biological units initiate planning, make decisions, command."

"Then why isn't Hilary or Kevin commanding?" So asked. "CPUs."

He turned to Tyler. "Eh?"

"Central Processing Units. That's all they may be, all they can be. Kevin was . . . drafted, and the ship might not trust him. Hilary may not be capable; it probably has a built-in set of acceptance standards. Or they may not be taking any stored programming too well. The ship might not be at all picky about who is selected for the tanks, but it probably has a minimum set of standards for performance. They may be trying to do something that contradicts those standards."

"Such as communicating with us," Daggit said, voice low and distant.

Before the silence grew pregnant, Tyler said, "I'd like to make one more suggestion before passing out," she stifled a yawn, "and it fits with what Pamela said. I think we should check the morgue tomorrow, first thing."

Dubois looked confused. "Why?"

"Because how could the mechanical computers interpret our atmosphere requirements and make a suitable, breathable environment? That process appears to be a function of a *biological* unit."

Dubois jumped ahead. "You mean—"

"I think we'll find a fresh alien body in the morgue tomorrow, the last one that was alive, within a container, that let us in and sealed us up."

Forsythe lay on his bunk, a frown creasing his forehead. Nan worried him. No woman in years had made him feel as she did. He imagined it was love. It could be, though he had faked that emotion for so long he often felt he had forgotten what it truly was. But Nan Poullard was special. He knew she was dying, would be dead in all too short a time, but that made her all the more precious. During the short time left to her, the two of them could live as boldly as possible.

Live life to the fullest, he thought. He could do that for Nan. And what would he gain in return?

Perhaps nothing, and that was the true indicator; he didn't care. He loved Nan and was determined to have her for as long as possible.

His frown changed to a smile and he stood. The others were asleep all around him, wherever a space could be found. He looked forward, to where Dubois snoozed on the flight deck. She had decided that sleeping in shifts was no longer necessary.

Dictator, he thought.

He pushed her from his mind. Nan was all he should think about now. She was in one of the cubicles, and he quietly pushed the curtain aside.

The cubicle was empty, the bed painfully neat. Lying on it was one of the maps Dubois and Tyler had made. Marked in red was the shortest route to the ship's computer room.

One more body . . .

Tyler's asinine suggestion and Nan's reaction to it slammed back into his consciousness. He was too late.

"No," he whispered. He grabbed up the map and committed the route to memory. Once though the right-hand door it was a fairly straight-line trip.

He ran.

Nan Poullard meditated with good success. The fears that had assailed her when she first arrived at the marked doorway were almost under control. Satisfied, she stood. Breathing deeply, eyes half closed, she began to slowly remove her clothes. Frances had said naked, and Buchanan's struggles, his suffering, had been drawn out because the ship had had to strip him. It seemed reasonable that any suffering would be minimized if the machinery did not have to waste time removing any garments. She tried to keep her mind clear, mumbling her mantra. More than anything, she wanted it done quickly.

More than anything? a voice in her mind asked. *Look at what you are giving up.*

She was dying, and therefore, had precious little to lose. *Quite the contrary,* she thought, *I have much to gain. More, I may be able to save the others.*

She stood naked, the center of the design in front of her. She opened her eyes slowly, gaze relaxed. She could feel the throb of the ship falling into step with her own heartbeat. She nearly smiled. It was so . . . relaxing. . . .

One touch, one outstretched hand, and she would be committed, never to return. Her eyes snapped shut, her heart suddenly pounding.

You've always sacrificed your own needs before, she thought. *The greater good. Why the fear now?*

More than fear—terror! She raised her right hand. It was shaking, and a cold sweat gave her arm and the rest of her body a glistening sheen. She trembled.

"Get it over with," she said aloud. The hand, as if it were detached from her, reached out.

"Nan, *no!*"

She turned, startled. Roger Forsythe came charging up the corridor. In a shimmer it went from functional brown to pastel yellow. Poullard looked about her. Hilary was exerting her own control over the interior again. She liked her work. She would let her pick the colors, even after—

"Nan, please," Forsythe said. He was a jump away, afraid to come any closer.

Why does he try and stop me? she asked herself. The answer came back immediately: *He cares for you.*

She looked into his eyes. So much pain there. *More than that. He* loves *you.*

Perhaps . . . A natural suspicion held her.

She turned towards him, arms extended, a relieved smile

coming to her lips. She breathed his name like a spring breeze. "Roger."

He came into her arms and they kissed for a delicate eternity. She fumbled with the closures of his garments and they fell away. They stood there, entwined in each other's arms.

"Do you love me?" she asked, a husky whisper into his throat.

"Yes, yes, yes."

"Why . . . why did you stop me? I could have helped the others."

He ran his fingers through her hair. "We can escape, Nan, and *live*. You and I, we—"

"But what of the others?"

He pulled his face from her chest. "They're fools. We'll get out of here, Nan, alone if necessary. We'll give the others to the ship."

She held him close once more, nodding. "I thought as much." She paused, then added, "My dear, dear Roger."

The corridor pulsed around them, catching him in its beat as she bent her knees, her lips playing across his chest, his stomach. As one they did a slow pirouette. He closed his eyes, carefully balanced as they turned, relaxed. Her lips moved lower and he forgot everything.

"Oh, my dear Roger," she whispered, "*we* can help the others."

She stood, arms going around him. Her legs straightened, shoving her against him.

He stumbled back, startled and off guard. Nan was still pressing tightly against him when he realized what was about to happen. He screamed once, trying to brace himself.

He might have succeeded, giving a few more centimeters of room that weren't there. His buttocks touched the wall dead center of the symbol, penetrating the doorway. She looked into his eyes, a smile of triumph on her lips, no longer frightened of what was coming.

"My dear Roger . . ."

The ship took them.

14

Further Explorations

The rumblings of the ship woke them. Dubois sat up in her seat and looked about in alarm. She jumped up, moving towards the rear of the boat. Tyler was already there, looking surprised and concerned. They opened the hatch.

The hangar ceiling was in confusion, the lights rippling in constantly changing patterns and colors. The deck was no better, sometimes flaring into a blinding white; squares, circles, and hexes marching around. The air seemed to crackle as the temperature ran up and down the scale, breezes coming from everywhere, rising to a roaring wind, only to die away again.

"I'm sealing the hatch," Dubois decided. "Something's gone berserk."

When the entrance was secure, Tyler said, "Looks as if Hilary, Kevin, and the ship are having an argument over the decor. I wonder who will win."

The decking shuddered, rocking the lifeboat and knocking them both down. The others sprawled around them. Daggit wiped blood from a gash in his forehead while So clung protectively to Quont. Marito alone stood, braced near the bow, hanging onto the overhead handholds.

Dubois's eyes widened in realization. "Where's Nan?"

Tyler frowned and said, "Where's Forsythe?"

Memory plays funny tricks. Dubois suddenly remembered how serious Poullard had been when questioning Tyler about her "one more body" suggestion. Considering the woman's condition, that should have been a waving red flag alarm, especially when she wanted to know how long someone would live within one of the containers.

Dubois paled. *What have I done this time?*

And what about Forsythe?

"Where's Poullard and Forsythe?" she yelled.

The rumbling settled slightly, and they quickly searched the boat. The two were gone. Marito pointed to the maps on the floor and said, "They were secured when we went to sleep."

Dubois picked one up, saw what it showed, and said, "I can understand Nan going there. I should have kept an eye on her. But where's Forsythe?"

"After her," So said. "He was the only one aboard who talked with her much. He was flipped for her."

"Forsythe?" Tyler asked, unbelieving.

Dubois said, "They've gone to sacrifice themselves to the damn ship."

"Not Forsythe," Tyler said. "It doesn't pay enough."

"Whatever. We've got to stop them." Bracing herself as well as possible, she moved towards the storage room and her pressure suit.

The boat heaved again. Tyler looked about and muttered, "I think we're too late."

The heaving of the deck stopped long before they reached the entrance to the computer core. They found two sets of clothing lying on a false wood floor. The yellow pastel walls, Kahn's choice of decor, lent a macabre air to the scene.

Dubois fingered the finer fabric of Poullard's pullover and sighed. She couldn't think of anything to say. All she felt was an overwhelming sense of guilt.

Tyler tossed Forsythe's clothes aside, cursing loudly. "I feel responsible for the fool. He was a bastard and all, but he wouldn't've been here if not for me."

"Don't be stupid, Frances. Forsythe was a grown boy. He came *here* voluntarily." She grimaced. "Though I don't think he went in *there* the same way."

Tyler nodded and motioned towards the now-normal doorway. "You know, if worse comes to worse, we can go in there and just blow the crap out of the mechanical computer, destroy it. We could even rig some sort of explosives and—"

Dubois cocked one eyebrow. "And kill Hilary and Kevin, and now Nan and Forsythe? I've thought of that, but dismissed the notion on two counts, one unimportant. That one is Marito. I think he'd kill *us* before letting us kill this ship. Second, more important, we don't know what that action would cause. If we assume you're right—that this is a warship—blowing its brains out may trigger a self-destruct sequence. And what if this isn't the only computer center? You, me, and whoever else was near the explosion might get sucked off to 'auxiliary mind control,' or whatever it might be called."

Tyler shrugged. "It was just a passing thought."

"Yeah." Dubois looked at the door and added, "Maybe, as a last resort, but I'm not that desperate. Not yet, anyway."

"I suppose there's no point in going in there," Tyler said, after a pause.

"I . . . I don't think I could take it just now."

"Then I've an idea. You wide awake?"

"What else?"

"Good. Our suits have been fully recharged, both air and power. Let's search the morgue now. I've got an insatiable itch to *know*."

Nothing in the morgue seemed new or rearranged. They walked to the left wall and began a careful search, going from one end to the other, shifting slightly, then back again. Sweep by sweep they covered over half the room, counting over four hundred alien forms, before finding what Tyler had suspected.

It was more than just color, though that originally caught their eye. The shape was different, bigger, fuller. In comparison, the others were dehydrated in appearance.

"You were right," Dubois said, voice low. "The last link."

Tyler shook her head, a feeling of sadness in her voice. "The poor soul. Don't you wonder how long he must have laid in that tank, waiting for rescue? For company? For *anything* to break the tedium? He must have been near the end when we stumbled along. He grabbed us as his salvation. When the ship had a replacement, it let him die, mercifully, and placed him with his long-dead comrades."

Dubois blinked rapidly. "You're damn poetic, aren't you?"

"It *feels* right."

Dubois looked about them. Tyler's theory lifted some of the gloom out of the air, allowing her to envision a more noble race of beings than their shrunken corpses showed. She let the moment linger, then sighed. "What now?"

"I'm not sure. Shall we talk about *our* lost comrades?"

"You're getting morbid again, and if you must, let's go up to the bridge and into some light."

They leaned against a couple of control stations, helmets removed. Tyler sucked a moment on her suit's water nipple, then said, "Have you noticed this ship's sexual preference? I think the last link was a she."

Dubois smiled. "What makes you say that?"

"Because Kevin suppressed Hilary when you tried to communicate, but the ship only suppressed Kevin. It didn't interfere with Hilary at all."

She laughed bitterly. "Superiority at last. Whoopee."

"No joke," the engineer said. "I bet the builders of this ship were predominantly female, and so was the crew." She took another drink, this one of liquid protein. "Note that the interior colors are now of Hilary's choosing. Smell the air. It's her perfume again."

Dubois unconsciously sniffed. "I think I preferred Kevin's."

"Puppet. Nevertheless, I think what we felt a while ago was a power struggle. Forsythe would have been a bitch for the ship to assimilate. He's probably controlling only minor functions. Nan, Kevin, and Hilary probably ganged up on him as he tried to wreak vengeance upon the rest of us."

Dubois laughed again. "This is too much."

"The ship contained Kevin after Forsythe was made to tow the line," Tyler went on, face serious. "Then it was between Nan and Hilary, the latter's personality being much more domineering. She won. Hilary's running the show."

"Through the ship and within its constraints."

"Exactly."

"You spin so wild a yarn, it could be true," Dubois said, having a "meal" of her own. "I'd like to think you're right, except for Kevin. I think the ship snapped down on him for trying to communicate with us, unauthorized and all that. Hilary and Nan would have been sufficient to contain Forsythe." She clucked her tongue, shaking her head. "But poor

Kevin. I got the impression he would have preferred being in command of the lifeboat, rather than me."

"Then you're a poor judge of character. You didn't see him when you first went through the hangar wall. Starman Buchanan would *never* want command."

"The voice of experience?"

"In more ways than one." She hesitated, then said, "You've got to stop blaming yourself for all this, Pamela. You can't afford the stress."

Dubois stared at a wall. "Meaning I've got more important things to worry about."

"Meaning you're in command and that's all you should think about."

She closed her eyes. "I don't want it. You take it."

Tyler shook her head. "I wish I could, but I can't. Like it or not, you're stuck."

"You've had more experience, as you've said. You're more qualified."

"I *command* people, Pamela; I never mastered the knack of *leading* them. *You* lead."

"Crap!"

"That too. Why do you think Kevin never mutinied? Why doesn't Marito try and take command? Because neither would have succeeded. Not as it stands, anyhow. You lead, we follow, period. You're a fine leader, Pamela. Your only problem is in controlling your guilt."

"Go to hell, Frances. If I'm in command, then my guilt is none of your affair. The subject is closed."

There was a long pause. Tyler asked, "What now?"

Dubois stood. "The ship's got four of us. I liked your earlier question: How many does it take to bring the ship up to a minimum operating level. I think we can safely say it needs more than four."

"Maybe five."

"Maybe the *correct* five. I don't think just anyone will do. If you don't measure up, you're nothing but a CPU." She took a breath. "Let's get back to the boat."

"No." Tyler shook her head, standing. "There's somewhere else I want to check."

"Yes?"

She pointed forward. "That weightless area in the bow. I want to see what's in it."

• • •

They stood on the brink of darkness. Dubois looked out into
the pit and asked, "Why did you want to come here?"

"To confirm a hunch and prove Marito wrong. We'll leave a
strobe here and float down."

They attached the brightly flashing light just below the edge,
clearly visible from the cavern below. Tyler took a deep breath
and stepped out. She floated, not half a meter from Dubois.
Curling into a ball, then straightening, she reversed herself,
now hanging upside down. Her fingers brushed the metal and
she said, "We're in luck. It's gridlike. we can use it to push 'n
pull."

She pulled one hand and fell out of sight. Dubois stepped off
quickly, keeping her light on the woman before her.

Down they went, the strobe becoming smaller and smaller
behind them. It was impossible to estimate the distance.
Dubois guessed at least a hundred meters. In so much darkness
the figure was meaningless.

Tyler stopped. She spun and looked back at Dubois, nose
crinkling. "*Whew*. Do you smell it?"

Dubois got a whiff, like rotting eggs, just before their suit
and scanwand "bad air" alarms went off. Both snapped shut
their faceplates.

"Do you think we breathed enough to kill us?" Tyler asked.

Dubois noted the question's emphasis. Any other time and
Tyler might have used the word *harmed*. Here, aboard this
derelict, it was *kill*.

She shrugged. "We'll soon find out."

"Not necessarily."

Dubois shrugged again. Either way, it was too late to worry
now.

They waited five minutes, growing more and more restless.
Dubois finally said, "I think we'll live. Let's move on."

Tyler drifted ahead once more, only to stop half a dozen
meters later. She pointed at her scanwand's display. "I'm
getting a bottom scan."

Dubois took her own reading, then fanned it away from the
floor directly below them, out towards the center of the cavern.
She frowned. "I get an irregular pattern."

"Same here. Different shapes."

"Keep moving. We'll get a clearer picture when we get
closer."

The bottom was less than thirty meters away. Their lights flickered off something liquid when they were still several meters away. Dubois anchored herself and grabbed Tyler's ankle, stopping them both.

"I don't think we want to step in that," she said, looking at the light mist that hovered over the fluid.

Tyler unhooked a transponder ball and tossed it down. It hit the liquid with a plunk. To their surprise it rippled like water, only more slowly. It appeared to be blue.

"Funny," she said. "Without gravity it should have flown off in all directions."

Dubois said, "There could be a gravity layer, or a magnetic field, if the fluid's metallic. You get a signal from the ball?"

"None. It's dead."

"Like I said, we don't want to step in that." She raised her wand, scanning the darkness of the cavern. Her light beam bounced off huge shapes, the display showing them to be no more than half a dozen meters away.

She pushed off gently, sailing towards one. As she got closer, her light picked out more details, showing a handhold, or what she used as one. She braked herself to a stop, calling back to Tyler, "It looks like a tall tube, on some sort of mount. Lots of 'em."

Tyler kicked off and sailed gently by, light flashing all around. "*Huge*. More up here."

Dubois flew in pursuit. Both stopped at a forward wall, the lake of blue fluid still below. The ensign motioned a thumb upwards. They moved in that direction until they were level with the top of the nearest tower. Aiming carefully, Dubois kicked off.

She caught the rim and stopped, flashing the okay to Tyler. She came over a moment later, catching Dubois's outstretched hand. They looked about quietly.

"What do you think?" Tyler finally asked.

Dubois hesitated in replying, studying the tower. It was a good three meters in diameter and seemed hollow. When she scanned the inside, she got nothing but a confused image, not even one showing a cylinder.

"I don't know," she said.

"The ship's forward weapons battery."

Dubois nodded agreement. Perhaps she was being too Earth-orientated, too anthropomorphic, not taking the "galactic" viewpoint, but the things around them had no peaceful air about them. They seemed to radiate hostility, danger, violence. Nothing else on the ship even came close to the feelings of threat she got here.

"And it's too big to be a defensive battery for an explorer," Tyler said. "And I don't care what Marito might think of my narrow-mindedness."

"Don't try and convince me," Dubois said. "Marito's going to be the problem." She paused before asking, "What tipped you off? You've thought this for a while."

Tyler nodded. "Some parts of the ship didn't change. The corridors did, along with the staging room and all the lighting. But not the bridge, not the morgue, and I was sure not here. Those areas are set in concrete, no doubt self-repairing, but immutable by the controlling computers." She turned to Dubois. "One of those twelve containers is meant to control these things, Pamela. Is it the next one, number five? Is *that* what the ship needs? And if it is, and it gets it, will it move out, under power once more, back off to war?"

"You're leading up to something again."

She nodded. "I don't think we can just leave this ship here. Assuming we get out of here, I think—" She stopped. Something shifted around them.

They could hear the noise through their helmet sound disks, like a sucking drain. Then a gurgle. Tyler looked at Dubois in alarm as the tower they clung to trembled.

Dubois flashed her light down. It barely reflected off the liquid, showing ripples of motion. The mist was gone.

"What's going on?" Tyler asked.

There was another gurgle, and the tower moved, tilting forward slightly. Slots along its height opened.

"Jump!" Dubois shouted, pushing off with her arms. Tyler followed suit, both of them drifting upwards as, behind them, the slots gushed dark blue fluid. The openings faced downwards, shooting the elected flow in that direction. It was caught in a field, and kept going down until it dropped into the lake with a loud splash.

They rose out of the range of their lights and radar. Tyler looked at Dubois and asked, "What was that?"

Dubois said, "I think we've just seen some routine mainte-nance. I'll bet that was their equivalent of oil, probably magnetized. That's why it fell, rather than drifting around, weightless. It's probably all automatic."

Tyler looked grim. "The whole bloody ship's automated. It even takes care of its guns by itself."

"Marito won't like what we tell him," Dubois said, shaking her head. She didn't especially like it either.

"Weapons?" he shrilled. "You're convinced they were *weapons*, not some variety of observation devices?"

"Guns, Marito," Tyler said. "Weapons, *offensive*. If you'd've been there, even *you* would have been convinced. It's the only part of this ship that's really *felt* hostile."

"'Felt hostile.' If you only knew how silly that sounds."

Dubois looked at Tyler. "Let's take him up there and throw him in, make sure that lake is really just lubricant."

"Yes, let's."

Before Marito could look too horror-struck, Tyler plunged into her conviction of what they should do with the derelict, if, *when*, they left. Marito looked even more horrified.

"You can't be serious. *Destroy* this magnificent alien artifact because you're afraid it might rage out of control? Where's your proof, woman? Where?"

"No, not because it might rage out of control, Marito. Because I don't want to think of some other poor bunch of fools stumbling into this system, and thinking like you, watching their crew get absorbed into this ship one by one. And when it has twelve, what then? What will it do? Resume its mission? Just what *is* its mission?"

Marito blustered. "Well, er, we don't—"

"And I don't feel we should take the chance. Even if this ship is, as you say, a 'harmless' explorer, there's no crew. But it will continue on its merry way once it has those twelve containers filled."

"*Enough!*" Jeanine Quont cried. They all looked at her, surprised at the outburst. "Can't we just get out of here? If we can make it back to Earth, let *them* send someone to destroy this . . . *thing*. Just let *us get out of here*."

So coughed and said, "I think she's right. Escape should be our number-one worry. If we can carry out Frances's suggestion and still get clear, fine. But let's get out first."

Daggit chipped in with them, as did Dubois. She added, "I

don't particularly care about the next guy right now, Frances. It's *us* I'm worried about."

Tyler nodded. "So be it. Any commands for now?"

"Yes. Sleep. Tomorrow we search this hangar from front to back, side to side, to see if we can't find some hatchway controls."

"Don't hold your breath," Marito mumbled.

Dubois frowned. "Is that supposed to mean something?"

"Only that I don't think we'll find the controls here. The bridge is a more likely locale."

Dubois shook her head but said nothing. She was suddenly too weary to argue with Marito any longer, especially to ask why a "peaceful" exploration ship would have a warship's setup for the hangar's deck. Without a word she turned and went forward, slumping into a flight-deck chair. The others separated and went their own ways. She watched them go, wondering if they could act on Tyler's suggestion.

What could we destroy? she thought. Her eyelids felt heavy, and she nodded once more. As she jerked back away, she could see Marito talking in a low voice to So. She felt mildly disturbed by it, unsure why, noting the boy's intense expression. It was as if he was listening to something he didn't really want to hear.

Dubois's mind drifted. Her eyes fell closed again and she was asleep in moments.

15

"But if you're so reluctant . . ."

The six of them stood in a semicircle outside the lifeboat. All but Marito were armed. Each also held a scanwand.

"We'll split into parties of two," Dubois said. "Marito, you go with Daggit. Frances, you've got Jeanine. Kelly, you're with me. I'll go to the far side, Marito takes the other."

Tyler finished, "Leaving the middle for me."

"Right. Do it quick, but don't miss anything. I want to know as much about this hangar as I can."

They walked quickly, each to their assigned area. The search poked into every nook, every opening, every curve. Hull sections were touched, alien shuttles examined (on the outside only), the alien derelict humming about them all the while.

"I've been considering our plight," Marito said to Daggit. They were near the door seam, or where it should have been, and Daggit was looking under an especially large shuttle. It still only had room for one, though, and he thought of it as a bomber.

"I said, 'I've been considering our plight,'" Marito repeated.

Daggit straightened up. "I heard you. So what else is new?"

"Only that I'm beginning to understand what this ship *needs*, what it wants, and why."

That caused a curious expression. "Oh, really? And what have you figured out?"

"That if we give it what it wants, *I* may be able to free the others *and* get all of us out of here *and* leave the ship intact for a proper exploration team. That is, if it's still here when they arrive."

"Why shouldn't it be?"

Marito smiled indulgently. "Because if it gets what it needs, there won't be any reason for it to stay within this star system."

Daggit leaned against the "bomber's" landing gear and crossed his arms, expression thoughtful. "And free the others?"

"Yes."

"I . . . I think you'd better explain."

Marito's smile turned expansive. "Gladly . . ."

"Do you think Miss Tyler is right?" So asked. "That this is some kind've warship?"

Dubois nodded. "Yes. The forward section mounts some sort of weapons array. Both of us agree on that point."

"Then what happened to the crew? Why isn't there any exterior damage?"

"There may be. We'd never see it because the ship's hull 'healed' itself. As for the crew, they died and the ship put them in the morgue, all nice and neat."

"Mr. Marito seems to feel we should leave the ship alone. Or give it what it wants."

Dubois sniffed. "Mr. Marito doesn't know what it wants."

"If he did, would you go along with giving it?"

"Depends. I wouldn't give it one of us."

So looked thoughtful. "What if it wants just one more of us? Another body, as Miss Tyler said. That would make five, almost half as many as it can take. That may be enough."

Dubois poked at the rear wall, wishing it would open for them. "I'd blast my way out first, Kelly, taking my chances with whatever defenses there may be. Is that enough of an answer for you?"

The boy didn't reply. They continued their search in silence.

It proved futile. They met back at the lifeboat for a dry lunch, all despising the taste of canned and dehydrated foods.

When the meal was finished, they sat outside the boat, frustration hanging in the air.

"I've been thinking," Daggit said, "about what the ship wants. Has anyone any ideas?"

"It wants meat," Tyler said, "just like me. Oy, for a steak!"

"Seriously. This is important. I think we should get free of this derelict as soon as possible. If we can find out what the ship wants, that end is better served."

"Served . . ." Tyler murmured, almost drooling.

"Okay," Dubois said. "Let's hear your idea."

"Simple." Daggit cleared his throat and continued. "It currently holds four of our companions. Of the four, only Starman Buchanan has any experience in ship design and the like. None of the others really knows much about star travel, navigation, astrogation, command, et cetera. Starman Buchanan is the only one who comes close to fulfilling what the ship's . . . biological computer links were supposed to be, what they *need* to be."

Dubois felt the hackles on her back slowly rise. Marito was looking pointedly at her, as were Daggit and So. She remembered the boy's questioning earlier.

Last night. She remembered. Marito had taken So aside. And he had been with Daggit today, the latter obviously coached for this speech. The facade faded.

She looked directly at Marito and said, "So what does the ship want, Mr. Marito?"

He looked annoyed that his subterfuge had failed, but replied, "I've surmised that the bio-link, the containers for the alien bodies and brains, is there because the alien mechanical computers have no sense of initiative. They do not *think*, not even on the level of our own computers. They can only react in a preprogrammed manner to the proper stimulus. The bio-link is necessary for initiation, for planning, for drive, for control."

He held his silence for several heartbeats. Tyler took a sip of water and said, "Is there a point to this, Mr. Marito?"

"Yes. Starman Buchanan is the closest the ship has to fulfilling its needs. But he was only in engineering, not even a career officer. He, like the machines, *takes* orders; he does not *give* them. He is not a leader, not an astrogator, not a ship's commander, not at all like you, *Captain* Dubois."

"You make it sound noble," Dubois said, voice low and cool. "You're suggesting that I *sacrifice* myself to this ship."

"You make it sound gruesome, Captain," he said. "You would only be acting in the best interests of us all. Is there anything higher in a captain's obligations? Your duty lies in protecting your passengers, in this case us. You can do that by—"

"By being plugged into some mindless machine?" Dubois snapped, voice rising. The thought was sickening, and everyone's calm acceptance of the suggestion only made it worse.

I lead, wasn't that what Frances said? she thought. Marito seemed to have changed that overnight.

But was he right? Rank has its privileges, but also it has its obligations, foremost among them the safety and security of command and passengers. Looked at in a pragmatic light, it was only logical that she should give herself up. In that same light, though, the question had to be asked, *Will it work?* It might.

Her subconscious rebelled at the thought, drowning out any other argument. Thoughts of possible responsibility were shoved aside.

She shook her head. "No, Mr. Marito, I'm not going to calmly walk up and give myself to this ship, not for you, not for anyone. You didn't hear Kevin's screams. You didn't watch as the ship placed him into one of those tanks. No thank you. I won't do it."

He opened his mouth to argue, but she cut in. "Beyond my personal revulsion at the suggestion, there's the simple matter of how do you know it will work? As you said, my responsibility is to my passengers, to you. I would be abandoning you if your scheme failed."

Marito said, "But—"

"Shut up, Marito!" Tyler shouted. She had held her peace while Dubois replied, thinking that that would be enough. Now it was clear that Marito intended to argue the point further. She stood and glared down at him.

"I won't even try and be polite to you, *sir*. Let's get this clear: no one else gets taken by this ship! No one, not for any reason, least of all Captain Dubois. You pigheaded fool, don't you realize she's the only one who could navigate the lifeboat out of here? Kill her and you trap all of us." She paused, eyes narrowing. "But then, that's what you want, isn't it? The ship could come to life and, if you're right, return to its home system, and you would meet the aliens face to face. Correct?"

Marito tried to hide it, but his manner betrayed him. Tyler

nodded in victory. "So forget the idea, all of you." She looked at Daggit and So, each in turn, until they gave way. "The idea is closed to discussion."

"No, it isn't," Marito said. "If need be, *I* could navigate this vessel, the lifeboat. Then—"

"If you can navigate," Dubois said softly, "then let's give the derelict *you*."

Marito sputtered. "I . . . but you . . ."

"Enough," Tyler declared. "On to other matters. . . ."

Dubois ran the alternatives through her mind once more. She could feel herself becoming desperate.

Of the others, only Tyler talked to her. So and Daggit sulked; Quont clung to herself, afraid of alienating So. Daggit had apparently believed everything Marito had told him, no matter how ludicrous it must have been. At the worst moments she imagined even Tyler wanted to give her to the derelict.

Marito held his peace, no longer mentioning the subject. His surrender had been total. Still, it was plain that the others thought of it continuously. No one spoke. It was left just under the surface, a growing tension.

She sat on the flight deck, her fingers playing with the controls. Could any of the others pilot them back through the hellhole? Tyler, certainly. Marito, maybe. None of the others. *Don't fool yourself.* Her fingertips brushed a large key marked INSTRUCTION. Pushing it gave the viewer a crash course in boat functions. Plus there were the preprogrammed maneuvers, each activated by a plainly marked key. If they sat down and concentrated, they could feed the destination coordinates into the computer and let it fly the boat. Their only problem would be one of supervision; there wouldn't be a human to double-check the computer, to ask the proper questions. "Does this orbit cut through the star?" "Does this orbit cut too close for safety?" If they programmed wrong, the results would be wrong.

"So don't worry," she muttered. "They *need* you."

Which was the problem. Too many people needed her. She could trust Tyler to keep reminding them. For now.

She looked at the lifeboat's computer console. *You're much like your derelict counterpart. You both require something human to command you. The only difference is that here I am a temporary master; out there I'm a permanent guest.*

Her eyes stared at the input board. Similarities. Both had their own security programs and procedures.

Security.

Her fingers danced on the keyboard.

"I wish to apologize," Marito said.

Dubois still sat on the flight deck, reclining and half asleep. He stood in the separation-panel doorway.

Dubois looked up. "Don't worry about it. You thought you were right. Who knows? Maybe you are."

"I hope there are no hard feelings. I just felt that—"

"Don't apologize. My feelings are none of your business."

He bowed acceptance. After a pause, he said, "I wish to see the alien morgue, then the computer room once more. If we succeed in leaving here soon, I want my own personal observations brought up to date."

She had a moment's fleeting worry. It passed. After all, she would be the only one armed, and she was confident she could take him in any physical contest.

She nodded. "Okay, but let's make it quick. I'm exhausted."

She felt it in her bones. The emotional stress of the past few hours had left her drained.

She led the way, her feet seeming to rise and fall through thickened air. The suit felt uncomfortably binding. She wished she could strip it off.

In the morgue he looked down at the fresh body, poking at the alien skin and the decking with which it blended. "I wonder how long this one waited for relief. I believe it was he who adjusted the lights and altered the atmosphere for us. The mechanical computers couldn't have done that."

"You could be right," Dubois said, too bored to remind him he was repeating Tyler's ideas. "I wouldn't know."

"I wish to see this so-called 'weapons array' in the bow."

She was about to say no, but considered his expression. He was simply curious, and he didn't want to believe that this was a warship. Dubois nodded.

They stood on the edge and she waved him on. "I'll wait up here, if you don't mind."

"No. I won't be long." He stepped off, turned, and pulled

himself down. Dubois sat and set the strobe as a beacon. She tried to shift the suit's backpack around for support, only partially succeeding.

He was back in half an hour. Dubois was almost dozing when he came up next to her. "Fantastic. They could be some sort of research tools. Massive radio arrays and the like."

Dubois shrugged. "Whatever you say. I don't think so and neither does Frances."

"Because both of you have a decidedly negative attitude towards this vessel. Let's go to the computer room, and this time try to understand the design."

The mechanical units were still the same, working easily in their vacuum environment. Their inner workings were unfathomable, and she didn't see how either of them could "understand" their design by simply looking at them.

Buchanan, Kahn, Poullard, and Forsythe were laid out in a row, each container alive with its own golden aura. Dubois waited in the mechanical area, allowing Marito to probe the bodies on his own.

"I wonder how long they'll live like that?" he asked after he came out. "Perhaps for centuries. We've no way of knowing. It's possibly not such a bad existence."

"Then join them," she said. "Don't ask me to."

He smiled. "No, of course not. I'm ready to leave."

They went through the exit. To her surprise, Marito took the lead, moving quickly. She felt apprehensive, hand twitching by her laser. Within minutes they were back at the entranceway again. It held the striped symbol of a normal door.

"What are you doing?" she asked, annoyed.

"I wonder if one must be wholly undressed to activate the assimilation process," he said.

"Hilary wasn't. Kevin took his suit off completely to check it. We've never tried just in between."

"That's another point, about Miss Kahn's absorption. Another proof that the last alien converted the ship for us. He must have waited until he was sure the ship could handle us, then trapped Miss Kahn. That would explain why we never saw the warning symbol until after she was in place."

"Could be. Makes sense."

Marito touched a hand to the wall, pushed through, and pulled back. "This fascinates me. See how it flows with your arm, forming a seal? Incredible."

She only nodded, sagging in boredom.

He stepped around her, ostensibly for a better view. She didn't feel the slight tug, but noticed him move in a hurried manner. She spun, too late.

Marito smoothly unclipped the laser from her belt and leveled it at her. He smiled and said, "Now, Dubois, I think we shall see if my theory is correct."

Dubois's throat went dry, adrenaline pumping into her system. Fatigue vanished as her mind screamed, *Fool! Fool!* She said, "I'll let you kill me first, Marito."

"Spare me the melodramatics. Do not mistake revulsion for inexperience. I have had my share of handling weapons. I can burn your leg off quite neatly, leaving the rest of you intact for the ship. Don't force me to maim you senselessly."

"Just allow you to make me a mindless hulk."

His face hardened. "If that's how you prefer. Remove your helmet!"

"No."

He aimed at her left leg. "I won't hesitate."

Dubois considered her chances, and slowly undid the restraining band for the suit helmet. She gave the entire affair a quarter turn, the locks coming free and allowing her to pull it off. She held it loosely in one hand.

To her left the symbol shifted. The ship was ready to accept the sacrifice.

Marito was all smiles. "Excellent. I've come to the conclusion that Miss Poullard had the correct idea about removing her clothing. I believe she wanted to be 'hooked in' with the ship as quickly as possible. You reported that it had to take time to remove the good Starman Buchanan's suit. Why don't you do that now, saving yourself the suffering."

"I won't go in there," she said.

"You have very little choice. But if you're so reluctant . . ." He raised the laser again.

She tossed the helmet and ducked to one side in a single motion. The helmet struck on target, deflecting the beam into the floor. A meter-long gash opened, puckering and peeling back. The ship roared around them, its equivalent of an alarm.

Dubois tackled Marito low and they tumbled back down the corridor. The section of tunnel around the doorway turned dark blue and the tendrils took form, writhing in wait for the violator to come within reach.

Marito looked at them and cried out. Dubois glanced back, distracted, and he slammed a gloved fist into the side of her head.

She tasted blood and rolled free, trying for space between the two of them. He grabbed one arm and tried to twist, but she was in better shape, slipping free, and swung a punch into his helmet.

She hissed at the pain and moved away. Both regained their footing, her back to the tendrils. They were less than a meter away, lashing at the gap between them. Anything entering there would be grabbed. One good shove by Marito and she would be gone.

"Surrender yourself," he said. "I know it will be easier."

She glanced at the fallen laser, then charged, ignoring it and catching him off guard. Her foot lashed out, hitting his chest piece. The machinery there was never meant to take such abuse, and the plate collapsed. Multiple circuits shorted, sparks popping. Marito spun into a wall, gasping for breath as the oxygen feed was closed. He succeeded in snapping open his faceplate and taking half a breath before Dubois was upon him.

He landed another blow to her head, and she wildly tried to knee him in the groin. She twisted and their positions reversed, his back now to the tendrils. The grunts of the ship's alarms grew deafening as they tried to summon long-dead personnel.

Dubois got in one clean rabbit punch to his kidneys, jamming another fist through his open helmet, cracking his nose. He reeled back, balance gone.

"Don't!" he screamed.

He was falling, his fingers slipping along her suit arms. Their hands met and she tried to grab him.

Only for a moment. It flashed through her mind to let him go, and she did, even before considering the results. Marito tumbled backwards. The tendrils took him.

His hand fell onto the laser as he fought the bands wrapping around him. A crimson bolt sliced into the ceiling, blue fluid gushing out. His arm was pinned and his suit's helmet was torn off. Marito fought on, shouting in terror. A tendril whipped around his neck half a dozen times, ending in a mitt-sized hand that enshrouded his head, cutting off his cries. His body went slack and he was yanked up through the ceiling.

The corridor, already beginning to heal itself, returned to

normal, the white lights and yellow walls making everything
too cheerful. Dubois felt the edge of hysteria working on the
back of her mind, and collapsed to the deck, gasping back the
tears. She squeezed her eyes shut.

*What do I tell the others? "No more will be sacrificed."
Hadn't I said that? And now . . .*

The ship throbbed about her. The lights and colors shifted,
stark red, then orange, before settling back to yellow once
more.

Dubois struggled to regain her composure and stood. She
picked up her helmet, securing it back into place. Marito was
now a part of his ship.

She frowned. She was beginning to realize that he could
possibly be the most dangerous part.

A chill swept through the hangar. Quont shivered and So
protectively wrapped one arm around her shoulders. He
whispered, "It's all over, it's all over."

Daggit and Tyler looked around. She overheard the boy and
understood. She spun towards Daggit and said, "He did it,
didn't he?"

Surprised and frightened, Daggit stepped back. "It . . . it
had to be done if we were to get out of here. And if it gets the
person it needs, it may release the others."

Tyler suddenly understood why Daggit had been so willing
to go along with Marito. "He told you the ship would release
Hilary, didn't he?"

"He said it was possible."

"He *lied*, damnit! If you had seen those containers, you
would have known that. Good Lord, man, the metal *absorbs*
the skin. It's a one-way process."

"You can't know that. You can't!"

The overhead lights flashed through the spectrum before
settling once more on white. So said, "I think . . . Captain
Dubois is fighting."

"Wouldn't you?" Tyler yelled. Her eyes burned and she
blinked back tears. "Damn you all to hell! Didn't you stop to
think what it must be like? What the hell got into you?"

She unclipped her laser. "I've a good mind to . . .
to . . ." She stopped, unsure what she had in mind to do.

Daggit took a step forward. "Please, Miss Tyler, it's for us all. If we get out of here, even if the ship doesn't free the others, we can return with help."

"Assuming we can even get out of this star system. Remember the hellhole, Daggit? It killed two of us coming through."

"We survived. We'll survive again, if only—"

"Forget it, Daggit." She stepped away from him, seeing a course of action. She quietly said, "I hope we do get out of here, I really do. And when we get back, I'll have you and Marito arrested. If there's any justice I'll—"

"She was sacrificed for the common good," Daggit cried. "You—"

"She was *not* sacrificed!"

They all turned, their heads snapping around as if pulled by strings. Pamela Dubois stood just inside the hangar, framed by the striped entranceway. She looked at Daggit, expression distant.

"On the contrary," she said, "I think Mr. Marito is having a hard time joining his precious damn ship."

Daggit looked stunned. Tyler's mouth twitched into a broad smile and she said, "Welcome back, Captain." There was a thin waver of emotion in her voice.

"Thank you."

"What did you do to Mr. Marito?" So asked. "You've killed him!"

"Oh, really?" She looked at the boy narrowly. "And what did he have planned for me?"

Daggit and So fumed briefly, then were silent. Dubois flicked her gaze back and forth over them and said, "The fool fell into his own trap. The ship now has five of us, with five more remaining." Her voice tightened, hardening. *"There will be no more!"*

The color in the room shifted, holding an angry red. The ship rumbled before the light was white again. Dubois looked around the hangar, thinking that Marito should be right at home. She added, her voice lightening only slightly, "I don't think it *needs* any more."

16

Demands and Challenges

The others had little to do with her that night. If they had been cool earlier, they were icebergs now. Even Tyler. She was reluctant to press for what had actually happened with Marito, whether he had forced Dubois's hand or she had decided that *he* was to be sacrificed.

The solitude suited her for the moment. Every time her mind turned to the problem of escape, the odds against it seemed to increase. And now exploration of the ship had to be strictly limited. They only had one suit, and Marito might prove to be a threat, depending on how well he could integrate with the ship.

The ship itself felt restless. Several times the deck lurched as some new adjustment was made. She did not want to think about what changes could be going on.

Unable to sleep, Dubois slipped out of the lifeboat and blinked at the now-glaring overhead lights. The temperature was up, humid and uncomfortable. She saw that the deck had returned to its original shape, black and finely hexed. Nothing else seemed out of the ordinary.

"Ordinary," she snorted. How quickly they had come to accept this derelict hulk as "ordinary," as a home.

She did a once-around-the-boat inspection, looking at the

smooth-lined hull, the expansive double-delta wings. It had been designed for space travel, for space survival. It was equipped for landing on a planet with or without an atmosphere. It could glide, in the unlikely event that all three modes of propulsion failed, for a distance eleven times its height above the ground. There were wind-driven turbines for emergency electrical needs, along with ample auxiliary power units. In addition there were dozens of other intricate little items for survival, for redundancy, for durability. It was even equipped with a storage closet holding seeds for growing foodstuffs in an alien environment. It had everything except an offensive capability. The only weapons available were those that could be carried by her crew and passengers, the hand lasers.

"If you only had a bow gun," Dubois mumbled, patting the blunt nose cone. "Can you stand ramming that door?"

She felt that very soon she would be putting that question to the test.

The next "day" Daggit and So again made it a point to ignore her. Tyler came over and tried to make idle small talk, but Dubois's attitude made it clear that, at the moment, such banalities were not welcome.

A short while later she announced, "I'm going up to the bridge."

"Why?" Tyler asked. "There's nothing more to—"

"Because I want to be *sure* there's nothing more to learn," Dubois snapped.

Tyler paused, then nodded. "I'll go with you. No one should go anywhere in here alone."

"No. I'll go alone on this."

Before Tyler could argue, Dubois grabbed a laser-equipped utility belt and went out the aft hatchway. A moment later she pushed through the wall and was gone.

"Good riddance," Daggit said.

Tyler was coolly threatening. "You have a reason for saying that?"

"It's obvious she killed Marito. She's a killer, and we're better off without her."

"'Killed' Marito? How?"

"She fed him to this godforsaken ship, that's h—"

Tyler cut him off with a sour laugh. "You hypocritical sonuvabitch! And what was Marito trying to do, *save* her?"

Daggit grumbled for a moment, and said, "That's not the point. She said *no one* would be given to the ship. She evidently changed her mind."

"We should leave now," So said. "Leave her behind."

Tyler was surprised at the venom in his voice. The boy's harder side was coming to light.

"This is pointless," she said. "We're not leaving now and we're not leaving Dubois behind. Can either of you pilot this boat?"

"Marito said it was mostly computer-controlled," So said. "An idiot could fly her."

"Did Marito tell you how *far* that idiot could fly? Did he tell you how to properly navigate an anomaly? No? Face it, Dubois is the only one who can get us out of here. Understand that if nothing else."

Daggit's eyes narrowed. "*You* could fly us out of here."

"Maybe, but not without Dubois on board. Any other way and you can forget about having me as a pilot. Understand?"

Both nodded, Daggit adding, "All too well."

She disliked their looks. She doubted if she had convinced them.

The corridors were once more yellow-walled, wood-floored. The bridge hadn't changed. Dubois looked at the blank control panels and walked over to the center one. She felt a sudden urge to experiment, and raised a hand. *To hell with the risks.*

A touch of a finger on the panel's center brought a square of light to life. More touches, more lights.

Nothing seemed to do anything. Marito's assumption must have been correct. There were no mechanical linkages. Everything was done through direct thought control. From "helmsman" to biological computer to mechanical computer to control. It was a lengthy chain of command which didn't allow for one link to be missing. Dubois wondered if there was an actual helm station, if the computer center did everything.

She touched a last square. There was a shift in light and she stepped back, awestruck.

The front of the bridge vanished. In its place were the heavens. To the left was the raging star, its halo of discarded matter glowing wickedly under the continual onslaught from the solar furnace. It drifted out and around the derelict, causing all the colors of the spectrum to dance about them.

To the right was the blazing firmament, only the brightest stars visible, and those only because the derelict was so close to the halo's edge. They stood out like diamond points, daring to pierce the star's rainbow veil.

She thought for a moment, and realized that by this time the derelict should have shifted through enough of its orbit to allow visual sighting of the hellhole. She closed her eyes and did some mental mathematics, remembering where the derelict had been and where the hole was. An answer appeared, and she opened her eyes.

"It should be right . . . *there*," she said, pointing a finger to the upper right.

Nothing.

The stars in that direction thinned out and an eddy in the halo allowed a clear view. The hellhole should have been visible as a bright amber star, one flickering for attention. There was nothing.

Dubois felt something inside her collapse. All this time there had been the hope that they could get out of the alien ship and chance a transit through that rip in space. Buchanan had to be right. Those alive would survive again. The vulnerable ones were already dead, victims of the accident that had landed them here.

Now the rift was gone, and with it, the way home.

There was still the possibility that the hellhole had merely been a visual phenomenon. It could have faded and left behind a normal, invisible anomaly. The lifeboat had the basic equipment for finding and using such a point. There was still that hope, though she had little faith in it.

Dubois squared her shoulders. Why not have a little faith? The "hellhole" effect might have been a temporary side-effect of a permanent rearrangement.

Maybe, she thought.

She fiddled with the controls for a moment but failed to turn the massive viewscreen off. She looked at the painfully clear view once more and decided not to tell any of the others until they were off the derelict.

She was still staring at the view when the overhead lights pulsed, then flickered. There was a pause, and they flashed again.

And again.

Dubois frowned. There was something rhythmically familiar about the flashes. She thought for a moment, then it hit her. A cold sweat covered her as she ran from the bridge.

The lights were sending code, and the first pattern kept repeating itself.

S-O-S.

The same signal kept up until she was back inside the hangar. The others were standing about, confused by the lights. Tyler, however, had understood. She looked at Dubois and quietly said, "I haven't told them."

Dubois nodded. "Who do you think it is?"

"Same as you. Marito."

Dubois looked around, eyebrows arched. "If he's getting away with this, then the ship's accepted him better than any of the others."

"Which means he can control more than the others." Tyler's eyes reflected concern. She understood what that meant.

Dubois nodded again, turning to the others. "This flickering is a code."

Daggit deigned to talk to her. "I've assumed that. It took me a while to remember the intervals, but it's saying S-O-S, isn't it?"

"Yes."

"How do we answer?"

"We spoke to our people once before, using the radio. We can try that now."

She climbed into the boat, tossing her belt on the dining table. She ran to the flight deck and adjusted the lifeboat's transceiver to the frequency they had used before. She returned to the hatchway and unlocked the secondary communications set. Licking her lips once, she spoke into the microphone, "We understand your S-O-S. Who is this?"

The flickering stopped as the others came up into the boat. It started again quickly, a new pattern. Tyler spoke the letters at first, then stopped and translated them as words.

"'Marito,'" she said.

Dubois's grip on the microphone tightened. "Have you found any way for us to free you?"

Again Tyler provided the translation. "'There is no release.'"

Daggit choked down a cry of despair. Dubois felt a moment's pity for the man, but other considerations pushed it from her mind.

Why was the ship allowing Marito to communicate? Either it didn't recognize his light works as communications, or . . .

Her mouth became dry. Or Marito had taken over. He was now running the ship.

Or only halfway there, she added.

She asked, "Is there a way for us to escape?"

A long pause, then: "Yes."

"How?"

Lights flashed. Tyler paused, licking sweat from her upper lip. " 'The crew is long dead. The civilizations that built this vessel conquered light, but the drive for that is long destroyed, as is the center for its control. The sublight engines are still intact, under this center's control. The ship . . . wishes to go . . . home.' "

Dubois fidgeted, waiting for Tyler to finish. The tone of Marito's "conversation" was ominous. She said, "Repeat: How do we get out of here?"

" 'The ship wishes to go home.' " Tyler turned to Dubois. "Do you understand what he said? 'Civilizations,' plural! And FTL. We've never even—"

The lights rapped for attention, and Tyler translated, repeating, " 'The ship wishes to go home.' "

The derelict growled. There was a pulsing from deep within, starting far astern and rolling all the way to the bow. They all looked around, waiting for Marito to give them the answer.

The lights flickered again, this time with an insistent and rapid pattern.

" 'Do not listen,' " Tyler read. " 'Marito is—' Just two letters, T-R. It's been cut off."

Quont asked, "Who was that?"

"Kevin?" Dubois whispered. She spoke into the microphone. "Who was that?"

One letter: "B."

"Buchanan," So said. "Why didn't he finish?"

Dubois said, "He was cut off—by Marito."

"You don't know that," Daggit said.

"It was heavily implied!"

"Implications aren't enough—"

"More," Tyler said. The lights flashed for attention and the translation resumed. "'This is . . . Marito . . . The ship needs to go home . . . and report . . . In order to . . .'" She stopped, frowning. "It's as if he's fighting someone."

"The others," Dubois said.

The message continued. "'I . . . it wants . . .'" She stopped, face blank.

But Daggit's face lit up. He knew the code well enough, and So could guess what the pulses spelled.

D-U-B-O-I-S.

"He was telling the truth the first time," Dubois said quickly, seeing the malice in their eyes. "It's not the ship that wants me, it's Marito. Revenge, pure and simple. That's why the others are trying to cut him off." Her words tumbled out, one on top of the other. It was useless. She had lost whatever control she had had over them.

"'Deliver Dubois,'" Tyler said, translating with a tremor in her voice. "'I will handle . . . everything.' The man's gone insane."

"No," Dubois said.

"I suggest," Daggit said, "that you have little say in the matter."

Tyler turned her attention back inside the boat, seeing what was happening. She said, "I would suggest your silence."

The lights went on. This time Dubois translated. "'This is . . .' Garbled there. 'Nan . . . you must now . . .' She doesn't know the code fully. I think that last word was 'not.' I'm only getting bits and pieces."

"'Give me Dubois,'" read Tyler. "'Give me Dubois!' He's getting insistent."

The ship rumbled, the deck shifting under them. They could hear the air whistling by outside the open door. Marito was depressurizing the hangar.

Just before the air grew thin, he stopped. The pressure rose back to normal quickly. The temperature shifted to bitter cold as the lights changed to an eye-aching orange.

Dubois's jaw twitched. Her second fear had been correct. *Marito* now controlled the ship.

"*Very* insistent," Tyler said.

The temperature and light stablized, and the flickering code said, through Tyler, "'Give me Dubois . . . give . . . the . . . ship . . . Dubois.'"

"You must go," So said. "He'll kill us all."

"There are no offensive weapons inside the ship that can hurt this lifeboat," Dubois said. "We're safe here."

"And trapped," Daggit said. "You *must* go."

"*No.*"

Daggit grabbed for the laser on the table, but Dubois's toe was faster, kicking his hand away. So tackled her, knocking her down. Daggit succeeded in grabbing the gun.

"It's a foolish threat," Dubois said. "Marito tried it just before we fought. He lost."

"*I* won't. Stand!"

Tyler jumped forward, knocking the gun from his hand. Daggit backhanded her as Dubois straight-armed So in the throat. He writhed to the floor, gagging, and she bolted for the flight deck.

Daggit slammed Tyler's head into the after bulkhead, using all his weight. She slumped to the side, stunned, and he recovered the laser.

Dubois reached the flight deck and leaned across the command chair, brushing the hidden panel. The laser fell out into her palm. She straightened up as Daggit yelled, "Stop!"

Her shot was wild, carving into a chair and setting it on fire. Daggit flinched as molten plastic sprayed. In that moment Dubois kicked the release switch, the separation panels snapping into place and locking.

There was a scanwand and utility belt on the right-hand chair, where she had left them. She scooped them up and reached overhead. There was a recessed handle marked in red, EMERGENCY. She yanked it. The boat's escape hatch snapped open, the inner section dropping to deploy a short ladder while the outer sprang up and to the rear. Dubois ignored the ladder and jumped, grabbing the edge and pulling herself up. She straddled the nose for a moment, listening to the pounding on the flight-deck door.

There were recessed handholds in the hull to the right. She slipped down, dropping the last few meters to the hangar deck. The wall into the ship was straight ahead. She ran for it and pushed through.

Daggit fired at the closed door. Metal flew, the lock dissolving. They pried the doors apart and found themselves staring at the words EMERGENCY USE ONLY stenciled on the dangling cover.

"Damnit," Daggit hissed. He ran for the aft hatch and out onto the wing. So, rubbing a bruised throat, followed.

The hangar was empty. They went down the wing ladder, from there to the staging room. It, too, was empty.

So moaned. "She could have taken any of the three. We'll never catch her."

But Daggit was smiling. "We don't have to. Remember what Marito said? *He'll* handle her."

17

Skirmishes

I am alive.

The thought was, at first, disorienting. It had no physical reality. He thought of colors, shapes, trying to fix himself in time and space. As he settled in, accepting where he was and what he had become, the turmoil subsided. John Marito was part of The Ship.

They were with him: Kahn, Buchanan, Poullard, and Forsythe. None of them understood The Ship's basic workings. They remained half out of sync, a part of them denying their new existence.

Marito had no such distractions.

He slid into unity with The Ship like a man pulls on a pair of well-worn gloves. He began to comprehend as stored data flowed into his brain.

Home was *there*; duty was *there*; The Ship must go *there*. It needed to.

Somewhere in his conscious mind, Marito smiled. *I cannot see, yet I know everything.* He stirred. How to communicate? Sound systems for The Ship cannot duplicate human speech. A radio link is too much strain. Therefore . . .

The lights. Code . . .

I want Dubois.

Was that desire his or The Ship's? His, because of revenge; *she* should have been in the cells instead of him. The Ship's, because it still needed a navigator, someone who understood spatial relationships and the mathematics necessary to travel between the stars. Marito could recognize The Ship's home star, could even "see" it. He could never plot a sublight course for it.

But *he* wanted her as well. He could thank her for opening *this* for him. He flexed The Ship's muscles; the engines rumbled with might, having accumulated more than enough power from their close proximity to the Wolf-Rayet star.

But that was all. The limit of his control over the drive ended with a test. He didn't know enough to use them. Dubois did. Dubois would be chief engineer, as well as astrogator. Starman Buchanan would be her assistant. Miss Kahn would be her apprentice astrogator, Miss Poullard in charge of . . . environment.

And Marito would be captain, commanding them all. The thought brought a feeling of warmth. He continued his introspection.

Security. With difficulty he managed to work The Ship's internal manipulators, the tendrils. His control was minimal, but it would improve with time. He could bring Dubois to him.

For revenge? Very possibly, but The Ship needed home, and for that it *needed* Dubois. *It* did, not Marito, though the two were now one, desires entwined.

He couldn't see, but The Ship had its own array of sensors. He knew where people within The Ship were. He sensed the conflict within the lifeboat. He felt the fear, the panic. And he knew.

Dubois was free, in his domain.

Marito could almost laugh.

But, of course, The Ship had his mouth.

Dubois ran several dozen meters up the right-hand corridor before turning. She aimed her laser, ready to blast Daggit to hell. No one followed, though.

I've made it, she thought. She glanced at the ceiling. *Or have I?*

She was in an alien ship, one that was under Marito's control.

Panic seized her for a moment, and she took several

shuddering breaths before regaining control. *Okay, Marito can control the ship. What does that mean?*

So far there was no evidence of any internal-beam weaponry. There was no threat of a laser burning her down. What *did* the ship have for internal security?

She felt chill. It had the tendrils, the ones that lashed out from the walls, unseen until the last moment. Kevin and Marito had touched off those hidden hands. She had to be careful not to. More, she had to avoid them, if possible. Marito could probably exercise more initiative with them.

But how do I know where they are?

Good question. She needed an answer, fast. The section of wall containing them turned blue before they came out. That wasn't enough warning. There was only one place she already knew where they were, just outside the computer room.

She was already on her way. Laser in hand, she continued, eyes flickering from side to side.

She arrived without trouble. She stopped several meters short of the door and raised her scanwand. She first tried a radar scan. Perhaps the security areas gave off a different echo pattern.

No such luck. The reading was of a smooth-walled corridor.

Sonar. She got a curious response, the walls absorbing most of the transmission and cutting down on the return echo. The walls seemed farther away. Other than that, no difference.

Ultraviolet scan. The walls were an eerie green, but the color was uniform. No distinctions.

Infrared . . .

She looked in horror as the image cleared. The regular corridor was a dull red. The security patch was bright white, warmer than the rest.

"I found you," she said.

Beyond the doorway, by several meters, was another patch of white. Another security trap.

Well, she thought, *Very high security conscious. They've bracketed the—*

Something tingled along her spine, a chill.

Dubois threw herself forward in one convulsion, collapsing to the floor. The yellow corridor behind her turned dark blue, the tendrils lashing out. One nearly had her foot as she fell out of reach. She leaned against the wall as the patch in front of the doorway turned dark, its own coils extending. She was trapped.

Too close! She gasped for breath, the blood pounding in her ears.

The lights flickered. She counted the pulses, but they didn't make any sense. Either someone else was trying to communicate or Marito was . . .

Laughing?

"You won't get me!" she screamed. "You won't!"

The lights continued their flickering, laughing.

She forced herself to calm down. She could see that all three patches were now alive, their tendrils swaying like massive jellyfish, waiting. She counted an easy dozen per section and was sure more lay in reserve.

The section she had just evaded stiffened. The tendrils straightened out, forming bars. Beyond the door she could see that section doing the same. Only the one in front of the computer doorway remained active, taunting. The symbol pulsed, x-on-cross, and the corridor throbbed its beckoning.

The lights flickered again, this time in coded regularity. Dubois read the letters easily.

S-U-R-R-E-N-D-E-R.

"Never," she whispered.

She slowly got to her feet, careful to stay between the two sections and out of reach. Marito had unwittingly supplied her with several pieces of important data, not the least of which was that the tendrils were short on reach. Second was that the sections did change colors just before the tendrils appeared. That gave her two edges. The ship, Marito, was predictable, in that they wanted her. Her actions, formed only around the conviction to remain free, were less predictable. That gave her three edges.

"Never," she repeated.

She fired the laser in one long blast, sweeping it like a scythe. The tendrils hissed and fell apart, leaving the way down the corridor open. She dove through, firing blindly into the ceiling as she went because it was from above that the tendrils came. More tried to grow, and met her ruby beam, spraying alien machinery oil. Sparks sizzled and died.

Dubois rolled down the corridor, out of reach of the few surviving arms. She felt a warm, sticky fluid on her face and arms and wiped at it. The liquid was blue and had a dead odor, like the lake in the bow. Despite the color, and its source, she could easily convince herself it was blood.

She cleaned herself as well as possible, then made an infrared scan of the way ahead, back towards the hangar. There were no white areas. The way was clear . . . for now.

She needed a place to rest, somewhere she could relax, if only for a moment. She could not return to the hangar. Daggit and So would gladly turn her over to Marito.

Where, then?

The interior of the computer room, the mechanical section, was free of tendrils, but that room lay in vacuum, and the sections outside its doorway lay in wait. So where?

"The bridge," she said aloud. It, the morgue, and the hangar were the only areas of the ship that never changed. Marito could alter the corridors, he could snap off the lights, but he couldn't change the bridge. The biological computers held no threat over the bridge personnel.

So how do I get there? She grimaced. *Very carefully.*

Scanning ahead, she moved slowly down the corridor. She had to return to the staging room, then enter the center corridor. If she ran into Daggit or So . . .

I'll kill them.

There was no hesitation. Her passengers' best interests had been supplanted by the instinctive drive to survive. She would do whatever she had to in order to ensure her own survival. To hell with anyone who stood in her way.

And she knew. Doubt had been haunting her ever since they had first become trapped inside the derelict. Now she knew it as a certainty. She would never command a great ship; she never could. When it came down to the wire, her first thoughts were for herself and her own survival. Above all else a ship's captain must hold his or her passengers. Ensign Pamela Dubois had come to that crossroad and turned. She would kill them to survive. Perhaps under normal, or more expected, conditions she would act differently. It no longer mattered. The drive for command was gone.

And knowing that, she also knew that if she succeeded in surviving, she could have to plot the deaths of the others. Marito would have to die, and with him Kevin, Hilary, Nan, and Roger. That would seal her career forever.

Dubois forced these thoughts from her mind. Survival was of paramount importance. The future, for now, must wait.

She reached the end of the corridor without finding another tendril patch. She scanned the center corridor, looking over her shoulder and waiting for one of the two men to come in and find her. She kept the laser pointed at the striped doorway.

The corridor was clear. She stepped in as the lights flickered for attention.

S-H-E I-S I-N T-H-E . . .

She broke into a run and was a dozen meters along the way when she heard the shout behind her.

"Dubois."

Daggit stood there, laser in hand. He hesitated, and she took full advantage, falling flat and shoving her laser back. The beam sliced the wall behind and above Daggit, blasts of oil spraying him with flashes of sparks. He cringed, then dove back into the staging room. Dubois got up and ran.

And stopped.

Racing down the corridor towards her was a dark blue patch of wall, ceiling, and floor. There were no tendrils, but she knew they would lash out soon.

She dropped to one knee and fired. She held the beam steady, letting the patch's momentum split it through its entire length. The ceiling fell open, fluid machinery spilling out. A slight steam rose from it. Dubois felt a tinge of nausea as she jumped over the heap on the run.

The lights went out. She stopped again, flicking on the infrared scanner. Another patch was coming down the corridor, unseen now except for its white screen image. She raised the laser and fired, the beam ripping into the ceiling behind the patch.

She adjusted, the beam painting itself cleanly on the scanner—*short*. The patch continued its charge.

She could almost feel the tendrils as she adjusted a last time and fired, holding the trigger. She heard the thing split open, the dull splat as the mechanism fell.

Dubois turned on the wand's light and looked. Not a meter away the mess sat, blue fluid oozing down the corridor.

She scanned the corridor behind her. Nothing. And the way ahead was clear once more. Moving slowly in the dark, she resumed her flight.

The rest of the journey was less hectic. She engaged and defeated several more security patches, all stationary. It was growing habit-forming and almost easy. She couldn't help but wonder how good they had been against the alien crew members.

Of course, they might not have had lasers. Slug-throwing weapons would have been ineffectual. Judging from the way the corridors absorbed sound and radio waves, they probably had a high resistance to maser fire. What defense could the crew have had?

The bridge was as dark as the rest of the ship. The viewscreen still showed the heavens about them, all the more clearly in the blackened room. Dubois felt relief flooding over her before she remembered that Kahn had vanished from the bridge, the destruction of the radio. She moved slowly around the room's front, the stars behind her, until she could scan the left-side corner. It glowed there, pulsing white. She could feel the throb of the beckoning ship, Marito calling to her.

She ignored it. One long ruby cut and the patch went dark. The bridge was secure.

She moved to the center of the room and collapsed to the floor. She turned her torch off, luxuriating in the starlight coming from the screen, only her breathing breaking the quiet. She needed time, time to think.

What do I do now? She had to return to the lifeboat at some time, if for no other reason than to eat. They would know that; Marito would know. So how did—

The lights came on.

She frowned and muttered, "Always spoiling my privacy."

The lights grew bright, and brighter.

Dubois squinted and shielded her eyes. The heat began to rise. Sweat exploded over her body.

The lights flickered, the laughing pattern, and she realized that Marito could win. He controlled the lights, the heat. Both were still increasing. She could feel her skin begin to tighten.

Get out!

It was too bright, everything dazzling. She couldn't see which way to turn.

She turned on the scanwand. The heat was at the upper end of the scale. The luminosity was blinding. She sat on the floor, bent over in a huddle, eyes closed and covered.

The heat became a thing, beating on her, slamming the air from her lungs. She had to straighten out to breathe. The light fell off as she did so.

"You don't want to hurt me," she mumbled. "You . . . don't want to . . .

The heat kept coming. Every breath seemed to burn into her lungs, and she felt her stomach cramp in endless nausea. It had to be over fifty degrees and still rising.

It became difficult to breathe. Marito was hitting her with everything he could, short of killing her. The air was slowly drained from the bridge, not to a critical level, but enough to bring on the effects of oxygen deprivation. Dubois grew dizzy and her vision blurred. The nausea that gripped her worsened, and she gagged. The ship spun about her.

She couldn't think and she couldn't move and she couldn't lie still. She writhered on the floor and she knew that Marito had won had won had—

Her body went limp.

In the hangar the lights flashed for attention. Daggit read the message clumsily, then turned to So. He grinned.

"The bitch is caught," he said. "Kelly, come with me. She's on the bridge."

"She's armed," So said.

"Don't worry. Marito subdued her."

Tyler grunted through the gag they had stuffed in her mouth. She was bound to a chair in the lifeboat's aft section, the bonds chafing her wrists and ankles. She tried to draw their attention, but Daggit ignored her. He led So out of the boat, leaving her behind with Quont. The young girl sat across from Tyler, silent. She avoided looking at Tyler.

What's wrong with them? Tyler wondered. So was just a kid. Daggit had been a fine man when they first arrived. Now both were reduced to sacrificing another, and for what? For another man's revenge?

Marito controlled them all, just as surely as he now controlled the derelict. He had won Daggit to his side by wooing him with a promise of a freed Hilary. When that lie had been revealed, he had turned to the same story he had fed So. *Give me Dubois and I will set you free.* And they believed him; they had to. Marito had ascended himself to godlike status, controlling their futures. There was little they could do but believe him, believe *in* him.

She grunted again, trying to get Jeanine's attention. The girl studiously ignored her.

This is insane!

Tyler couldn't cry. She was too numb. She could only wonder which one of them Marito would ask for next, who would be the next holy sacrifice. Who would he ask for, and get?

It was cool, blessedly cool.

Dubois's mind tried to focus but was having a difficult time. Her skin was pale and clammy, her muscles refusing to cooperate as they twitched in ragged spasms. She forced herself to lie still and take slow, deep breaths, willing strength back into her limbs.

Why is the heat off? Why—

She knew. Marito had blasted her into oblivion, then turned the heat down to allow Daggit and So to get her. The lights were at their normal level, ready for them.

She rolled onto her belly. A fumbling hand sought and found her laser, bringing it to bear on the door they would use. The first one through would lose his head.

A scanwand poked through. As a warning, she fired, the sensor array exploding. The stick was hastily withdrawn.

"Ha, ha," she said without humor. "Come 'n get me."

The heat began rising again. She could feel it assaulting her back. No doubt Marito had learned how to discriminate with such things. Daggit and So were standing out there in wonderful comfort while she again began a slow roast.

It took an eternity to get to her knees. She knew the temperature was over forty again. *Never mind. Get out!*

She went to the forward door. Wonderful coolness lay on the other side. She had to get there.

She more or less fell through. She lay there, half in, half out of the bridge, gathering strength to pull the rest of her body out. In one motion she did so, giggling at the relief. She felt cool and wonderful . . . and . . . so . . . tired . . .

"No!"

She shouted, snapping her eyes open. The temperature in the bridge would be dropping off. It might start rising here. In either case, Daggit and So would soon be coming through. She had to keep moving.

Standing was too much like work, but she succeeded. She leaned against the wall until the corridor stopped spinning, then began walking.

Warning, warning . . .

It gonged in her mind. Slowly she unclipped her scanwand and waved it ahead. All clear. She began moving, gaining speed, knowing where to go now.

She heard something behind her. She turned and could see, fifty meters behind, Daggit and So come through the wall. She fired wildly, beam slashing down the length of the corridor and tearing into the walls. The lights vanished, and she could hear Daggit's loud cursing in the dark. His own laser beam winked, and she cringed as the crimson tube flashed by her. So began yelling at him to hold his fire. They needed her *alive*.

But I don't need you, she thought. She raised her scanwand and got an infrared reading. Aiming by luck, she fired. The beam sliced across the screen and tickled one of the ghostly figures. A scream echoed by her, and she smiled. "Got you, you sonuvabitch."

She continued moving forward, Daggit yelling at her. He was begging, and she was ignoring him. She knew where to go, where Marito would have no control. None at all, because it was a vast nothing.

One last scan. The end of the corridor was just ahead, darkness and the pit beyond. She would much rather drift in the dark and suffer the odor of the machinery than deal with Marito-the-ship, Daggit, or even So. She needed rest.

But it wasn't fair. The end of the corridor shone bright and white on the infrared scan. She watched the image shift, and the longest tendrils she had ever encountered formed, reaching for her . . .

So bit down on his lower lip, hissing in pain. Dubois's beam had carved into a wall, and hot shrapnel had sliced into his leg and side. The wounds were superficial, but the worst he had ever suffered.

Daggit groped for his near-crying partner and said, "Will you c'mon. She's just ahead."

"Where? I can't see a damn thing. And she damn well ruined our only scanner."

"Remember the maps she made? She can either jump into the pit or divert down into the morgue. Either way she's trapped. Come *on*."

They had taken three steps when a blood-curdling scream came from ahead. Laser light flashed and they could hear the sizzling as it carved into alien metal. Something splashed and the scream came again.

Then it was gone, fading away.

The ship throbbed.

So felt sick, his stomach churning. Daggit said, "It . . . it must have got her."

"God, did you *hear* her? Oh . . . oh God, what have I done?" His stomach cramped and he retched violently.

The lights came back on and Daggit blinked at the glare. He looked in disgust at the teenager and said, "Come on. We can go back now."

So looked ahead, wiping his mouth on a sleeve. He could see the corridor's end and many shattered tendrils. "Shouldn't we be sure? Looks like she did some damage up there."

"You want to look, go ahead. I'm goin' back to the boat."

So took a step towards the bow. A tendril twitched. He turned away. "Wait for me."

The two walked away, several tendrils still waving behind them.

The ship throbbed again.

18

Respite

They returned to the lifeboat weary to the bone. Daggit took it easily, accepting what had to be done. For So, however, reaction was setting in, eyes twitching, breathing ragged. He alternated between hysteria and tears, trying to justify the need to *feed* someone to the ship.

Tyler looked at their expressions and slumped in resignation. Daggit came over and undid her bonds, stepping back and letting her remove the gag. She looked at him with open disgust and said, "So, Marito has her."

"The ship has her," he said, nodding. "It . . . it had to be done."

"You pompous jackass! Nothing *had* to be done. How do you plan on getting out of here now, fool? Are *you* going to pilot this boat?"

"If need be, yes, but I think you'll do that."

Tyler suddenly felt very shrewd. Her mind plotted and came to a decision, one that struck her as appropriate to the situation. A smile played on her lips and she said, "Yes, I think I will."

Very slowly, she stood. She walked to the water tank and drew off a glass. Sipping it, she looked at Daggit, then So. The boy would be no trouble at all. Her attention refocused on

Daggit. The old man was stretching out in a chair, closing his eyes.

He opened them again, somewhat faster. The muzzle of a laser was pressing into his right ear. Tyler whispered, "If you move one iota too fast, I'll burn your brains out."

Daggit froze, heart pounding. "I . . . I . . . I . . ." He seemed unable to carry on a sentence.

Tyler stepped back. "Stand!"

He obeyed. She waved the laser towards the hatch and worked the controls. The doors slid aside. They stepped out onto the wing, and Daggit saw So and Quont huddled together on the deck below. Tyler motioned him to join them.

He walked over quickly, turning to see Tyler standing on the top of the ladder. She smiled, this time a hideous gesture. "You gave Pamela to the ship, I give it you three. Jeanine has opted to stay with you, Kelly. I consider it a poor choice. I don't know if I'll succeed, but I intend on trying to ram my way out of here. If I fail, I don't care. Either way, you three will remain here. I suggest you three vacate the hangar. When I hit that wall, this place is going to be open to vacuum."

She moved towards the hatch. The hangar lights flashed for attention, and surprise came to Tyler's face. She yelled, "Go to hell, Marito. You're not getting any more sacrifices." Then she laughed. "Well, you'll not get me in any case."

The code came rapping out. It was an insult.

F-O-O-L-S, S-H-E E-S-C-A-P-E-D

Tyler's heart leaped. Pamela escaped?

"How?" demanded Daggit. *"How?"*

"We heard her scream," So said. "We saw the tendrils that were—" He slapped his forehead. "Damnit! Most were burned away. She must have fired at them, screaming to throw us off, and double-backed down to the morgue. She's still somewhere in the ship."

His face hardened, the guilt of a moment ago forgotten in a rush of anger. He had felt anguish over Dubois's sacrifice. Now she had avoided that, making a fool of him. His sorrow had been over a trick. Blind rage, at being made the fool, blotted out the guilt.

Daggit ran towards the lifeboat. Tyler aimed. "Freeze! You're not going anywhere."

"Neither are you," Daggit said. "You won't leave without Dubois. I'm coming aboard."

"No," Tyler said, unsure of herself. She couldn't leave now. Nor could she burn Daggit down in cold blood. Whatever measure of desperation that took, she didn't have. And Daggit knew it.

"Don't move another—" she began, stopping as a wind stirred around her. The ship grunted and the lights went out, leaving her neatly silhouetted by the light spilling from the lifeboat's interior. Beyond, all was dark.

Damnit. Marito's working wi—

She took a step backwards, lifting one foot. A hand grabbed the other and yanked, tripping her. Her head slammed into the ridged supports for the solar cells. Daggit jumped up to the wing and slammed a fist into her head, making sure she was unconscious. He dragged her into the boat's interior and retied her. Grabbing two lasers and another scanwand, he slid down the ladder to the hangar deck, tossing one of the weapons to So. The lights came back on.

"Thank you, Marito," he said aloud, unsure if the man could hear them or not. He gave So a stern look, then pointed to the wall. "We've a job to finish. Let's go."

So nodded, some doubt creeping into his expression. "Why doesn't Marito get her? I thought he said leave everything to him."

"Remember what they said before. The morgue can't be touched by the computers. It must be a blind spot to him." He waved the laser. "But if we flush her out, he'll have her."

So nodded again. Quont tugged lightly on his sleeve as he left, her cheeks moist. Oblivious to her, he didn't realize how close she was to the breaking point.

"Kelly," she whispered, afraid to speak any louder. Marito would hear and Marito could punish, more effectively than any god her childhood had ever known. She, Kelly, and Daggit were all his puppets, and she didn't know how to fight it.

She didn't speak again. With great care she walked back to the lifeboat. The two men pushed through the wall, leaving her alone, powerless.

Dubois floated, and it felt wonderful. She had burned her way through the final obstacle by all-out attack, jumping through and out into the darkness beyond. One tendril had caught her leg, causing her to scream in surprise. She had

barely burned it away in time. She screamed again, letting it
drag out, knowing the sound would be fading to Daggit's and
So's ears, as if she were being carried away. The corridor lights
had come back on, and she could hear them talking, someone
being sick. Then they were gone and Dubois floated . . .
wonderfully.

After a while she bumped into the bow wall, the corridor a
distant point of light. She worked her way up until she was
against the ceiling, above the corridor landing. She hovered
there, just . . . relaxing.

Marito had no control over the bow area. She had gambled
on that. Assuming that Tyler and she were correct, that below
her were massed weapons, Marito's revulsion should cause the
ship to deny him control over them. Better, it was probable that
he was blind in the cavern. To him, she had vanished.

That she had guessed right became apparent. No one came
for her. Nothing happened. Apprehension faded, and she
thought how the lack of data must be frustrating the hell out of
Marito-the-ship.

She closed her eyes, secure at last. Now she could sleep,
recover, plan.

She dreamed. She held Marito by the throat, carefully
placed a laser to his head and fired, burning his brains away. It
felt good in the dream. It was the thing to do.

Marito was frustrated, and the ship throbbed because of it.
He had probed for Dubois and failed to find her. How had she
escaped? *Fools!*

There were too many dark areas in his knowledge, too many
areas he was blind to. The ship had sensed his capabilities and
had given him reign accordingly. He was not absolute. He
commanded Daggit and So to continue the search, into those
areas where he could not see. They would be his eyes and ears.

His servants.

They, unlike the others, obeyed him. With the others it was a
constant struggle for control. They did not understand the
fusion they had undergone. He did. He exercised that knowledge to the fullest, maintaining dominance.

But he was tired. Even the brain grows weary, and the ship's
mechanical computers began sensing his fatigue. They knew
he was the strongest of the five they had been able to gather,

and by that same measure he was the most important. He must not burn himself out. But the mechanical link could not allow the other bio-links to upset his programming. In their own simple way they accepted Marito's commands as supreme. The others were kept dormant until needed. Marito could feel the fatigue coming on, and instructed the alien computers.

Blocks were put in place. Active control passed into a passive mode. The ship was now effectively dead, as if it did not have a biological link-up. Marito could rest without the others taking advantage. They, too, slept.

Marito drifted away, no dreams, no thoughts. The machinery kept them all alive.

Tyler came to, face down, gagged, and with a splitting headache. She dimly remembered what had happened and tried to roll over. She felt hands gently grab her shoulders and roll her onto her back. Quont looked down, tears streaking her cheeks.

"They don't know what they're doing," she cried. "They think they're doing right. Kelly's just trying to protect me, to save me. Can you understand?"

Tyler mumbled into the gag, openly gesturing to be untied. Quont shook her head. "And you would have left us here, left us behind. How can you expect me to help you?"

Tyler went slack and felt dry, uncontrollable sobs racking her body. The situation, she realized, was hopeless. . . .

"Christ, this place is spookier than I thought."

Daggit looked at So and snorted. "What's so spooky about a morgue? Just a buncha dead bodies. Don't let 'em bother you, kid."

Kelly nodded, not at all reassured. "Where do we go from here? She's not here, and Marito hasn't told us he got her. Why doesn't he tell us where she is?"

"I don't know. No, she's not. I don't know," Daggit answered. "We're on our own, Kelly. It's that simple."

"Do you know how much space there is inside this ship? There's over a billion cubic meters. No way can we search it all."

"Not unless we start now. Remember, a good portion of that space is vacuum-filled. She'll only stick to corridors she knows. And wherever we find burned tendrils, we'll know we're on the right track. Let's go."

He led the way across the morgue to the exit doors. They picked one and pushed through, leaving the alien dead to their own.

19

Desperate Measures

Dubois came back to life and looked about. All was dark. For a moment she thrashed helplessly in panic. Remembrance flooded in. She stopped and took a precautionary scan around her. There was nothing.

She had no idea how long she had slept. Far below her a patch of light marked the corridor landing, the way out.

A dim part of a dream filtered back into her consciousness. She had burned out Marito's brain . . .

Dubois stiffened. She knew what had to be done, what she had to do, and it sickened her. No more running, no more reacting and fleeing. It was time to go on the offensive, to attack.

Maybe as a last resort, but I'm not that desperate, not yet. The words haunted her.

The situation had changed. Now, she was *that* desperate. There was only one problem.

She had to go back into the ship, back to the lifeboat.

She drifted just outside the slack tendrils' reach. They didn't move. Wary of a trick, she moved closer, laser at the ready. They didn't move.

I must have shorted out the system, she thought, landing.

She stepped through quickly. They didn't react, and she moved off without a backwards glance.

The bridge was unchanged, only now it was as cool as the rest of the ship. She moved through, down the corridor she had used before. The way was reasonably clear, since she had already destroyed most, if not all of the security patches. She stepped by the twisted debris, the blue fluid hardened. It still looked like blood to her.

She didn't stop to think why the ship hadn't already "healed" the destroyed portions of the corridor.

Nothing moved. The ship seemed still, lifeless. Only the ever-burning lights told her different, that and the fresh air. Dubois didn't debate the point with herself. She took advantage of it and moved faster.

Riding down the "elevator" gave her one bad moment. She had no control over her progress and was at the ship's mercy. She sighed with relief when it set her down, untouched, in that first corridor she and Frances had explored so long ago. The brief flash of nostalgia passed.

The staging room was quiet, deserted. She moved more cautiously now, pushing her scanwand through the wall and into the hangar. A quick scan showed only the lifeboat. No one stood about. She went through and looked around. Nothing. She moved towards the boat.

The hatch was open. She climbed up onto the wing, then moved in a crouch towards the hatchway. Leaning in, she saw Tyler lying in a heap. Quont sat over her, looking startled at Dubois's sudden appearance. She leveled her laser and smiled.

"Don't move, Jeanine."

Quont didn't. Dubois stepped in and worked the hatch controls. The triple doors slipped shut and she threw the manual lock, cutting off the exterior controls.

"Hello, Jeanine," Dubois said, voice far too pleasant. "Where are the others?"

"Out . . . out looking for you."

Tyler grunted in shock and rolled over, eyes sparkling. A moment later she was untied and standing, embracing Dubois in a bone-straining hug. When they separated, she was all smiles. An awkward grin played on Dubois's lips.

"What's next, Captain?"

"You can't leave without them," Quont said. "You *can't*."

"I don't intend to," Dubois replied, tone becoming mechanical. She handed Tyler the laser and stepped over to the storage room. She pulled out the last pressure suit and began putting it on, making sure the air tanks were fully charged.

Tyler's smile dimmed slightly, unsure of Dubois's attitude or intentions. "*I* intended on leaving them," she said, "when they told me the ship had you."

Dubois stopped and looked at her oddly. "Really?"

"Yes."

"And how would you have gotten out?"

The smile faltered and died. "I would have rammed the doors and—"

Dubois shook her head. "You would have done nothing. The moment it was clear that I was becoming persona non grata, I made plans. The control board for this boat is locked and keyed to my release code. Even if you knew the sequence, it wouldn't work. It's keyed to *me*, period." She resumed pulling on the suit and grinned wryly. "It was my insurance policy. Unfortunately, it didn't work. I never had a chance to tell anyone."

Tyler's jaw was slack. "But . . . but then if they had succeeded and you—"

"None of you could have piloted this boat out of here. Not ever."

The designer's face tightened. "Then you didn't trust even me."

"No. I assumed I could rely on you, but we were both outnumbered, myself especially, as what occurred shows."

After a long silence Tyler said, "So, what's the plan?"

Dubois's voice was flat, again mechanical. "Very simple, really. I intend on blowing this ship's brains out."

"*What?*"

She sealed the final opening and stepped back into the storage room. She returned a moment later with a small box marked in red, DANGER.

"This boat is supplied with most everything some bonehead decided would be needed for survival," she said, opening the box. "That included survival on a planet. We've six lasers for defense and two airguns for hunting. Seeds for planting and the necessary tools. And there." She pulled out a ten-centimeter ball, flattened on opposite sides, one flat spot smaller than the other by half. "Low-yield explosives, variable focus. They're for moving medium-sized boulders or tree stumps, or for

general defensive purposes. They don't take up much room and
they're not very heavy, so they were added just to round things
out. We've got six."

She replaced the charge and sealed the lid. Standing, she
secured it tightly to her suit's thigh utility hooks. She began
slipping on her gloves. "I'm going to the computer room. As
near as I can remember from my last visit, there are no tendrils
in that room. I intend on going into the tank room and planting
these charges around . . . around the occupied tanks.
They've got delay timers, so I'll have plenty of time to get out.
That and—"

Tyler said, "You're going to kill them."

Dubois looked at her, face hard. "Yes, I am. Do you see any
other way?"

Tyler hesitated, not meeting Dubois's eyes. She shook her
head once. "No. I just wanted it said."

"So now it has been. Once the biological units are gone,"
she couldn't call them "people" anymore, "the mechanical
units will be helpless. We've already established that they
cannot act on their own. They react. If there hadn't been one
last alien in the tanks, we never would have been trapped here
in the first place. When I blow those tanks, the ship will be a
mindless hulk, a *real* derelict. I'll—"

Tyler's eyes widened. "Wait! There *are* tendrils in the
computer room, a set over each container."

Dubois remembered. She said, "Those are just placement
arms, not security related. Marito will have no control over
them."

"You can't believe that."

"Why should they be tied in with security? Besides,
everything seems quiet now. Maybe I can sneak up on him if I
hurry."

Tyler snapped, "You're committing suicide."

And Dubois yelled, "I'm tired of running, of being some
sort of victim. I won't be Marito's toy!"

They stared at each other for several moments. Tyler asked,
"What do we do once it's done?"

"We get out of here. Either we burn through the hangar
doors or we ram 'em. Whichever. We get out of here."

"And back through the hellhole?"

Dubois hesitated, then shook her head. "No. There is no
hellhole."

She told them how she had turned on the bridge viewscreen and how the hole had apparently vanished. "Perhaps my calculations were off, but I wouldn't hold too much hope."

"So where do we go?" Quont asked in a small voice.

"There's a possibility that the hellhole resolved down to a normal anomaly. The boat's equipped to check that. When we get out there, we'll see."

Tyler held Dubois's helmet. "What if you're wrong? This could be our ticket home."

"It's a dead ship, Frances," Dubois said, conviction firm. "I'm only completing what started no one knows how many centuries ago."

They looked at each other for a heartbeat, then Tyler reached over and secured the helmet in place. Dubois took a laser, a heavy-duty tool kit, and a scanwand. She checked the explosives pack once again.

"Good luck," Tyler said.

"And to you. If I run into Daggit and So, I'll send them here. Other than that . . ." She let her voice drift off.

"We can't leave them," Quont said.

"If I can't find them on my way back, I won't wait."

She didn't wait for an argument. She was out the hatch and down the ladder in a hurry. She turned to duck under the wing when Daggit and So came through the wall, exhausted from hours of being lost.

Dubois raised her laser and yelled, "Don't move or I'll cut you down!"

Both men looked stunned. Daggit recovered and went for his laser. Dubois had plenty of time and fired carefully. The beam blew his weapon apart, scorching his hand.

"Kelly," she said, "drop your laser, *now!*"

Tyler came out the hatch, another laser aimed, and So saw defeat. His laser clattered to the deck.

Dubois ran by them, saying, "Get into the lifeboat and wait. I'll be back and we'll be getting out of here."

Both men nodded, resigned to defeat. They moved towards Tyler. Dubois didn't give them another thought. She went through the wall, back into the ship.

Tyler suddenly realized and shouted, but it was too late. Dubois was gone, without freeing the lifeboat's controls. If she failed . . .

Tyler looked at the striped wall as Daggit and So climbed up onto the wing. She hoped the ship remained dormant long enough.

Marito's mind was reactivated. He reaffixed himself into the derelict's computers and mentally smiled. He felt refreshed, renewed, ready for—

Impulses flowed in. Something was wrong. There was no one outside the lifeboat. Where were Daggit and So?

Wait. There was something, but only a glimmer. It was as if someone *was* inside The Ship, but something was blocking The Ship's sensors. A glimmer, though. A person wearing a pressure suit, with the faceplate open . . .

Dubois.

He tracked her and for the first time felt fear. She was walking straight towards the computer room. With a pressure suit.

She had to be stopped.

"We're all going to die," So said, slumping down next to Quont. "Marito will kill us."

"If she succeeds," Daggit said, "the ship may self-destruct. You said so yourself."

"It's the only way," Tyler mumbled, still thinking about the controls. She turned to them and said, "Both of you, shut up."

There was a pause. Daggit said, "We could leave now. Just leave, then come back and see if she's succeeded or not."

She suddenly smiled. Dubois hadn't *forgotten* to free the controls at all. She began, "Ignoring the problem of getting out," and told them about the locked controls, finishing, "so you need Pamela alive if you want to fly this boat out of here."

Daggit scowled, face flushed in confused anger. Outside, through the open hatch, they watched the lights flash, then snap out. The ship roared and grumbled.

"What?" asked Kelly.

Tyler said, "It's begun. Marito's discovered what she's up to." She turned to Daggit. "If he kills her, we're trapped here forever."

"I know. And if she succeeds, she'll have killed the last person I ever loved."

Tyler blinked. She had forgotten how close Daggit and Kahn had been. "You know she's trapped forever. You prefer that?"

He looked torn between two choices. "I . . . we don't know that. Marito only *implied* that was so. He never *said* it."

"If Pamela dies, we'll never leave here."

"So?" Daggit swiped at his eyes. "I . . . I'd rather . . ." He stopped.

Tyler turned to So. "We can help her, you know."

The boy frowned. "You mean go out . . . out *there?*" Tyler nodded, and So said, "What if Marito depressurizes the ship? We've no suits."

She stood, checking her laser and scanwand. "*I'm* willing to chance it if it improves the odds of getting out of here."

Daggit said, "You *can't* kill Hilary!"

"She's already dead, Ben."

So stood, unsure of himself. "It's the only way?"

"Yes."

He nodded. "All right, we need her alive. Let's go."

Tyler smiled and tossed him a laser and a breathing mask. She took another for herself. "Short-term protection."

He only nodded again. He gestured for Tyler to lead on. She didn't move.

Laser nonchalantly aimed, she said, "After you."

So's grin was tight.

Daggit buried his face in his hands, caught in the agony of indecision. The thought that they were killing Hilary rang again and again in his mind.

Tyler and So moved out into the ship quickly, out into the war zone.

20

War

The lights went out. She had been expecting it.

Dubois snapped on her torch light and the infrared scanner. She took a reading behind her, then to the front. Wherever Marito's mind had been, it was back now, and he knew where she was going, if not what she was doing.

She could feel the corridor change around her. The infrared display grew distorted, senseless. Her torch didn't catch the overhang until her head nearly slammed into it. Marito had altered the corridor into a series of low overhangs. She ducked under it. On the other side was a short wall. Evidently Marito couldn't cut off the corridor completely. He could, and was, making it more difficult for her, though.

She slipped over the wall and under the overhangs, feeling inexorable. She came over a wall when the next overhang came to life, flashing white on the infrared screen.

She fired, falling back as the tendrils lashed out, over her head. She continued firing, waving the beam back and forth. Blue oil sprayed her suit, covering the faceplate. Hunks of tubing fell on her and she slipped to the deck. Then all was still, the only sound the hissing of her own breathing. She wiped off her faceplate as well as possible and continued her advance.

The corridor turned into a square sitting on one edge. She had to walk with one foot on each side of the V. It began to revolve. She fought to retain her balance, still moving forward.

The obstacles formed again. She waited until a wall rotated up to become an overhang, then ducked underneath. And she kept moving forward.

Wall joined overhang, sealing the corridor.

So much for what Marito can't *do.*

She blasted her way through. The lights came back on, but in bands of the rainbow, first rushing away from her, then racing towards her. All the while the square corridor spun, faster now. She fought a rising sensation of vertigo.

The suit's faceplate compensated as much as possible for the flashing colors as they rose from the barely visible reds to eye-searing ultraviolets. Her suit readouts flashed for attention. The exterior temperature was rising, already over forty degrees Celsius. The suit was rated to over one hundred, so that was the least of her worries. And still she moved forward.

The corridor was suddenly round again, and jerked to a halt. Dubois fell at the change and fought to catch her breath. She looked ahead, a last band of rainbow colors vanishing in the distance, leaving only the dark. The temperature fell off to normal. For a moment all was quiet.

Her skin crawled. She swung up the scanwand. A marching white patch was racing for her. She raised her laser, aiming via the scanner. She fired and missed.

Something rumbled in the dark, the ship's grunting alarms. Only now they were like some hideous laugh. Dubois whirled around, scanning behind her. Another patch raced towards her from that direction. She fired, a glancing hit. Fluid gushed out, brilliant white on the screen.

She turned towards the one in front of her. She could hit one or the other, not both.

The front.

She ran towards it, crouching and hoping for distance from the one behind. She fired, holding the stud. The ceiling burst, the mechanism spilling out. Perhaps . . .

She spun and dove for the floor, laser coming up—

Too late!

Two beams sliced into the ceiling. The unit blew apart, falling out and steaming at Dubois's feet. She looked stunned, staring at the two bobbing lights coming towards her. They resolved into Tyler and So.

"He figured you'd need help," Tyler said, motioning towards the boy. Both were bathed in sweat, breathing hard.

Dubois looked at him, guessing the truth but willing to accept the lie. She took deep breaths. "How did you aim?"

"You gave it away by firing at it. I made a full-spectrum scan and found it on the infrared. As I assume you did."

Dubois nodded. "Okay, okay, now get—"

Something whirred through the air and slapped Tyler in the back. She jerked foward with a grunt, falling on her face. A hunting dart protruded from her shoulder.

So looked shocked. "What the hell's that?"

Dubois raised her wand, scanning the corridor. A figure was crouched less than a dozen meters away, bent over and working with something.

Her voice was flat. "It's Daggit."

So looked, squinting into the dark. A faint glow, as if from a shielded torch, gave the older man away.

Tyler groaned. "What . . . hit me?"

Dubois examined the wound, leaving the dart in place. "Lucky for you he didn't find the poison that goes in these. It hit the muscle. A bandage and rest and you'll be just fine."

So crouched down, then went prone. "Why doesn't he fire again?"

"Takes time to pump the airgun up. You have to—"

A dart whistled by her ear, causing her to flinch. She raised her laser. "Throw it down, Ben, or I'll burn you!"

"I'm not going to let you kill Hilary," he screamed. "I'm not!"

So turned and said, "Don't move, Captain."

Dubois looked. His laser was aimed at her head, rock steady. "Drop it."

She hesitated. There was a note of urgency in So's expression. She tossed down the laser and he said, "Come on up, Ben. I've got her. We'll give her and Tyler to Marito, then he'll let us go."

Daggit jogged into the light, still trying to recharge the airgun. "Great, great," he muttered. "Marito'll let Hilary go too."

So stood, nodding. "Sure, sure."

He turned and kneed Daggit in the stomach, chopping his neck with the flat of his hand. The man dropped, unconscious. So looked at Dubois, terror and uncertainty plain in his voice. "You'd better be right about this."

Dubois stood, helping Tyler up. "Can you walk, Frances?"

"Yeah, yeah. It's kinda gone numb."

"That won't last long. Kelly, you'll have to carry and/or drag Daggit. Get back to the boat in a hurry." She looked around the dark corridor, scanning to make sure there were no patches sneaking up on them. "I think Marito assumed you were coming after me. Once it's clear that isn't the case, there's no telling what he'll do."

Tyler and So nodded. The boy stooped and lifted Daggit by a shoulder, half dragging, half carrying him. Tyler reached around to the dart.

"Leave it in," Dubois said. "You'll only worsen the bleeding if you pull it out now."

Tyler nodded and followed So.

Dubois waited until they were out of sight, then turned back towards her objective. She listened to the ship. A dull throbbing could be heard, and a light pulsing came up through the deck. She moved forward slowly.

She reached the first of the doorway's security patches without difficulty. She scanned it and the other two, then lasered them all from a distance. Though she had already destroyed the first, she refused to take any chances. Marito might have repaired it.

The doorway was now clear. She took one step towards it and the typhoon began.

The corridor turned icy smooth and the air started rushing out. Marito was depressurizing the ship. Dubois thought fleetingly that the others might not have made it back in time, then realized her immediate problem was to stay in one place. She was losing ground.

Her hand fumbled at the tool kit, extracting a short-handled pick. She fell, slamming it into the deck. The material yielded around the hook and it dug in. Dubois held on with one hand, the other making sure the explosives stayed secured at her thigh. The winds continued, the temperature plummeting.

The gale slowly slackened off to nothing. She was left in a hard vacuum, temperature just above zero. A chill swept through her before the suit's heaters kicked in. Dubois stood carefully, rotating her scanwind on its wrist thong so she could grab the grip. She reached for her laser.

It was gone.

She raised the scanwand and flicked on the light. No dust motes danced in the beam, no air to support them. The walls absorbed the light, giving off no reflection. It was almost as though she hadn't turned the light on.

She looked around. The laser had vanished, sucked away by the winds. She licked suddenly dry lips. Care would have to be taken. No one could help her now. She walked forward.

She stood before the doorway. No tendrils reached for her. The scanner picked up none coming. On the other side of the door was nothing. From the wall, through the scanwand, she could feel a methodic throbbing, a calling. Dubois hesitated, then went through.

The room was the same, gold and amber lights flashing and glowing. The shine from the container room was brighter, and she peered in. Five tanks were active, five naked humans secured within. Four of them looked tense, straining, as if fighting an unseen force. The fifth was also tense, but in concentration. Its glow was fiercer than the others, enough to make them appear subdued. That one was Marito. She knew what he was concentrating on.

She looked up. Over the tanks were the same slack tendrils. This was her only doubt. Stating confidently that they were only for placement was easy, back on the lifeboat. Facing them and believing it was another matter. She knew they would become active if a body was turned over to them by the exterior tendrils. Now that she was inside, they *should* remain inactive, no threat to a "workman"—*if* she was correct.

Marito would be fighting to change that. She had only one way of knowing if he succeeded: when they grabbed her.

How best to proceed? She had six of the explosive charges. One in each tank would be more than enough. Marito would be "honored" with two.

She took a deep breath and pushed through the transparent field. In the room's atmosphere she could hear the steady throb of the room maintaining its charges. There was something more, a humming intensity. She looked up at the still-slack tendrils for a moment, then swallowed to wet a dry throat, moving towards Marito's tank.

Dubois leaned over the side and looked, the man's expression covered and unreadable. She couldn't resist poking his side. He jerked.

"I'm here, Marito," she said softly, not knowing whether he could hear or not. "I've come to kill you."

She pulled out a bomb and adjusted the blast focus for tight field. She set the timer for two minutes and pressed the larger of the flat sides against Marito's chest. She did the same for the second charge, placing it on his forehead. A tight focus would, for the most part, keep the blast wave limited to one direction. That focus was straight down, through Marito and into the container mechanism. She tripped the timers, the digits beginning to run down. She moved her lips, softly counting down, and moved towards the other tanks.

Over Marito's tank, unseen by her, a tendril twitched. Another joined it. And another . . .

She planted the charges on Forsythe and Poullard in quick time. She set the fifth charge, standing over Buchanan's container, and reached out to place it. Her hand stopped.

Ohmigod, she groaned to herself, *what am I doing?*

She remembered his joking manner, his serious times, his active self. He hadn't deserved her overbearing manner, her insistence on perfection. Buchanan hadn't wanted any of it. Just get through the bare minimum, get it on your service record, and on to a less-hectic merchantman.

And now he was trapped in an alien machine.

Time was running down. She mumbled, "I'm sorry, Kevin," and placed the bomb.

She put Kahn's in place quickly, not daring to look at the woman too closely. She knew she couldn't go through with it if she thought about it much longer.

It's better this way, it's better this way . . .

When she stepped away, she hesitated for only a moment. There were a few seconds between each explosion. She had less than thirty seconds before Marito's went off. She moved towards the door—

—and bounced off. The light amber had hardened to glowing firmness, trapping her inside. She pushed against it, uselessly. There was no way out.

She turned back to the tanks. She had to find cover, as far from the explosions as possible. She turned to look for cover when a movement caught the corner of her eye.

A tendril lashed out, whistling through the air, and wrapped itself around her helmet. Dubois screamed as she was lifted off the floor, clawing at the cord wrapped tightly around her faceplate. Marito had succeeded in gaining control over the room's arms. The one that had caught her carried her above the containers, more coming to life and whipping around her. She was held rigid against all struggles. Dubois screamed and fought as the tendrils drew tight, squeezing her chest, cutting off her breath. They felt like pulsing snakes, and her body jerked in spasms. The alien mechanism was oblivious to it all.

They held her poised over the sixth tank, next to Marito's, and she could feel them begin to work on her suit. The container glowed to life, its golden field enveloping her. The room throbbed, working to calm her. Dubois went into hysterics, gasping for breath, knowing that if Marito succeeded, she would be alone, the others destroyed by her actions. And the ship would go on, working through her, after those still in the lifeboat—

The explosives! How much time to the first blast? She tried to squirm around, bringing her back to face the concussion. It had heavier armor, and she fought to curl into a ball.

The tendrils began lowering her towards the tank. Her vision began to tunnel, graying out from lack of oxygen. A wave of lethargy swept through her. Her gasps for breath became spasmodic. She grew faint, cares fading.

The helmet lock bank flew away, the hardhat twisting the one-quarter unsealing turn. It separated from the suit—

The first blast blew Marito in half, the second vaporizing his head and tearing apart the fragments. The tendrils dropped Dubois into the tank as the shockwave pounded her head, knocking the helmet free and clear. Her ears roared in pain. She lay there, stunned, lungs sucking in disinfected air, as succeeding blasts slammed her into darkness . . .

21

". . . any time."

. . . slowly increasing light.

There was a drumming in Dubois's head. She opened her eyes slowly, the pain behind them stabbing into her. Her ears felt numb, as though stuffed with cotton. As her vision cleared, she could see the slack tendrils dangling down at her.

She jerked in reflex action, then stopped. The tendrils didn't move. She was safe, which meant . . .

Nothing about her moved. Her face felt damp, and she wiped a hand over it. She looked at her hand.

It was red.

She groaned and squeezed her eyes shut. Her mind was a rush of confusion, and she muttered a string of pseudoprayers. Her eyes opened wide.

Her ears felt stuffed.

"Hello."

Her voice sounded in her head, not in her ears. She slapped her gloved hands together and heard nothing.

I'm deaf.

A vague sucking sensation yanked her from this realization. She lifted a leg in horror. It had almost fallen into the proper slot, and the tank was trying to absorb and fuse with her suit's fabric. She recoiled in horror, jumping from the tank. She

slipped on something and fell against Marito's tank. She turned
and—

Her eyes bulged in horror, then snapped closed. The carnage
within and about the room was absolute. Her knees felt weak
and she fell onto them, mouth tightly clenched, fighting back
sobs and bile.

After several minutes she felt in better control of herself.
She wiped off as well as possible and recovered her helmet. It
was intact and serviceable, as was the rest of her suit. One air
cell had ruptured, but the others held more than enough. She
twisted the helmet back into place, securing the lock band, and
stood. She glanced about, orientating herself towards the door.
Her stomach heaved and she tightened her jaw again.

Don't look around, don't look around, leave!

She walked to the doorway, the field again a normal hue. She
left the room, never looking back.

The mechanical computers seemed the same, other than a
flashing battery of green and blue lights on several panels. No
doubt the computer was aware that its biological links were
now scrapes of—

I will not think about it!

Knowing that Marito could no longer touch her, she began
experimenting with the computer controls. Bizarre symbols
told her nothing. She understood none of it.

A great weariness engulfed her, and she stumbled towards
the exit. Her ears began ringing painfully, in time with the
stabbing in her head, and she realized the effects of the
concussion were not permanent. It made the next step slightly
easier to take.

The ship was dead. Kevin, Hilary, Nan, Forsythe, and
Marito were gone. Now came the next step. She had to get the
survivors out.

The corridors were silent, an empty vacuum. More than
silent, though, they were dead. She could no longer feel even
the normal life throbbing of the ship. There was nothing. It was
evident that some circuits were still functioning, but without
the continual guidance of the biological link computers, that
would soon fade, falling into decay.

A dingy yellow patch of light followed overhead, the
original ship's lighting. It provided little useful illumination.
She had neglected to recover her scanwand, and she had no
intention of going back. She fumbled along without it.

She found her way to the staging room after an inordinate amount of time. Nothing was the same anymore. More exactly, except for the boat radio gear, everything was as it had been when they first arrived. The corridors had shrunken back to two-meter tubes. The deck felt yielding again. Again, this time more forcefully, she realized how familiar the alien vessel had become. Now all familiarity was gone; it was unknown and alien once again.

The doors still worked, to her silent thanks. By whatever process, they were independent of computer control. She looked about the room she had, such a short time before, accidentally fallen into. And Kevin had been ready to charge to her rescue.

That brought a smile, then a tear. She had saved him by killing him. The thought was blunted only slightly by the knowledge that he had already been worse than dead. She didn't feel any better.

She pushed through the wall. The lifeboat sat in a dingy puddle of yellow light. With a silent flare the boat's floodlights came on, illuminating the area around it and Dubois. Her suit radio crackled and someone said, "I see you succeeded."

It was Tyler. Dubois felt relief that the engineer had made it. She activated her transmitter. "Yes. Is Kelly there?"

"We all made it. We've rigged the airlock. You can come aboard any time."

"Not yet. Put a laser and a scanwand into the lock. I need them."

She had them a few minutes later. After resealing the outside door she stepped around the lifeboat's stern and walked towards the closed entranceway.

"Are you going to cut our way out?" Tyler asked.

"I'm going to try." She turned and studied all sides of the lifeboat. "If this doesn't work, we've enough room to turn the boat for a ramming attempt."

Dubois looked at the black door, fifty meters away, and raised her scanwand. She pressed for an infrared scan and looked at the screen. It was clear. She scanned the ceiling.

It was covered with dull, yellow patches, hundreds of them. She knew what they were for: maintenance. And they were yellow, not white.

"Dead," she mumbled. Dead and cooling off. She turned back to the door, this time raising her laser.

The beam hit the hull and vanished. There was no backsplash, no flare, no glow. She had expected it to be as easy to cut as the interior walls. Instead, it simply absorbed the beam with no effect. She held it on for a good minute, the laser beginning to overheat, without improvement.

She understood. The derelict's hull absorbed the terrific assault of a Wolf-Rayet star as though it were nothing. What more could a laser add?

"No good," she reported. "Start securing the boat. I'm coming in."

By the time she had cycled the airlock and stepped inside, most of their makeshift living quarters were secured away. Loose objects were bound together and stuffed into lockers. Tanks were strapped against bulkheads. No one greeted her as she entered, everyone up front. She went into the rear compartment and stripped off her suit, ignoring what clung to it. She hid it away in its case. She grimaced and washed quickly. After pulling on a standard orange jumpsuit, she went forward to where the survivors now sat.

Daggit was slumped in his seat, safety web locking him in. His mouth moved but she couldn't hear what he was saying.

"The others are dead," she said without preamble. "This ship can no longer initiate actions. It can no longer hold us. I don't know how, or if, it will react when we hit it, but I intend to find out. Arguments?"

She looked them over. So and Quont wouldn't look at her. She knew he was still questioning whether or not he had backed the right side. He wouldn't be sure until they were outside the derelict.

Daggit had no doubts. His head rolled back, eyes shut, and his mutterings became a shout. "You killed my Hilary, you killed my Hilary . . ."

More for her own relief than for his, Dubois took out the syringe she had prepared. Daggit's eyes fluttered as the drug took effect. She hoped he would find some solace in the temporary oblivion.

She turned and stepped through the separation panel, glancing at the door's melted lock. She climbed into the left-hand seat, the command chair, savoring its feel for a moment and closing her eyes. She felt her body screaming for rest, for its own escape.

Tyler slipped into the right-hand seat, wincing slightly as she settled in. Her jumpsuit was unzippered partway, and Dubois could see the bandage drawn over her shoulder and around the back. The engineer looked over at her and said, "What can I do?"

"Sit tight," Dubois said, voice just above a whisper. "I'll handle it."

She looked overhead. The emergency hatch had been resealed. "You did that?"

"Yeah. When the air went out of the hangar, I figured it was the prudent thing to do."

Dubois missed the jovial tone and reached behind her. A tug on the handle and the doors snapped shut, closing off the flight deck from the rear compartment. She didn't bother with the ruined lock.

Tyler looked alarmed. "Why—"

Dubois activated the intercom. "Don't worry. I've sealed the bulkhead in case the hull ruptures up here." She turned and began rigging a temporary lock. She said to Tyler, "This thing won't hold pressure as it is now. I just don't want them changing their minds."

"Oh." She nodded and remained silent.

Dubois looked at the center computer console and smiled, as if thinking of a dark joke. She pressed the main power switch and the control boards winked to life.

Alarm and surprise again came to Tyler's face. "It . . . it was all a bluff? The controls were never locked?"

"All you had to do was turn them on to find out." Her fingers danced and the lifeboat came to life. "I had planned to, but didn't go through with it. I'm sure it helped you convince *them*, though, especially with Jeanine as a witness to my ruthless nature."

She activated the main viewer and the assortment of auxiliary screens. Range information appeared, distances and clearances. She unlocked the attitude jets and the main engines. The lifeboat hummed.

"Activating null-fields," Dubois said. She keyed the intercom again. "Strap in. If the fields fail, we'll get one hell of a jolt."

She looked over at the seating diagram next to Tyler. Three green lights. Tyler and she made five.

Five out of ten, she thought. *You've killed half your passengers, your responsibility.*

Her hands shook.

The belly jets lifted the lifeboat easily. She slaved in the flight computer and it held them five meters above the deck. She fed in another order and the boat slowly began turning, degree by degree, and soon they were nose-on with the closed entrance.

"I'm backing us to the wall," she said. "I want lots of running room."

"Shouldn't we try and nudge it first?" Tyler asked. "Just as a test."

Dubois considered, then agreed. She eased forward on the stern maneuvering jets, retracting the landing gear as she did so. The lifeboat moved ahead. The wall was 150 meters away.

She backed off on their accumulated speed at seventy-five meters. Abruptly the belly jets were no longer needed, the derelict's artificial gravity fading out as quickly as it had come on. Dubois looked dismayed as they began to rise. The flight computer caught the motion in the next instant, firing topside maneuvering jets. They leveled out.

"Fifty meters," Tyler said. "Want to slow up?"

Dubois said, "I'm just going to kiss it."

Tyler activated the intercom. "Brace yourselves!"

Fifteen meters from the wall they were moving at one meter per second, a good walk. The lifeboat represented a great deal of mass, however, speed converting that into momentum. Dubois steadied herself, securing her own restraining harness. Tyler blinked rapidly, concentrating on the main viewer image. Only the computer readout told them how close they were to the black wall.

When they were ten meters from impact a slit appeared. It grew rapidly into a slot. The hull bulged upwards, slipping into the great shape of the derelict above them, giving way to open space below. The door opened and the lifeboat slipped out into its natural element, having hit nothing.

Neither woman spoke for a moment, then Tyler asked, "What the hell happened?"

Dubois blinked once, then began laughing. She broke into a fit of near-hysteria, and Tyler looked at her in concern. She made certain the lifeboat was free and clear, falling away cleanly. They were in no immediate danger, their path lying within the ship's solar shadow. She turned back to Dubois.

"Are . . . are you okay?" she asked.

Dubois wiped the tears from her eyes and managed to choke. "Yes, yes, I'm fine. Just . . . just a second."

It was nearly a minute before she was able to talk, hysteria changing to sorrow. "Don't you understand?" she asked, upper lip twitching slightly. "Other than specific ship functions, *everything* on that ship *reacts*. The lights, the doors . . . *the doors.*"

Tyler fell back, stunned. "The hangar doors were automatic. They react to anything that approaches them."

Dubois nodded, grimacing. "They closed the first time because we tripped them. A ship coming at them from the inside would have caused them—" She broke off, voice breaking for an instant. "Would have caused them to open." She looked at the engineer, expression wide. "We . . . we could have left *at any time*."

The bubble protecting her popped.

Dubois's mind shifted to automatic. The events of the last few hours began piling up. Her fingers trembled ever so slightly as they programmed the computer, checked the astralscan, setting course and acceleration.

"To the hellhole?" Tyler asked.

Dubois nodded. There was a slight quaver in her voice when she said, "We've a few days till we get there."

Tyler played with a control. The viewscreen shifted to view aft, the derelict an unmoving dark shape silhouetted by a revolving hell. She said, "What happens to the next group that stumbles upon it?"

"They'll find what we thought we had," Dubois whispered. "A d-dead ship with a dead c-crew. I doubt if the computer can hold out for long without reaffirmation by a b-biological computer. It'll . . . fall into the sun."

Tyler nodded and unhooked her harness. "Well, shall we break out the rations and celebrate?"

Dubois was blinking rapidly at the tears in her eyes, mind in turmoil. She fumbled at her harness, muttering, "Celebrate what?"

She bolted for the rear. In the stern compartment, door sealed, her reserve collapsed. She fell into a corner and wept.

22

Life

They were a day out from the hellhole point when the sensors went berserk. A beacon call, loud and clear, broke the silence. Dubois, feeling better after a day's sleep, jumped into her command chair and told the computer to show and tell.

On the main screen was printed a green square, indicating the position where the hellhole had been. Coming away from that point, slow but accelerating, was a flashing red target star. Dubois took another reading, a look of apprehension crossing her face.

"Hey!" she yelled. "We've got a ship here."

She turned on the radio. The speaker hissed for a moment, the receiver scanning for signals. One broke through loud and clear.

". . . vessel *Cousteau* calling lifeboat, come in lifeboat. This is Exploration Vessel *Cousteau* calling lifeboat, please reply."

Dubois keyed their transmitter. "Attention *Cousteau*, this is *Goddess* Lifeboat 2-2-7 responding. Where the hell are you from?"

"*Goddess*? Another one! One moment, 2-2-7."

Tyler said, "What's he mean 'another one'?"

"Who cares?" So asked. "We've been rescued!"

195

There was a chorus of shouts, almost drowning out the *Cousteau*'s next message.

"Attention Lifeboat 2-2-7, this is Captain Dennison, commanding *Cousteau*. Do you receive?"

"Affirmative, Captain. This is Ensign Dubois, commanding 2-2-7. What are you doing here? How—"

"Stand by, 2-2-7. We are tracking a large spacecraft in your orbital wake. Can you identify?"

Dubois's mood turned somber. "Affirmative, Captain. It is an alien derelict. We'll tell you the whole story when we link up."

"Alien?"

"Yes."

"And a derelict, a dead ship?"

Dubois's grip on the microphone tightened. "Yes."

"I think we'll have much to discuss, Ensign Dubois. Tie in your computer. Stand by for orbital data conference."

Dubois did so. In moments the two ships' computers were deciding which were the best orbits to effect the quickest rendezvous.

"We're going home," Tyler said softly. "There's an anomaly here. *We're going home!*"

Quont threw herself at So, both laughing in joy, both crying in relief. Even Daggit stirred from his near-catatonic state, a slight smile on his lips. Home.

Unlike *Goddess*, or even the derelict, *Cousteau*'s hull lines were bluff and square. She was a vessel of space and nothing else; aerodynamic sensibilities hadn't played any part in her design. Though shorter than *Goddess*, she had nearly the same amount of interior room, for carrying her myraid research and exploration vessels, the science departments, the living quarters. She was a glittering city in the sky.

The lifeboat slipped into one of the ship's larger receiving bays. Dubois's eyebrows arched in surprise as the lifeboat locked to one of the access tubes. Four other *Goddess* lifeboats lined the bay.

Pressures equalized. She opened the hull hatch and let her four passengers move down the short access tube ahead of her. In the receiving room stood six men and women, uniforms crisp and clean. *Cousteau* smelled clean, airy, and fresh, compared to the lifeboat, or even the derelict.

Dubois came last, walking slowly, unsure of where she was headed, of what lay ahead. A tall man stepped forward, his chiseled face contrasting with soft, warm eyes. He smiled, extending a hand. "I'm Will Dennison, captain of the *Cousteau*."

They shook, a longing grip. His was the first new human she had heard in so long. "Pamela Dubois, formerly of the *Goddess*."

Dennison looked at the other survivors, then back down the access tube. He frowned. "Only five?"

"We started as ten," Dubois said. She looked at Daggit. "That man needs a doctor." She rubbed her forehead. "Maybe we all do." She suddenly felt very weary again.

Dennison motioned two of his crew forward. They helped Daggit into a float chair and guided him and the others into the ship proper.

"Just a second," Dubois said. The chair turned, Daggit looking at her with hollow eyes.

This man tried to kill me, she thought. *I could ruin him with a word*. She said, "Take care of yourself, Mr. Daggit. Everything's okay now."

A touch of life reappeared behind his eyes, and he nodded slightly in understanding. They pushed him away.

"What happened to the others, Ensign? Transition shock?"

"What?" She frowned.

"Several of the other boats reported that some of their numbers didn't survive the shock of transiting the anomaly. They—"

"Where did these others come from?"

"It's what we're here for. We were in final approach to the anomaly when you came out and exploded. They still haven't figured that out. Last theory I heard before we transited was a fusion field failed.

"As I was saying, we were the closest ship to the disaster. We aborted our approach and began picking up survivors, what few there were. Not too many boats survived the final explosion."

Dubois leaned against a white bulkhead. "How did you find us?"

Dennison shrugged. "S.O.P. We tied into the anomaly traffic-control drones. They got orbital arcs on nearly every lifeboat that was sucked through the anomaly. We've been tracing them ever since. Two more to go."

"And then?"

He smiled. "Back to Earth, and probably a commendation for all of us."

Dubois's stomach jerked at the thought.

"And now, Ensign, what happened to your passengers?"

"Two by . . . transition shock. Killed."

"And the other three?"

"Five. We started with twelve. They died so soon, the first two, I . . . I barely remember them at all."

Dennison's scowl grew. "What happened to the other five, Ensign?"

Her knees felt weak. "Can we go to your cabin? It's more private. And I think I need a drink. It's . . . it's a long story."

She sat at one of the *Cousteau*'s many observation bubbles. Her recovery was continuing. Some day she might be able to think about all the past events without crying.

That had been embarrassing, strangely so. Dennison had been comforting, but firm. He had to know all the facts.

He got them, or at least most of them. She shaded out Daggit's actions, and So's. She presumed that Tyler had understood what she had said to Daggit in the airlock, absolving the old man. Tyler had backed up Dubois's story, equally shading Daggit and So.

There really wasn't any point to vindictive actions. Daggit was an old man, doomed to die in a short while. He wouldn't live long, remembering Hilary. And So was young. She could ruin his life, his career. Maybe, instead, he would learn.

She sat looking out at the alien derelict that had tried to make her a part of it. She had even saved Marito's reputation. None of them remained wholly sane inside that ship. It wasn't forgiveness she felt. It was a driving urge to forget.

Dennison had finally relented. He had wanted to reboard the derelict. She, and the others, had convinced him otherwise. Their compromise had been this, a quick pass-over, a photographic run before heading for Earth. The rescue of the other lifeboats would have to wait while news of the alien discovery was transmitted to higher authority. The excitement the news would cause was already sweeping through *Cousteau*. It was, after all, one of the prime reasons the ship existed.

Dubois felt little excitement beyond the thought that she would soon be home, on a planet. She never wanted to space again.

She looked at the derelict, an empty and dead ship. It was now a true derelict. More than just adrift, it was abandoned.

"Forsaken," she mumbled. She closed the bubble's protective covers and went back to her cabin. She tried to forget.

She never succeeded.

MORE SCIENCE FICTION ADVENTURE!